Mouse's Dream

Kerrera House Press

Mouse's Dream

by

K. Scot Macdonald

Kerrera House Press

K. Scot Macdonald is the author of:

Novels

The Shakespeare Drug

In Justice Found

Non-Fiction

Rolling the Iron Dice

*Propaganda and Information Warfare
in the 21st Century*

Macdonald, K. Scot.
Mouse's Dream/K. Scot Macdonald—1st Edition
p.   cm.
ISBN 978-0-9859650-9-9
Kerrera House Press
Culver City, CA
www.KerreraHousePress.com

First Printing: 2014
Printed in the United States of America

10 9 8 7 6 5 4 3 2 1

"He who believes in his dreams is mad,
and he who does not believe in them—
what is he?"

—Lorenzo Da Ponte,
Librettist for Amadeus Mozart

"Follow your desire as long as you live…"

—*The Maxims of Ptahhotpe*
(c. 2350 BC)

To Kippi,
for encouraging me to follow my desire
all the days of our life together.

Chapter 1

Anthony Maas opened his front door and froze at the sight of the two men on his doorstep.

Tim Cooper, short, broad and without a hint of emotion in his voice, announced, "You owe me," then snapped his stubby, nicotine-stained fingers and closed his black eyes, waiting for the number to come to him.

"Four thousand, three hundred ninety-five dollars and seventeen cents," Daniel Lindhe, tall, well-dressed and bespectacled, read off his personal assistant. "Principle only."

"It's Sunday," Maas wailed, raising his hands in supplication. After a furtive glance inside to make sure his family was not in sight, he closed the door gently behind him.

"We work seven days a week," Cooper said. "A habit you might consider adopting."

"I paid—"

"Last week," Cooper cut Maas off with an admonishing wave of a scarred right hand that was missing the last digits of the fourth finger and pinky. "Let's stay in the present, shall we? This week, you owe your weekly vig."

Maas frowned.

"Vig is short for *vigorish*," Lindhe explained, mistaking Maas's frown for a lack of understanding. "It's Yiddish or possibly Russian slang for a moneylender's interest or the house's take in a casino."

Distracted for a moment from his worries, Maas said, "You

know some obscure facts."

"It pays to know all facets of your particular business," the accountant advised. "Terminology, history, current trends, new technology, customer service, advertising."

"Whatever it's called, right now you owe me," Cooper cut in, his voice trailing off again as he snapped his fingers and closed his eyes, searching his memory for the number.

As Maas wondered if loan sharks advertised, let alone worried about customer service, Lindhe, suppressing a yawn at such an early hour, recited Maas's weekly interest payment, "Ten percent or $439.52."

"I'm on my way to church, for God's sake," Maas said, glancing back at the closed door and praying no one would open it. "My wife, my daughters."

"I need the money."

"I just need a few more days, Coop, for pity's sake."

"I don't loan pity. I loan money to sons who want to help their fired fathers—"

"Laid off, along with everyone else at the plant, and after 35 years."

"Mothers who break their hips."

"She needed a nurse and someone to cook for her and Dad or they would have starved."

"Fathers who need heart surgery in posh hospitals in Seattle."

"If he'd waited for the bypass operation in Vancouver he'd have been dead by the time he reached the top of the waiting list."

Coop shrugged. "Am I responsible for the ills of Canada's socialized medical system?"

"I didn't have a choice."

"Of course you did. Credit card companies are always eager to lend money."

"They charge 18 percent. You offered 6, at least for the first three months."

"Then it rose to a mere 8 percent."

"For three months; it's been increasing ever since."

"So pay off the principle."

"I was going to."

"Lindhe, did you receive full payment?"

Lindhe shook his well-coiffed head.

"Then I expect the vig, now."

"I get paid Thursday."

Coop frowned and shook his head. "Since you failed in your financial responsibilities last Friday, I took the liberty of stopping by to check your mail. You know what I found." He peered at Maas as if inspecting a possibly counterfeit C-note.

"You went through my mail?" Maas asked in disbelief, looking down at the diminutive, yet broad-shouldered loan shark. Their eyes met and Maas did not, for the first time in their relationship, look away.

"We found bills, bills and more bills," Lindhe reported.

"And?" Cooper prodded, his gaze still locked on Maas like a leopard on his prey.

"Ah, yes," Lindhe said, "we also found a rather interesting plain, grey envelope that appeared upon discrete fondling to contain a new credit card."

"You're transferring balances to new cards with zero-percent grace periods," Cooper said, poking a thick finger into Maas's chest as his aftershave seared Maas's nostrils. "You're desperate. I can't give you any more time. I need the money, today, this morning, now."

"I'm on my way to church, Coop," Maas said, almost plaintive as he hoped beyond all evidence to the contrary that the loan shark was a God-fearing man.

"I wouldn't recommend dropping anything in the collection plate," Cooper warned, his dark eyes slit. "I'd pay off those a lot closer to you than God, first."

"I don't have the money."

Cooper's lips turned into a thin white line at Maas's admission.

"Those are not words he likes to hear," Lindhe commented as he stared across the yard at a yellow rose bush that sheltered a weathered garden sculpture of a man leaning against a tree stump as he cradled a baby. "Isn't that *Hermes of Praxiteles*?"

Shocked, Maas stared up at Lindhe. "How on earth did you know that?"

"Art history elective for my MBA. The Greeks did some beautiful work; made marble look like fabric, right down to the folds." Lindhe paused to reflect, then added, "Too bad; barely make the rent churning out that classical realist style today."

"I need the money," Cooper broke in. "You owe it. I need it. If you don't have it, we'll have to make other arrangements—now."

"I just need a few days."

"Now."

"Just a couple of days."

"Now."

Maas sighed, glanced back at the closed front door and, resigned to his responsibilities, said, "It's Sunday. I can't get any money today, but I'll get an advance against this week's pay check tomorrow, alright?" As he tried to calculate his commissions for the current pay period, someone started a lawn mower down the street, breaking both the idyllic calm of the West Los Angeles neighborhood and Maas's frantic financial calculations.

Cooper cast a questioning look at Lindhe, who glanced at his gold wristwatch and said, "We *are* late for our next appointment."

"Tomorrow it is, then, but we'll have to arrange something to cover the unfortunate and completely uncalled for delay." Cooper surveyed the front yard and his dark eyes alighted on a red mountain bike. "That should be worth a few bucks at Rashid's to tide me over through your tardy times," he said, stalking across the lush lawn toward the bike as if he had just discovered the lost treasure of the Aztecs.

As Cooper picked up the bike with one hand and headed for his SUV, Maas managed to yell, "That's my daughter's bike." His voice, however, betrayed that he had already written off the loss. The last thing he wanted was for an argument to ensue that would bring his wife and daughters out of the house in their Sunday finery to hear the sad details of his financial dealings with Cooper.

"I wouldn't press it," Lindhe whispered, slipping his personal assistant into his inside suit pocket and straightening his jacket. "At least he didn't take the Hermes."

"Thank God for small favors."

"He'll break one of your ribs if he doesn't get at least something for the delay in payment."

"A rib?" Lindhe's presence brought just the hint of aftershave to Maas's nose. Unlike his boss, Lindhe was never one to overdo anything.

"I thought you guys usually broke knee caps."

"I never injure anyone," Lindhe said, rearing up to his full six-foot-six height. He seemed genuinely taken aback at the mere thought of committing an act of violence. "But don't worry. Your legs are safe. A broken leg slows you down too much; takes longer to get to work, let alone the time it takes to hobble into the trading room with a trade."

Maas's fear eased from his body—slightly.

"Now a broken rib hurts like a hot poker in the side, but you can work," Lindhe stated with clinical detachment. "Believe me, you can work with a bust rib, I've seen it many a time."

Maas's gut clenched at the thought.

Chapter 2

"Paul, Tony Maas, here," Maas said over the phone at 6:45 the next morning. He had been calling clients since he was the first broker to arrive when El Dorado Trading Corporation opened its glass doors at 5:30. For more than an hour Maas had tried to convince, cajole and coax his clients on the East Coast to buy, sell or trade something, anything to generate a commission. So far: nothing. "I've got an excellent opportunity in the corn market. I'm putting all my clients into it and I'd kick myself if I didn't put you in it, too."

"I can't afford it right now," Maas's client said. He could hear his client's fingers typing on a keyboard.

"I'm looking at a healthy return in just six to eight weeks. In fact, I'll be shocked if we don't see a 100 percent return on this one." Maas forced excitement into his voice but he didn't believe what he was saying. He was desperate and every client heard his desperation as soon as he uttered his first word.

"Maybe another time."

The phone went dead. The dial tone reminded Maas of the flat-line tone they use in movies when someone in a hospital dies. Having exhausted his list of East Coast clients who would be awake, Maas spent two futile hours cold calling, desperately trying to convince someone to open a new account before the voice of Nickel, co-owner of El Dorado, boomed over the intercom,

"Mouse, get in here."

Everyone called the diminutive Maas, Mouse. It was a name he loathed, but he could do nothing to change it in the nickname-addicted brokerage firm.

The background clatter of the big board accompanied Maas's walk across the now broker-filled bullpen to Nickel's office. As the markets in New York and Chicago had opened in succession between 6 and 8:30 a.m., the big board that ran from wall to wall across the front of the office had come to life, clicking and clacking as it displayed the rapidly changing prices of everything from gold, silver, platinum and palladium to pork bellies, oats, corn and wheat, with the currencies and energies in between.

When Maas appeared at his office door, Nickel looked up from analyzing a chart on his computer and asked without preamble, "Opened any accounts this month?"

"I sent charts and information to three—"

"Open any?"

"I think a couple will open tomorrow or the next day."

"Did you open any?"

"I'm sure one of them will definitely open."

"Did...you...open...any?"

Maas stared at Nickel, not wanting to say the "n" word. Finally, he capitulated to the inevitable, "No."

"I need your desk."

This could not be happening. "What? Why?"

"Of the three guys who survived Sam's course and sat the Series 3, two passed; we only have one desk open."

"You want to give my desk to a cherry? They don't even have their license yet."

"Their licenses will come through in a couple of weeks and until then I want them bird-dogging for the top brokers."

"You're giving my desk to a guy who's bird-dogging, not even opening accounts?"

"He can pass leads to a broker who will open accounts."

"And I can't?"

"Not lately."

Maas saw his life collapsing, his value as a broker and as a man gone. Rage bubbled up within him like a cauldron coming to a boil. "Nickel, I can open accounts. I have a few that are close to opening right now."

"Then open them. Now. Today."

"Christ, Nickel, I need a little more time than that."

Nickel leaned across his desk, elbows resting on its top. "Mouse, the new brokers are champing at the bit. They're young, eager and they can sell. They sound good. Vinny agrees." Nickel and Vinny co-owned El Dorado. "I want to give them both a chance, but we only have one desk open. I need yours. It's as simple as that. It's business; nothing personal."

It was as personal as life got. "I'm not the lowest performing broker."

"You're always near the bottom. The others bounce around. Once a quarter they land a whale and make me a ton of money. You never do."

"I've had dozens of whales."

"It's been years since you landed one."

"Then I'm due. I need a month." From the look on Nickel's face, Maas was no more successful convincing Nickel than he had been cold calling. "A few weeks."

Nickel stared placidly at Maas. Nickel could outlast Buddha in the silent-waiting game.

"Nickel, I've made you a fortune for you over the years," Maas pleaded, hating himself and Nickel. Why should he have to beg for a job that should by all that was right and just be his for as long as he wanted it? "I can open accounts. I've done it before. I'll do it again. You and I both know I'm just in a slump. Everyone has slumps. You were a broker, you know that, and the only way out of them is to work through them. I just need the time to work through this one."

Still no change on Nickel's face. It was set in an emotionless, dark-eyed stare. It was all business to him; cold, impersonal and almost abstract—a math problem that required a subtraction.

"Give me a chance; a month, a few weeks. I'll produce. You'll see."

"I've been waiting to see you produce more than enough to cover a car payment for eight months."

Maas's mind scrambled for a way out, any way out. "Put one of the new guys in the storage room. There's a phone in there."

Nickel leaned back, sighed and said with great reluctance,

"That just might be an idea. We'll give it a try."

Maas felt the tension begin to ease from his body.

"But if I don't see any new accounts from you in a couple of weeks, one of the new guy gets your desk. Maybe in the storage room, the new guy will stay focused on cold calling and won't pick up any bad habits from the rest of the flotsam out there."

Coiled taut with anger, Maas floated back to his desk.

After a day of fruitless cold calling, Maas returned home in the mid-afternoon after the markets closed and noticed the light blinking on the answering machine. In a voice gruff and hesitant, his father asked Tony to call him as soon as he could.

"I found her in the garden."

That single sentence was all Maas remembered clearly from the conversation. While he had been wasting his time cold calling to try to save his job, his mother had died. A stroke had taken her life. The part that stuck with him was that she had passed away in her garden, in the spring sun, amidst her carrots and beets, lettuce and raspberries, peas and beans; her favorite spot on earth. Even with a hip that was still painfully mending, she would not be kept from her beloved garden.

Chapter 3

"I wish you could come," Maas told Maria that evening as she packed his suitcase. He stood at the bedroom window watching Robyn in the driveway pound a volleyball against the side of the garage. His head ached. He had found himself crying after he talked with his father. He had not even realized he had started crying, but had felt a wet spot on his shirt. Looking down in a daze, he had felt his cheeks. They were damp. By the time he called Maria and she rushed home, the tears had stopped but, with their end, had come a dull ache behind his eyes.

"I wish I could come, too," Maria called from the walk-in closet. "But I don't want to dump the girls on Dad, especially not now. Coralea and Marina cried until they finally fell asleep."

Staring out the window, Maas said, "Robyn seems fine."

Maria stopped briefly in her packing to glance out the window. "That's just her way of dealing with it."

Maas nodded, in a haze that only seemed to allow him to focus falteringly on one thing at a time; his attention a flickering searchlight struggling to pierce a dense fog. "Didn't we agree that she shouldn't hit that ball against the garage?"

"I don't like her going to the park alone after dinner," Maria explained. "She really loves her new bike," she added, as she put three shirts in his suitcase. Looking over at Maas, she said, concern in her voice, "Are you going to be alright?"

Maas nodded, pursing his lips as he wondered what 'alright'

meant when you had just lost your mother. The lump he had felt in his throat since he heard the news rose again, threatening to choke him.

"Isn't her wrist still hurt?" Maas asked as Robyn delivered an especially hard volley against the defenseless garage.

"I told her to take it easy."

Maas shook his head, but a smile flitted across his lips despite his devastation. Robyn's conception of taking it easy was hitting the ball a thousand times against the garage instead of five thousand times during her evening practice session. Even the passing of her grandmother didn't stop practice—or maybe that was why she was going at it with such dedicated, single-minded focus.

Maas wished he felt as passionate about something as Robyn did about volleyball. Maybe such passions naturally ebbed with age. Then a vision of his mother in her garden planting vegetables on a warm spring afternoon flooded his mind. Maybe some passions never ebbed, but remained at the flood for a lifetime, if you were lucky.

"I stopped at the ATM and got your hundred for the week," Maas said, as he turned from the window and stretched his sore back. Hunching over a telephone cold calling all day was not conducive to a pain-free back and, for some reason, his left shoulder burned. His whole body, in fact, ached. It had since he spoke with his father. "The money's in your purse."

"Thanks for doing that, Anthony. You shouldn't have."

"I stopped on my way home."

Maria nodded, understanding; he got the money before he heard the news.

"The gardener's coming Friday."

"Okay." She darted into the bathroom. "I'll make sure he fixes the sprinkler in the corner of the yard," she called out. "He didn't last week."

"It was raining, so he didn't show." Maas sat on the bed and watched her as she packed his shaving kit—he should be doing it—and then wrapped one of his dress shoes in a plastic bag and slid it into the bottom of the suitcase. "Make sure Robyn makes it to volleyball Thursday after school."

"I'm sure she'll remind me," Maria said with a faint grin.

"Malena has swimming every afternoon this week for the Van

Nuys meet on the thirtieth."

Maria nodded.

"Coralea has piano Saturday morning at 10. Make sure she takes both her exercise books, and Robyn has swimming every afternoon, right after Malena."

"Anthony," Maria said, stopping in front of him, holding his shoulders and fixing him with her teak-colored eyes. "You don't need to be worrying about any of this. I'm taking a few days off; I'll take the girls to all their activities."

"I know."

Maria tilted her head to the side with an appraising look like a physician checking a patient's eyes for disease. "Are you going to be alright? You've had a horrible day."

Maas took a deep breath, swallowed and, looking off over her shoulder at nothing, said, "I think so. I'm worried about Dad, and my job."

"Me, too."

"He's never cooked in his life. If I wasn't going up there, he'd probably starve to death by the weekend."

"What's he going to do after you come home?"

"I'll teach him to cook or he'll have to live off frozen dinners for the rest of his life." Maas shook his head, far from wanting even to consider such problems, not tonight, not yet. "He'll need someone to help him with the yard and cleaning the house. Maybe they can cook for him, too. I hope it doesn't cost too much, especially if I lose my job."

"Anthony, this isn't the time to worry about money or jobs or anything but you, your father and our family. Things will work out."

Maas wondered.

"If we need it," Maria said, "I have some money invested for a rainy day."

"What money?"

"The money my dad gave me when we got married and I've added a little I've saved from the shopping budget over the years."

"Oh," Maas said, his hopes at a windfall vanishing as soon as the hope formed.

"You'll make some commissions while you're away. Who's handling your accounts?"

"The Doctor's the only one I trust not to churn them."

Churning was when a broker traded clients in and out of positions not in hopes of making the client any money, but solely to generate commissions. It was illegal, but was next to impossible to prove since winning trades in commodities are rare even with an honest broker.

Maria smirked. "Remember that time the Doctor threw out his knee and Nickel gave your accounts to John Winter?"

Maas smiled at the memory. "We came back from vacation and Old Man Winter had traded every one of my clients in and out of so many contracts they were all beyond done; they were burned to carbon, through and through."

"You made nearly $20,000 that month." Fished the packing, Maria zipped closed the carry-on.

"But my run sheet was cleaned out. I spent six months rebuilding it. I barely made a grand the following month."

"We went to Europe for five weeks on part of that $20,000, remember? That black sand beach on Santorini? The sunset gondola ride in Venice with that wonderful Riesling? Walking the walls that spring evening in Rothenberg? That pub in the Wiltshires, the Royal Oak, with the succulent smoked salmon in whiskey cream sauce? Harlech, and hiking in Glencoe?"

"Great memories," Maas agreed with a forced smile. It was sad to think back to such times since they seemed so long past, yet happiness peaked through the sadness.

"It's been a while since you had a $20,000 month," Maria said with a wan smile at the memory of things long past.

"I know," Maas said. His shoulders slumped. He felt old and exhausted. "Maybe I'm getting too old for the commodities game."

"You don't look too old to me," Maria said, running her hand through his short, dark hair. She kissed him softly, her tender, warm lips lingering on his cheek.

"Besides," she said, straightening and adopting a serious tone. "You could always get a nice, stable 9-to-5 office job shuffling paper."

"Might be hard at my age. People think you're set in your ways and can't learn anything new once you're over 35, let alone 40."

"You could get one. If you did, our income would be more stable."

"We'd never see another $20,000 month."

He was relieved that Maria didn't ask if they would ever see such a month again even if he stayed a broker. Instead, she smiled and said, "We'll see a $20,000 month soon, and you'll keep your desk, right?"

"Right. Then we can afford to have Dad just eat out all the time."

"Or hire Wolfgang Puck to cook for him every night."

Maas laughed, then stood and hefted the suitcase. Maria hugged him. He put the suitcase down and ran his hands through her long, lustrous hair. He marveled at how black it had remained after 20 years of marriage. He held her tight, feeling her body, her warmth, her love.

"I wish you could all come," he said. "Mom would have liked that, especially seeing the girls." Then the tears came, again.

Chapter 4

Taking a break from accepting condolences and sympathy from the mourners who crowded the living room and kitchen of his childhood home, Maas stood on the back porch, breathing in the cool spring air and staring out across the backyard, glistening from a recent rain. Three trees, a lovingly pruned Japanese flowering cherry, a squat ambrosia apple and a spreading Black plum, grew along the left side of the yard, providing shade in the summer and privacy most of the year. A garden carpeted the right side of the yard, almost from the house to the back wood fence, which leaned toward the plum tree like an ardent lover. The garden had always been far too large for a family of three, yet his mom had maintained it with meticulous care. Now who would?

Turning, Maas looked through the kitchen window and saw Donna, Paul's wife, pouring tea for one of the guests. Maas's father was an only child and his mother's sister was too frail to arrange the post-funeral reception, so the wives of Maas's childhood friends had stepped in. He sighed as he recalled how very different his past visits home had been. Around thickly varnished pub tables cluttered with pints of local ales, pilsners and bitters, he and his friends would talk of old times, youthful dreams and the teenaged adventures that had grown more ridiculous and hilarious with the years and the retelling. They had grown up together and now, middle-aged, they knew each other better than their own wives.

With his old friends, Maas felt totally at ease and completely relaxed. When they saw each other for the first time at each reunion, the genuine happiness in the eyes of his friends filled Maas with a profound contentment. They were the best friends a man could have; his band of brothers. Maas had friends in Los Angeles, but you never seemed to make the same kind of friends as an adult that you made as a child. His friends in Vancouver had known him as a boy, when he had talked about his dreams. The friends he had made in Los Angeles only knew him as a commodity broker, husband and father. They had only met him, and he them, after as adults they had erected the walls of privacy that all adults construct around themselves like individual castles—or prisons. It seemed that adult friendships could only get so close; they always hit the walls, forming shadow friendships that rarely, if ever, delved deep to the place where dreams reside.

"Someone here to see you," Kraig said from the kitchen doorway.

Maas turned and, as Kraig stepped aside, Maas saw her: Sharon Calloway.

Maas stared as he beheld the girl, now a woman, whom he had dated throughout high school. She was still as beautiful as he remembered and in many ways even more so than 24 years before. A flood of emotion washed over him, filling him with an overpowering joy that brightened the day and warmed his soul.

"Tony," she said, stepping toward him. "I'm so sorry. You have my deepest sympathy." She hugged him, rubbing his back through his black suit and then, standing back just a half step on the tiny porch, said, "I'm so sorry I'm late. I wanted to come to the funeral, but I got tied up at work."

"It's great to see you," Maas said.

They stood and stared at each other.

After a long pause, she filled the silence by saying, "I had to stay to complete a sale. I could have left it to one of my assistants, but the buyer's a regular and I had to give him the VIP treatment, complete with me, the gallery owner, on hand to offer suitable praise for his impeccable taste in fine art. Made me miss my ferry. I'm so sorry."

"I'm just glad you came. You own your own art gallery?"

She nodded.

"That's fantastic. You always wanted to."

"It's just a small one in Victoria, but Victoria's the retirement capital of Canada," she said as Maas accepted a tea from Sunyoung, Bruce's Korean-born wife.

"Would you like some tea?" Sunyoung asked Sharon.

"Yes, please, with just a splash of milk. That would be wonderful."

Sunyoung nodded and stepped back inside.

"There are a lot of rich old people who love to waste—I mean spend or is it invest? I'm never sure what they call it these days—their millions on paintings, sculptures and anything else I can convince them is fine art."

"Business is good?" Maas asked, eager to talk—and think—about something other than his mother's passing, at least for a short time.

"There are good times and slow times—such as right now—but it keeps a roof over my head, food on the table and pays for a yearly buying trip to Europe."

As Sunyoung returned with a cup for Sharon, Maas sipped his tea.

After thanking Sunyoung, who slipped back into the kitchen, Sharon asked, "How's your father doing?"

Maas shrugged. "About as well as can be expected. They'd been married almost 50 years."

"Must be horrendous; like losing a part of yourself."

"You don't get over something like that for a long, long time."

"If ever." Her gaze met his, holding his eyes for a long moment.

Maas nodded, sipped his tea and felt its sweet warmth wash down his throat.

"Michael said you're a commodity broker down in LA," Sharon said. "I have to ask, what's a pork belly?"

Maas laughed. "That's the most common question people ask about commodities."

"And the answer is?"

"The part of the pig used to make bacon."

"Not a big market in Israel."

"Hard to cold call Israel anyway with the time difference."

"Do you like being a broker?"

Maas shrugged. "It almost pays the bills."

"Almost?"

"Three daughters can spend more than 10 men can make."

"Maybe they'd like to spend some of their dad's money on a few pieces of fine art," Sharon suggested with a sly grin.

"I better rack up a lot more commissions before I let my girls loose in your gallery."

Maas kept glancing at Sharon, fighting the urge to stare. When he looked at her, he was flooded by thousands of warm memories of their time together so long ago; a time when life was full of promise, newfound joys and periods of intense happiness.

He asked, "Did you ever marry?" She wore no wedding ring.

"Yes, twice; neither lasted."

"I'm sorry to hear that."

"Some things you have to put behind you. Now I can focus on my gallery and art. It's a pretty good life." Her voice was soothing and tender. "Do you still sculpt?"

Maas hesitated. She tilted her head to the side, inquiring.

"No, I haven't sculpted in years," he admitted, his voice a monotone.

"That's a shame," she said, sounding as if she had just been told of a great tragedy. Her eyes could still draw his in as if they were connected by a cord that had been bound tight between their souls decades before and had never loosened. "You loved sculpting and you were talented. Why didn't you keep at it?"

Maas shrugged. "My parents wanted me to go to university. I would have rather gone to Europe with you."

"I saw a lot of fantastic galleries that first trip," she said, a smile spreading across her face at the memories. "The National Gallery in London, the Louvre, the Hermitage, and the galleries in Rome: the Bourghese, the Colonna, the Corsini, and the Spada. All the great artists; Michelangelo, El Greco, Monet, Picasso, Courbet, and Masaccio, and so many others." Her voice took on a pleasing, gentle lilt; the very names of the galleries and artists bringing her great pleasure, like the names of old lovers.

"My parents said it would be a waste of money."

"It really didn't cost much. I didn't have much to spend. I bought a EuroRail pass, stayed in hostels, bought most of my meals from street vendors, and toured the museums in the evening or on days when they were free."

"I'm sorry I missed it." He felt a hole in his heart where those memories should have been. Since then sculpting had been sealed in a separate compartment, quarantined from the rest of his life, waiting for....for what? Then, remembering that time, so long ago, he added, "You came back....different."

She frowned.

"Before you left, you were interested in art and thought you might try to make a career of doing something with art in a vague sort of way. When you returned, you were filled with a passion for art and a determination to get involved in the art world no matter what."

"You make it sound like I was possessed."

"I admired that you had so much passion and certainty about what you wanted to do; what you should do. You had become who you really were."

"You'd changed, too."

Now it was Maas's turn to frown.

"When I came home you'd dropped your art courses and were taking business classes."

"I figured a business degree would let me make enough money in five or 10 years to retire. Then I could sculpt full-time and not have to worry if I ever sold a single piece." He snorted, shaking his head at the memory. "Silly, really."

"We were kids, what did we know?" She sipped her tea. "I was surprised you gave up sculpting that easily."

"It wasn't easy. I tried to make time to sculpt, but university was hard. I had to study a lot to try to keep up with Terry, Micheal and the rest of them. They're a lot smarter than I am."

"Terry and Micheal were the top students in the province in grade 12."

"I wanted to keep up; to be like them, and Paul and Bruce, Kraig and Ken. I didn't want to be the worst student."

"You were far from the worst."

"I was far from the best. In any case, I didn't have much time to sculpt."

"You could have got a part-time job after university and sculpted."

"I thought I'd be able to, but then I lucked out, got a scholarship to USC for an MBA, met Maria, and the girls came before I knew it. I thought I'd be able to get back to sculpting, but after we had Coralea, I had to drop out of graduate school to get a job and....and I fell into commodities. I always thought I'd get back to sculpting someday."

"But someday never came?"

"Not yet," he said with a forced grin.

As they stood close to each other on the porch, he looked at her and, feeling happiness for the first time since his mother had died, said, "You're a stunning woman, Sharon."

"Watch what you say. You an old married guy away from home and me a divorcee, footloose and fancy free—well, mostly." She smiled, filling his eyes. "When do you go back to LA?"

"Sunday afternoon. I'll be busy with Dad until then."

"I wish we had more time, in happier circumstances."

"Me too." He stared at her, feeling warmth spread through his body even as the world around them faded away, the sights, sounds and fragrances of the yard, the garden and the reception fading before her beauty and his memories. "You were the first woman I ever loved."

"I know."

"The first woman I ever made love to," he whispered, glancing over her shoulder to make sure no one in the kitchen was within earshot.

"I was there, remember?"

Maas grinned at the memory; a cold evening at Harrison Hot Springs, the conjoined sleeping bags in the pup tent, the awkward moments, the nervousness, almost terror, then seeing her stunning body, the bliss and far, far too fast, it was over.

"I'm a bit better at it now."

She laughed. "So am I. We got pretty good at it, though."

"Practice makes perfect."

She grinned, looked down and sipped her tea. "You were my first love, too, you know." She sighed and, looking deep into his eyes, said, "I still see you."

He frowned.

"I mean, when I dream at night, I see you."

"That's very flattering."

"Not all the time, though," she added quickly, as he started to puff up like a peacock about to display.

"Of course not."

They laughed.

She looked up at him, her wonderful azure eyes making him tingle all over, and said, "If you had married me, you could have been a sculptor and I could have sold your works in my gallery, just like we planned when we were in high school."

"Assuming any sold," Maas said with a self-deprecating chuckle.

"They would have sold."

"I doubt it."

"Tony, you were good. You had real talent. I'm sure I could sell your pieces now."

He pursed his lips and shook his head. "I have a different life now."

"Some people change their lives."

"Not many."

"You changed your life before from art to business. Why not change back?"

"That was a long time ago."

"You're not that old."

"I'm pretty set in my ways."

"You were born to be a sculptor, Tony, not a commodity broker. I was born to sell; you weren't."

"I have a pretty good life, Sharon."

"Pretty good?"

"I'd be easy if I was miserable, but I'm not. I'm doing alright."

Sharon looked at him and he knew she did not believe him. They knew each other too well to successfully lie to each other.

"Maria's a great woman and my girls are a joy." He pulled out his wallet, slid out a photograph and thrust it at Sharon. "That's Maria and the girls from last Christmas, so the girls are bigger now. They had it taken as a surprise...for me."

"They're adorable."

Maas carefully returned the photograph to his wallet.

"You don't have to convince me, Tony." She smiled, reassuring him like no one else could. "You just don't seem...."

"What?"

"Happy? Content? Fulfilled? I don't know the right word."

Her sadness mixed with disappointment was a presence

between them like an all-embracing fog. They looked at each other, trying to see back through 20 years of two separate lives.

"If you're ever in Victoria…"

"I'll look you up," he promised, then quickly added, "but I doubt I'll get a chance anytime soon."

"Victoria's not going anywhere."

"I know."

"I'm not going anywhere."

They stood looking at each other, silent, yet filled with memories and emotions, dreams and desires.

"If you ever change your mind…," she said, her voice trailing off into hope.

"You'll be the first to know." He hugged her and whispered, "I dream of you, too."

"All the time?"

"No," he laughed. "But a lot."

She smiled and they slowly, reluctantly let go of each other.

"Tony," Terry said from the kitchen door. "Your aunt is leaving and wants to say goodbye."

Maas nodded. Reality flooded back. He wanted to keep talking to Sharon about art and dreams and their youth, but he had relatives and friends to say goodbye to, and, in a couple of days, a plane to catch to fly home from the fantasy world of the past where people knew him for what he was meant to be, back to the real world where people only knew him for what he had become without him ever really having noticed that he had changed at all.

Chapter 5

On the flight home, Maas sat in a window seat, the arm rest up to enjoy the extra room provided by a rare adjacent empty seat. He was beat. The days after the funeral had been filled with battles with his dad. They argued over moving to an apartment, which would be easier and cheaper to maintain than the house. Maas lost that argument even before it began. They argued about whether his dad would need someone to cook, clean and do laundry. Maas partially won that argument. They argued over what to do with his mother's clothes, jewelry and knickknacks. Amidst the battles, Maas spent his days helping his dad with various financial and legal matters associated with his mother's passing, even while trying to teach his dad the rudiments of cooking. He thought his father would be alright, at least for a while. Thank God for microwavable meals.

Even with so many concerns about his dad, as his mind meandered back over the past few days, it focused on Sharon, which drew his mind back even farther into the past.

It was a sunny, warm June day just after school let out when Maas and his friends drove up to meet their girlfriends at a campground an hour and a half east of Vancouver near Harrison Hot Springs. They arrived at Sasquatch Provincial Park—named for the local version of Big Foot—met their girlfriends and pitched their tents. They swam in Harrison Lake, brimming with the first of the winter snow melt, icy but refreshing, marred only by Bruce being bit by a horsefly that took a chunk out of his stomach the size of a corn kernel. In the gathering dusk, dinner was hot dogs and chips. Ken was so eager to eat he started cooking his hot dog above the campfire as Maas, Sharon and Paul coaxed the smoldering wood into a blaze by thrusting loosely crumpled newspapers into the fire-pit. His hunger getting the better of his patience, Ken declared his hot dog cooked and started eating. After a few bites he announced with a disgusted frown, "This tastes funny."

In the twilight made darker by the firs that encircled the campsite, Ken peered at the uneaten portion of his hot dog. Jennifer, Terry's girlfriend, shone a flashlight on the half-eaten wiener. The hot dog was black.

"What the...," Ken exclaimed, grimacing.

"The newsprint from the newspaper burned up and settled on your hot dog," Maas said, laughing.

Ken gagged and stuck out his tongue, revealing a black tongue in the light of Jennifer's flashlight. For the rest of the trip they called him Chow after the black-tongued dog breed.

After dinner, the couples sat around the fire roasting marshmallows and drinking beers and wine coolers before drifting off to their tents. No one had known what would happen but Maas found himself alone in his pup tent with Sharon. They stared at each other, neither knowing what to do or say, let alone what the other would do or say.

"Why don't you grab us a wine cooler?" Sharon suggested, as she kneeled on the foam padding that held two sleeping bags side by side. "I'll zip the sleeping bags together."

Maas rushed out to an ice chest for a wine cooler. When he returned, Sharon was in the now double sleeping bag, fully clothed against the chill air.

"Get in," she said. "It's freezing." Even in June the lower reaches of the mountains that cradled Harrison Lake and the hot springs dipped into winter-like temperatures by the time the sun slid over the western horizon. There was snow on the mountains to the east and it would not melt for at least a month.

He slid in beside her and, resting on his elbow, looked down at her. Her hair splayed out around her face like a golden halo in the diffuse light cast by a lantern on the picnic table through the tent's blue nylon.

"Why don't we each take a drink, then remove one piece of

clothing?" Sharon suggested with a bashful smile Maas could still picture. "We can see where it leads us."

Maas thought it was the most wonderful suggestion he had ever heard.

The next thing he remembered was being naked in the sleeping bag with Sharon, their bodies pressed tightly together. She was warm and smooth, soft and firm, and they seemed to fit together so well. Even as they kissed and held each other, he did not know what to do. She did not know what to do. They kissed and explored, huddling down in the sleeping bag to avoid the chill night air on their shoulders. The world seemed to shrink to just each other.

He was on top of her and then inside her and he felt a warmth flood his body. It had been bliss; a bliss he would feel many times with Sharon, but never often enough.

"Drink, sir?" the flight attendant asked. "Sir?"

Startled, Maas jerked his head up and, after a jarring return to the present, replied, "Just some water, please, with ice."

Chapter 6

As Maas scanned the carousel at LAX for his bag, a gentle hand touched his forearm. Turning, he beheld Maria, flanked by a beaming Malena, a smiling Coralea and a bored Robyn, her arms folded. All four looked prettier than he remembered. It was a sensation he always had upon seeing them after a trip; as if absence made them prettier than the images in his mind's eye.

"Welcome home," Maria said, kissing him. "We missed you."

Maas kissed each of his girls in turn, earning a plaintive, whining, "Daaaaaad," from the eldest. A teenager, Robyn had recently developed an aversion to being seen with her parents, let alone being kissed by her father in public.

"How's your wrist?" Maas asked Robyn in an attempt to make amends as they walked from the terminal to the parking structure.

"Sore."

"If you lay off volleyball for a while, it'll heal faster."

"I have to practice, Dad," she replied, sounding as if Maas was an imbecile for thinking that a layoff was even a possibility to be considered.

During the drive home, Maria asked, "How'd it go?"

"The funeral was nice; lots of people. Mom would have liked it, seeing everyone."

Maria reached over and patted his thigh sympathetically.

"Dad's going to be a handful. He doesn't want to give up the house and I don't think he's up to maintaining it anymore."

"You said you got him to agree to have someone come in to help?"

"I pushed for a lady I found to come in and clean, do laundry and some cooking five times a week. Dad wanted no one—'a waste of money,' was how he put it—so we compromised on twice a week. That was all he'd put up with."

"Hopefully it'll be enough." They fell silent for a moment, then she reported, "The dryer stopped working. It wouldn't start Saturday morning. I had to go over to a Laundromat with all the sopping-wet clothes to dry everything since I'd already done the wash."

"I'll call someone about it tomorrow," Maas said, turning up Sepulveda on the way home.

"I'd do it, but it's hard to make calls from work."

"I know. I can do it."

"The doorstop on our bedroom door fell off."

"I'll take a look at it."

"Maybe soon," Maria suggested, looking over at him and lifting her eyebrows to emphasize her words. "The doorknob is marking the wall. I tried to fix it, but I couldn't figure out how to get the screw thing off. I think I used the wrong type of screwdriver head or something. It kept slipping. And the garage door opener is making a grinding sound, like its sick. I don't know what's wrong, but if you could take a look at it...."

Chapter 7

In bed that night, Maria snuggled against Maas's side.

"I'm sorry you had trouble helping your dad," she said, stroking her fingers across his chest.

"Wish I'd had a little more time with him. Maybe I can go back up there next month."

"I hope so, but I'm glad you're home now."

"It was pretty draining up there. I never sleep well without you."

"Me neither."

He kissed her hair and massaged her neck with one hand. He was tired, but he wanted to reconnect with Maria. He felt a strong desire to feel alive; to know there was life in the world and to forget about everything else, at least for a time.

"That feels good," she said, letting her head fall forward to allow him to reach the back of her neck more easily.

Maas resisted the old urge to just turn Maria around, kiss her and make love to her in a rush with all the passion that he felt. She liked to take things slow, so he took his time, slowly winning her over, as if they were making love for the first time.

"Did you see Coralea's drawing from art class?" Maria asked, her face masked by her long hair.

"No, not yet," Maas said, his mind far from thinking about art or a class, let alone one of his daughters.

"It's really good."

"I'll ask her to show it to me tomorrow."

Maria sat up, slipped off her loose nightgown and turned to face him. He knew how it would go now. She would roll onto her back and he would lie, perched on his elbow, kissing and holding her. Then, finally, she would acquiesce and they would move on to make love as they had hundreds of times before.

Afterward, Maas lay staring at the ceiling as Maria spoke of the kids, chores and things Maas could listen to with only half his attention. Usually Maas found sex relaxing and invigorating, tightening the connection with Maria. Now, however, he felt as if he had missed out on something. Maybe it was the endless portrayal of sex in movies and novels as earth shaking and life changing. Most sex was not, yet sometimes it was; more often early in a relationship, but once in a while in a relationship that was decades old. Whatever the reason, movies or just a relationship's natural progression, Maas felt as if he and Maria were missing something. The times when Maria would lose herself in the moment, her chest and breasts flushed red, nipples hard, fingernails digging into his back, occurred so rarely now he had trouble remembering the last time it had happened. She always needed some wine now before they had sex, something she had never needed before. Did she need it to even get in the mood? For her, had sex become some sort of a chore? He felt sad not only for himself, but for Maria. Shouldn't there be more passion between two people who for so many years had shared a bed and their lives?

Chapter 8

Early the next morning at El Dorado, after greetings and a brief discussion about Maas's father, Maas asked the Doctor, "How was business?"

"Let's see," the Doctor said, leafing through a pile of account folders on his chipped, gray desk. "I made two trades for your clients: seven hundred bucks for me; seven hundred for you."

"Great." Although he had hoped the Doctor had churned his clients as thoroughly as Old Man Winter at his most avaricious, Maas was surprised the Doctor had managed even two trades with Maas's overly done clients. At least now he had enough to cover Coop's vig, although he would have to make a lot more to cover the mortgage, the credit cards, Maria's $100 for the week's shopping, and their usual non-credit card spending, not to mention the new cost of his father's hired help. With a sigh he told himself his time off was over; time to get back to work.

Maas carefully checked the trades the Doctor had made for his clients. The last thing he needed was an error eating into his paycheck. True to form, the reliable Doctor had committed no errors.

Maas started cold calling. Within five minutes the funeral, Sharon, art, and the trip to Vancouver seemed to have receded years into the past, as if it was all part of a long-distant childhood dream.

After two fruitless hours, a dejected Maas surrendered to defeat and walked across the street to the ATM to withdraw Maria's $100 for the week. On his way back he followed two brokers, Hero and Chisel Chest, into the office as they appeared for work at 8:30, well after all the markets had opened back east and more than two hours after Maas had arrived.

"The Bible says, 'Thou shalt not kill,'" Hero said as the pair walked ahead of Maas down the hall toward the bullpen. Hero's last name was Hogan, so everyone called him Hero after the 1970s World War II prisoner-of-war camp sitcom *Hogan's Heroes.* "Capital punishment is immoral."

"And criminals who rape and murder aren't immoral?" Chisel Chest, nicknamed for his muscular physique, asked.

"Two wrongs don't make a right," Hero said, raising his nicotine-stained right index finger to emphasize his point.

"Exactly," Chisel Chest said. "Letting murderers back out on the street to kill a second time makes two wrongs and that's damn far from being right."

After another futile hour cold calling, with only one person agreeing to let Maas mail him some information "just to look over," Maas steeled his resolve and decided the time had come to confess his misery.

"Your daughters go on a spending spree again?" Sam, El Dorado's manager, asked with a knowing grin from behind his desk, the top of which was hidden beneath a jumble of run sheets, customer files and daily client position reports.

"You know my princesses too well," Maas replied as he flopped into a chair beside Sam's buried desk.

"Your daughters will have to learn restraint some day."

"They're not the only ones. My wallet has enough demands on it to make Bill Gates's accountant cringe."

"Sounds familiar." Tall, wide and in a constant battle between his desire to lose weight and his desire for Cajun cooking, Sam was a man who loved to eat. A former musician from New Orleans who realized music didn't pay particularly well unless your last name was Springsteen, McCartney or Petty, he fell into brokering and became the manager at El Dorado.

"On top of all my current financial demands," Maas said, "I'm trying to save to retire from this blissful place someday."

Sam forced a smile, then handed Maas an envelope. "Nickel and Vinny made a donation to the National Stroke Association in the name of your mother in lieu of flowers."

"Thanks," Maas said opening the envelope. It was a $4,500 donation. Maas was touched by the generous donation.

"They took a collection. Every broker chipped in."

"Thanks, thanks a lot."

Maas liked Sam. When the firm wrote more than $400,000 in business in a month, the owners took the top five brokers to dinner. Sam always rented a limo to ferry them all in style to Spagos, Asia de Cuba or Crustacean.

Sam checked a printout to determine how much money Maas had earned so far this pay period. "Did you do any business this morning?"

"Not yet, but I want to trade a guy out of crude and into the grains later. He lives in LA, so he's not up yet."

"Lazy bastard; it's almost nine," Sam said, glancing at his Rolex Submariner: a gift from a broker after a particularly prosperous month.

"He works ungodly hours; owns a nightclub. I'm pretty sure about the trade," Maas added. He knew every broker asking for an advance said they were about to put a big trade into the market, but he said it anyway—it was expected.

Sam found Maas's listing in the printout. "How much you need?"

"About $3 million."

"Don't we all?"

"The more relevant question is, how much can I get?"

"Somewhat less: $650."

"That'll have to do."

"So many of these guys just blow their money," Sam said as he wrote and then tore off a check. He gestured out at the bullpen where the brokers sporadically labored. "They never save. I'm always telling my son, save and invest. Find a good index mutual fund and add a little every month, just like paying the rent. Make you rich some day. Otherwise, you spend it as fast as you get it."

"Or your daughters spend it even before you get it," Maas said with a pained grin. "Maybe you could speak to them."

"Domestic disputes are the most dangerous calls cops get, so

I'll pass. Now, if you want to talk to my son about the dangers of spending I'd be all for it."

"Like you, I think I'll pass."

"That doesn't leave you much in your check this week. Better get out there and pound the phone."

Chapter 9

"Commodities? You've got to be kidding."

"Go to hell you bastard, and please take me off your list."

"I'm not a sucker."

"I told someone from your firm last month I'm not interested. Leave me alone!"

"You're my fifth sales call today."

"How did you get my phone number?"

Maas made 118 calls in the next two hours without a bite, his enthusiasm and confidence declining with every rejection and every hang-up, even as his frustration at the futility of trying to convince someone, anyone to open an account increased. Despite his frustration he kept calling from the stack of four-by-three inch lead cards on his desk. Purchased from a company that sold contact information for every business need, Maas had the feeling the leads had already been called by every telemarketer in the country. The rejections ate at Maas's soul, nibble by nibble, bite by bite.

"What gives you the right to call me in the middle of my lunch?" An irate shoe store owner demanded.

Calm, Maas asked, "Do you have an answering machine?"

"Yes, of course."

"Then don't answer the phone until you hear who it is. You'll never have to talk to a salesman again."

"I'll still have the phone ringing all the damn time, invading my privacy."

"A small price to pay for the American dream."

"What the hell are you talking about?"

"Every one of those calls is from someone trying to make a little dough, trying to get ahead and make something of themselves; pursuing the American dream."

"They should go out and get a real job."

"Like selling shoes in a store?"

"Yeah, not selling damn commodities over the phone."

"You sell shoes. I sell commodity futures and options. We're both just trying to sell something. What's the difference?"

"I don't bother people while they're having lunch."

"Point taken, but when we stop letting people try to make a buck, we're in trouble. Buying and selling are at the heart of America. Think about it. We bought most of this country from somebody; Manhattan, the Louisiana Purchase, Alaska."

"That's not the same thing as trying to sell me soybeans."

"If I had Manhattan to sell, I'd offer it to you."

"Instead you try to sell me beans."

"I sell what I have."

"What you have is garbage."

"Let's let the market determine that. If it's garbage, the price will go down—but whether it goes up or down, you can make money in these markets."

"Yeah, right."

"If you don't think so, I'll move on and find someone who thinks they can, but don't stop me from trying to make a buck or you'll destroy all our freedoms."

"Well, go make your buck someplace else."

"Alright, I'm glad we've been able to reach an agreement on these philosophical matters."

"Agreement? What the hell are you talking about?"

"You agreed I should be able to call someone else to pitch my wares," Maas said, then quickly added, "Good day," and put the receiver down. He shouldn't have done it. It was a waste of time. Even so, it gave him the boost he needed to make another few hundred cold calls.

Chapter 10

After another ineffectual hour cold calling, Maas decided to take advantage of an easier way to make some money; not a lot, but a little to staunch the bleeding from his wallet, although it would do nothing to help him keep his desk. After stretching his sore back and left shoulder, he sauntered back to the copy room off the rear of the bullpen. The brokers had computer terminals at their desks to track the markets, but no printers. They used the copy room's printer and copier to produce charts to use as another weapon in their arsenal to convince invariably reluctant clients to buy, buy, buy.

Maas, however, wasn't interested in the room's selling aides. He found what he was looking for in the form of Detective Kovic, Leadless Joe and John Ford. Well dressed in suits or sport jackets and slacks, although sans ties, the three brokers were debating the merits and demerits of a crude oil chart.

"It's gotta go up," Ford said. "OPEC's cutting production. Says so right here in today's Reuters: 'OPEC agrees to slash production 5 percent.'" He waved a printout of the news article in Leadless Joe's face.

"No way," Leadless Joe countered, grabbing at the paper but missing. "This is 2001, not 1973. OPEC doesn't control supply anymore. Norway, Britain, Venezuela, Canada, and the US will just pump more and the price won't budge a penny."

"Anyone care for some car roulette?" Maas asked, gazing out the 14th-floor window as the sun's early rays lit the empty, verdant fairways of the Los Angeles Country Club across the street, the hotel-sized mansions of Beverly Hills and the parched Santa Monica Mountains beyond.

"Sure, Mouse," Leadless Joe said as he abandoned his attempt to divine if crude would go up, down or more likely, meander aimlessly within a narrow range until his clients's option contracts expired worthless.

"I'll pony up to the table, Mouse," Detective Kovic said, pulling out his calf-skin wallet. Tall, lanky and with easy good looks, Kovic always wore a sharp suit and looked more like the popular image of a Beverly Hills cop than a commodity broker, hence the nickname.

"Me, too," John Ford said. His real first name had long since been forgotten. Since his last name was Ford, a trading room clerk had started calling him after the legendary director and the name stuck, even though the broker was black and the director had been white.

"Five on black," Kovic said, slapping a five-dollar bill down on the metal windowsill.

"I'll see you on red," Leadless Joe said, adding his five to the sill.

"I'll take blue," Ford said, his voice like broken glass covered with molasses.

"And I'll take white," Maas said, making the pot an even $20.

Maas folded his arms and, leaning against the wall by the computer, gazed out the window past the neighboring building down at Santa Monica Boulevard. "All bets are down. Next car?"

The others nodded and, waiting as the traffic light hidden behind the neighboring office tower changed, watched eagerly to see the color of the first car to appear.

"White!" John Ford yelled, slapping his hand against his thigh and grimacing at his loss as the first car appeared.

"Damn it," Leadless Joe said, stuffing his wallet back deep into his pant's back pocket.

"Easy come, easy go," Kovic said philosophically, rocking back on his heels as Maas reached in to snatch the four bills from the sill. The winnings would pay for Malena's night at the movies Friday.

"Again?" Ford asked, his pleading eyes seeking what he

appeared to believe would be a near certain chance to win his money back and put him firmly into profit territory for the day before he even looked at his run sheet. Ford never got an early start, except maybe on goofing off.

They agreed and the bets were placed once again. They each choose a color: yellow, red, black, and, Maas, white. This time it was a $10 bet.

Even as Maas calculated how much Robyn's day at Disneyland with her friends would cost that weekend, Goldstein, the resident source of useless facts, wandered in perusing a *Consumer Reports*.

"Car roulette, eh?" Goldstein asked. His real name was O'Reilly but he believed that people were more likely to entrust their investment dollars to a Goldstein than an O'Reilly, so he had changed his name. "I may have some information relevant to the game at hand."

"Bets are already down," Ford announced, leaning against the sill as he peered out the window, his hands hovering over the bills as if they might attempt to escape.

"Too late to change 'em now," Kovic added.

"White by a fender!" Leadless Joe yelled, doubling over with anguish. "Damn it! White beat red by the length of a bee's dick!"

"Width is more like it," Kovic observed.

"The Mouse wins again," Ford said, as Maas unobtrusively collected his winnings.

"Who the hell buys a white car anyway?" Leadless Joe demanded of his colleagues. "Boring as watching dried paint."

Kovic asked, "Isn't the saying, watching paint dry?"

"Watching dried paint must be even more boring than watching paint dry," Leadless Joe explained.

"Actually, it says here that almost half the people buying cars in the United States select a white car," Goldstein said.

"What?" Ford demanded, rearing up to his full six-foot-three height, which only accentuated his broad shoulders as they strained the fine stitching of his bright blue silk shirt.

"White?" Kovic asked. "You always bet white, Mouse."

"I don't believe it's against the rules to always bet white," Maas said, folding his winnings to better hide them in his hand.

"It is if half the cars are white," Leadless Joe said. "No fucking wonder you always win."

"I do not always win," Maas countered, retreating into a corner as the other brokers advanced on him. "You should remember that I always bet last, allowing anyone else to bet white, if they so choose." Maas did have his morals.

"When someone does, it's about the only time you lose," Kovic said.

"Actually I lose 42.6 percent of the time, not counting today," Maas admitted. It was always prudent to know the odds in games of chance.

"I want my money back," Ford demanded. He seemed to fill the room, leaving little space for Kovic to peer over his left shoulder and Leadless Joe to peer around his beefy right arm.

"It was a fair game," Maas asserted, "according to the agreed upon rules."

"Not with you betting white and half the cars white," Kovic charged.

"Give us our money back," Ford demanded, raising his over-sized fists.

"Using your knowledge should not be illegal in a game of chance," Maas argued.

"Give us our money back," Ford repeated.

"Alright, alright," Maas said, outnumbered and outweighed by at least 400 pounds. He returned his colleague's money.

The three angry brokers, their wallets restored to their former glory, stalked out of the room.

"You should really mind your own bloody business," Maas told Goldstein, wondering when the tide in the affairs of men would change and things would begin to flow his way.

"Business is what it is," Goldstein agreed. "I got five bucks a pop for that little piece of information from 23 brokers out there. Seems like you played car roulette with a lot of guys who regularly lost."

"You just destroyed a gold mine for a one time pay out of $115?" Maas asked, wincing. With a pain in his wallet, he thought of the hundred or more a week he had made on car roulette for almost 20 years that was now suddenly and irretrievably gone. Maas considered strangling Goldstein but could see no money in it. Worse, it would probably mean he'd lose his desk, so, after casting a brutal scowl at the Gaelic Goldstein, Maas stalked out of the room.

Chapter 11

"The death penalty is unevenly applied," Hero declared as Maas passed the young broker on his way back to his desk.

"Yeah, unevenly applied to rapists and murderers," Chisel Chest said, his $399 polished, black leather French shoes resting on his desk.

"No, unevenly applies to blacks, Hispanics and other minorities," the wiry Hero countered, gesturing wildly with his bony, nicotine-stained fingers as he emphasized his point.

"Look around the city, Hero, Whites are the minority in LA," Chisel Chest said. "Besides, tell me something that isn't unevenly applied in this world."

After a moment's reflection, Hero replied, "Death."

Just as Maas sat at his desk, Nickel's voice boomed out of the intercom on every phone, "Meeting in five minutes."

Not wanting to cold call for just five minutes, Maas called his father. In five minutes he had learned that the cleaning lady/cook did not do a very good job dusting, that she under cooked his carrots, and that his dad's car was making a funny sound when he turned corners. Nickel appeared at his office door and Maas said goodbye to his dad, promising to call the cleaning lady to ask her to clean a little more diligently and to cook his father's carrots longer. The car he could do nothing about, save ask his dad to let him know how much it was to fix. Then Maas would send a check to pay for part or all of the repair.

"Boatin' Bob! Put the damn phone down! We're trying to have a meeting here!" Nickel, tall, dark and with a greed for money that rivaled Midas was, Maas had always thought, the quintessential brokerage firm owner.

"I hope everybody had a great weekend," Nickel said, his voice carrying over the dozens of brokers slouched or reclining in their chairs at the 10 rows of chipped and worn gray desks. "I hope you're all ready to get back to work. This is a fantastic time for us with some excellent markets. There's a drought in the Midwest that's front page in the *Wall Street Journal.*" He waved the newspaper like a banner. "I'll have Genius make copies for everyone. Fax it to your clients. Use it to open new accounts. I'd buy out to September or even December. Buy the grains with both hands and both feet.

"In the energies, I think crude oil is almost done, but if the Mid-East flares up again, we could be looking at a nice spike there. But I'd get out of crude if any of your clients are in profit right now."

Maas smirked. The odds of any of their clients being in profit enough to cover the 35 percent commission the firm usually charged was a far smaller chance than that of any broker ever beating him consistently at car roulette—at least until Goldstein opened his yap.

"The Saudi's are threatening to cut production again and Iran is making threats, both of which will drive the price of crude up at least a few dollars, but not enough to risk leaving any profits on the table," Nickel warned. "The possibility of a war will also push up the metals, especially gold. Lastly, there's major flooding in South America, which has crippled their grain crop. If the grain is ruined, they won't have any feed for the cattle. So look for a run up in the grains, and then in cattle and the meats."

"War, famine and flood," the Doctor whispered, "great news for us. The only thing missing is the fourth horseman of the apocalypse; pestilence."

"Knowing my luck," Maas whispered, "a plague will strike and I still won't have any clients to take advantage of any of it."

Chisel Chest asked, "Isn't Death the fourth horseman of the apocalypse?"

"Nope," Hero said. "My wife's the fourth horseman."

"I also have the phone records from last week," Nickel

announced. "Some of you are making more than a thousand calls a week." Thin cheers from some of the brokers. "Good work, keep it up, but many of you may as well stay home and play with yourselves."

A few brokers laughed.

"Right, laugh while the grinders make all the money. In the long run, the grinder always wins."

Hero whispered, "In the long run, we're all dead."

"You think about death way too much," Chisel Chest whispered.

Hero shrugged. "I'm Russian."

"The more you call, the more accounts you open and the more money you make," Nickel said. "It's that simple. I can't believe we have to hold contests to get you guys to work." Nickel's face grew solemn as he adopted the tone of a kindly uncle who fears his favorite nephew is squandering his life. Forcing sincerity into his voice, he said, "You guys have a golden opportunity here. Don't waste it. Make hay while the sun shines. These markets are moving. They're in the news and you can make a ton of money. Don't waste time. Get your ass in your chair, put your head down and dial. I don't know about you guys, but I'm never satisfied with what I have. I always want more: a bigger house, a nicer car, finer food—"

"A hotter wife," Lost Wages, a broker who frequented Las Vegas, called out.

"That's right," Nickel agreed over the brokers's laughter. "I've traded up four times and each time for the better. But the key is, I'm never satisfied; my wife knows that"—more laughter—"and neither should you be. Keep striving for more: more accounts, more commissions, more money, and a better life."

"Not exactly a recipe for a happy or content life," Chisel Chest whispered.

"If Nickel wasn't always trying for more, he'd shrivel up and blow away," the Doctor replied in a whisper.

"Drives like his made the United States what it is: the largest, most dynamic economy on Earth," Hussein said, a young broker who had just started at the firm after his recent arrival from Jordan.

Maas wished he had a tenth of Nickel's passion and drive, if not for money, women and the finer things in life, then at least for something.

"So let's open some new accounts and make some money. Get

to work!"

Maas liked Nickel's closing sentiment but he had trouble mustering the courage to confront the tedious and depressing process of endlessly calling strangers, people who had been called a dozen times before, to ask them to invest in commodities. The rejections outnumbered the nibbles, let alone the bites, a thousand, sometimes two thousand to one. It was doubly hard to get back to work as he watched most of the other brokers stream outside for a cancer stick or a coffee from the gourmet shop on the first floor. Even so, his work ethic, debts and fear of Cooper won out against his frustration after only a brief struggle. He liked his ribs just the way they were. Maas picked up the phone and dialed the number on the top card of a four-inch stack of lead cards on his desk.

"Hello, B and A Roofing," a hard, toneless female voice answered. Most of the leads were small business owners.

"Hello, is Ron there?" Maas asked, reading the name off the card and sounding as if he and Ron had met in kindergarten and been tight ever since.

"Ron Baker?"

"Yeah."

"Junior or Senior?"

"Senior." A guess: senior could be retired, senile or, worse, dead. You could open retired and often senile, but never dead, although there were always heirs.

"He's not here right now."

"Then give me Junior, please. Haven't talked with him in too long."

There was a second's pause and then, "Just a minute." The pause said reluctance. The words said suspicion. Maas could be Junior's tenth cold call this morning.

Maas leaned back and fiddled with the card as he watched John Ford lob crumpled up order slips over Leadless Joe's head and into a garbage can 20 feet away. Ford made three in a row, but missed the fourth as Maas waited on hold.

"Hello?"

"Hello, Ron, this is Anthony Maas over at the El Dorado Trading Corporation. Do you remember me?"

"Ah, no."

"Well, we spoke—" (pause to show that he was not in a hurry

nor that it was his hundredth cold call of the past hour) "—just briefly, at the end of the last quarter about crude oil."

"I don't remember that."

"That's nothing to be ashamed of," Maas said, leaning forward and forcing a cool enthusiasm backed with immense confidence into his voice. "I forget half the people I talk to every day."

"Is this an investment call?"

"Damn right, Ron."

"I'm not interested."

"I wouldn't be either; you haven't heard what I have to tell you."

"I have work to do."

"Remember that crude we talked about a few months ago?"

"Not really." Maas could hear Ron shuffling papers in the background. He was losing the roofing czar.

"I do. I put all my clients into crude way back before that trouble started in the Middle East and you know how much my clients have pulled out of crude the past few days? Do you know how much crude went up?"

"No."

"Well, it's no secret. It's in all the newspapers."

"How much did it go up?" The papers stopped rustling. The hook was in.

"A lot, a whole lot. Not enough to retire on, but enough to finance a nice trip to Europe or buy the wife a new mink coat."

"Exactly how much are we talking about?" The hook bit deeper.

"An extremely nice return, but I'm looking at the grains right now."

"What about the crude?"

Maas stood. It was easier to sound confident, successful and rich standing than hunched over a phone. "I'm sorry to say you missed the crude rally, but it's nothing to beat yourself up over. It's not the end of the world. You can still get in on the grain rally. For $5,000 you can open an account and we can pick up a September wheat call option. You'll have all the way out to September for wheat to go up. Every dollar move up in the price of wheat returns $5,000 per contract back into your pocket."

"If it increases a dollar, I double my money?"

"You're getting the hang of this fast. Yes, just one dollar

doubles your money. Wheat's sitting at," Maas glanced up at the big board, "$2.65 right now for the September contract. All it would have to do is move to $3.65 over the next five months and you would double your money. In my experience, a dollar move is pretty common. In fact, a $2 move isn't exactly uncommon. Even a $3 move isn't as rare as a vegetarian on a Wyoming cattle ranch."

"What about those margin calls I've heard about?"

"Can't happen with an option contract. You'll have that in writing in the account papers. You can read it for yourself. Margin calls are only for futures and the accounts I open are not allowed to trade futures. I wasn't born stupid and I won't let any of my clients do such a dumb thing as trade futures. With options, the most you can lose is the amount you put up, no more, and that's only in the very worst case."

"Five thousand, huh?"

"Yes sir, just some play money."

"Five thousand ain't play money to me."

The dial tone assailed Maas's ear.

Chapter 12

"No luck?" The Doctor asked as he reached for the next lead card off the six-inch stack on his desk.

"Tons of it," Maas replied, "all bad."

The roofing pitch was the longest Maas made for the next hour. He made a hundred calls resulting in "No thanks," "Buzz off" and other less polite tag lines or just hang ups. At least those who hung up immediately saved Maas time. He could call the next lead that much sooner.

"You've never traded commodities before," he heard Detective Kovic tell a potential client. "Well, that's nothing to be ashamed of. I can walk you through it. Have no fear. I'll be with you every step of the way. That's my job. That's what I'm here for, but most importantly, I'm here to tell you when to sell. I make sure greed doesn't get in the way of your good sense, and it's easy to get greedy in these markets that can produce a 100 percent return in a week."

Maas wished he could sound as smooth, polished and relaxed as Kovic. You had to be born with it. They could say exactly the same words, yet Kovic would open an account and Maas would not. On his worst day, Kovic sounded 10 times more convincing than Maas on his best day. Worse, Maas's best days seemed fewer and farther between with each passing month. No wonder Nickel wanted his desk. Maas knew that most months he was near the top of the list for the number of phone calls made, yet he did not open nearly as many accounts as some of the brokers who were at the bottom, such as Leadless Joe, whose work ethic rivaled that of the laziest of sybarites. Maas shook his head at the injustice of it all. He had to devise a way out of the financial hole in which he found himself; cold calling certainly wasn't the way out.

"Any hot tips?" Maas asked moments later as he perched on the corner of Eddie Weinstein's cluttered desk.

Eddie glanced up from *The Racing Form* he was surreptitiously studying by holding it just beneath the top of his desk so Nickel wouldn't scream at him to get back to work. "Possibly," he said. Brokering was Eddie's dream job. It was not because he loved being a broker but because, since the markets in Chicago and New York closed by 1 p.m. Pacific Time, Eddie could make it to Santa Anita or Hollywood Park without missing much, if any, of the racing day. For Eddie loved horses above all other creatures on earth.

"Sorry to hear about your mom."

"Did you see my card in the lunch room? Thanks for the donation."

"Yeah. Nice note."

Maas nodded, staving off thoughts of his mom that threatened to bring tears to his eyes. Before they could, he admitted, "I'm in need of some cash, fast."

"I heard your car roulette syndicate got broken up."

"By that bastard Goldstein."

"Never trust the Irish. They're all blarney and drinking Guinness until they stick a dirk between your shoulder blades: ruthless, competitive bastards who are about as reliable as a Saran wrap condom. Exhibit one: *Irish Lady* last week at Pimlico."

"What happened?"

"I'm trying to work here," Hussein, the fierce young Jordanian broker hissed from the next desk, covering his phone's mouthpiece with his hand.

"Then stop yakking to us," Eddie spat back.

Maas and Eddie glared back at Hussein, who met their glares and then after a suitable pause returned to cold calling.

"An old buddy of mine put together a syndicate to buy *Irish Lady* in a claiming race," Eddie whispered. "She was in a $25,000 claiming race and he had a buyer interested in her for $35,000. He figured she was good for a quick turnover. I agreed and put a little in, just to keep my hand in, you know."

"Who'd pay 35 gs when you could get the horse for 25 in the claiming race?"

"Some Asian tycoon. Not the sharpest pencil in the drawer. Didn't know a gelding from a colt."

"How'd he become a tycoon then?"

Eddie shrugged. "Even a deaf, dumb and blind squirrel finds a nut once in a while; an inheritance or a lucky lottery ticket? Anyway, my buddy cobbles together a syndicate for the $25,000 and puts up the money to buy the filly in the claiming race. *Irish Lady* romps home easy and wins. The previous owner gets the purse, right?"

"That's what the rules say."

"And the second the horse was deemed a starter, me and the syndicate own *Irish Lady*."

"Sounds good all around."

"Not so good. The horse up and died not two strides past the finish line."

"You've got to be kidding."

"Not on your life. I lost five gs on that little deal. Today I get this." Eddie handed Maas a slip of paper.

"A bill?"

"For the removal and disposal of one horse carcass from the fine, upstanding and businesslike gentlemen who administer Pimlico Racetrack and the Maryland Jockey Club."

"*Irish Lady*?"

"The earthly remains thereof."

"Some people have no luck," Maas said, even as he told himself that at least his luck had not gotten as bad as Eddie's, let alone that of *Irish Lady*. He handed the bill back to Eddie. "About the races this afternoon…"

"A few possibles, but nothing I'd bet the farm on."

"I need three grand, fast."

Eddie peered at the racing bettor's bible, flipping pages between races and, after much intense consideration, shook his head. "Nothing today. Next week I might have something good at 20-to-1, but I'm not promising a lottery winner; the odds may change to single digits by then."

"I was hoping I could clear a few grand this week."

"You sound desperate, Mouse," Eddie said, concern in his voice. "Remember, always bet with your head, not above it."

"I'll keep it in mind," Maas said and returned to his desk to stare at his phone before he forced himself to start dialing. He had to keep his job. In the next 150 calls he reached two people who asked for application materials to be sent to them. Even with such uncommon success, he still felt exhausted and defeated by life, but he kept calling.

Chapter 13

With nothing promising in the equine world and car roulette demolished, Maas decided his LA nightclub owner would be awake by now and called him. As he rubbed his side, idly wondering whether you really could cold call with broken ribs, Maas recommended that the client sell his crude oil contract.

"You're up a nice 33 percent after commission and fees, Ken," Maas explained. "With the return, we can put you into two wheat contracts."

"But it might go up a little more," the nightclub owner said.

"You've got a nice profit already after being in the market for only six weeks, and the grains look fantastic," Maas said, trying to avoid pleading. "Let's get out of crude while the getting out's good."

"But crude's been going up."

"I know it's been going up, Ken. I've been sitting here watching it every day, but you have to know when to get out. That's what I'm here for; to tell you when to get out. Sure as ten dimes make a dollar, now's the time. Crude won't go up forever. Nothing does. You've made money. Let's get out."

"Maybe just another few cents."

Maas shook his head, exasperated. He had heard the same argument a thousand times; clients always wanted to stay in to make just a little more.

It took another 20 tension-filled minutes for Maas to convince Ken to sell. Maas finally transferred him to the trading room, grabbed the sell and buy tickets he had optimistically scribbled up before he placed the call, and ran out from his row of desks, down the aisle to the front of the room, past the big board, and into the trading room. He handed the tickets to Frank, who, already talking with the client on the phone, verified the trades while a computer recorded Ken's consent for use in arbitration if he ever complained.

Finished, the balding Frank hung up, time stamped the tickets in a machine with a metallic clang, and handed them down the counter to the younger Al, who, taking a break from reading Torah, already had the Chicago exchange on the phone to place the orders. The trading room was often quiet but the clerks still had to be at their phones in case trades came in, so Al studied Talmud and Torah when the markets were slow.

"An easy $650," Frank said, citing the broker's commission on the trade as he turned and grinned up at Maas.

"Yeah, easy," Maas said, slumping against the counter across the room.

In his fifties, Frank had worked as a financial advisor at a big investment company but had been downsized in the late eighties. Now he was an order room clerk, about a staircase worth of steps down in the financial world, but all he could get at his age, even with his several decades of experience.

"Why don't clients ever want to sell?" Maas asked. "If they're losing, they want to hold on in case the market reverses, and if they're in the black, they want just a little bit more profit. In the long run, they all lose."

"A lot of our clients are small-business owners," Peter observed. A bespectacled, math Ph.D. who had failed to find a teaching position, he wrote articles analyzing the markets when the phones weren't ringing. "A psych prof I had said everyone thinks the world should be just, so maybe our clients have more money than they ever thought they would have and want to make the world a little more just by losing some of it."

"No one wants to lose money," Frank said.

"Then explain Las Vegas," Peter countered.

"Maybe a few grand just isn't much money to some of our clients," Al said, having placed Maas's trades. "They get into commodities for the really big play."

"They all sign paperwork saying it's money they can afford to lose," Maas agreed. "Imagine selling any other investment that way; put money in our bank and the worst that can happen is that you might lose all your money."

"So, get a client to invest *all* their money, then they'll be willing to take a small profit for fear of losing it all," Peter suggested, laughing. "And make sure they feel like they deserved all the money they've made."

"I'm a broker, not a shrink." With a sigh, Maas turned his attention to the stack of newspapers that towered beside Frank. When Frank started at the then new firm, he had a lot of down time because El Dorado had few brokers and even fewer trades. Frank convinced Nickel to subscribe to 37 newspapers from across North America so Frank could find articles to copy to support the brokers' pitches. Now that the firm had more brokers and far more trades, Frank was often weeks behind on his reading, as evidenced by the teetering stack of newspapers on the floor beside him. Maas asked, "Anything happening in the world these days?"

"A few civil wars, some teetering governments, several juicy sex scandals, and the Fed trying to decide whether to lower interest rates again," Frank replied.

"Same old, same old, then."

Frank leaned back in his chair, stretched and, looking out the big windows that overlooked the golf course and Beverly Hills, asked, "I wonder how high a fly can fly."

Daniel Molina strode in, sat in his corner chair and, frowning, asked, "What did you just ask?"

Young and bright, Danny had been a broker but had tired of trading clients in and out of positions when he knew it would be better to hold a position or stay out of the market entirely and wait to buy when the market presented a more favorable entry point. Brokers, however, only made money when their clients traded. They could not let clients wait to buy or their clients would squander their speculative dollars somewhere else. Too honest or maybe not enough of a gambler to be a successful broker, Danny had transitioned to working in the trading room, first as a clerk and then as *de facto* supervisor.

"There's a fly out there on the window," Frank said, pointing.

"I just wondered how high a fly could fly."

"Busy day, huh?" Maas asked, rising from his perch on the counter. He had better get back to his desk while he still had a desk. "Wish I got paid to read newspapers and wonder how high flies fly."

"But we don't make $60,000 a month," Peter said.

Maas grinned, thinking back to a golden month his first year at El Dorado when he had opened 15 accounts and wrote more than $100,000 in business, taking home a tidy $61,329.42. He was famous at El Dorado for that long ago golden month. Those were the days. He did not know why, but those days were long gone. He prayed they were not gone forever.

"I shall return," Frank said, standing and hurrying out the doorway.

"Did you hear about that woman suing us?" Danny, his briefcase on his lap, asked Maas, who shook his head. Hispanic, Danny had black hair, a short, neat mustache and a compact, muscular build. "She opened an account, but she was handicapped and on a fixed income from State Disability."

"Not the best of clients," Maas observed, knowing he should return to cold calling but deciding he could reward himself with a break after earning $650. Maybe that would appease Nickel for a little while.

Peter, armed with three rolled up file folders taped together to form a bat, and Al, drawing from a pile of crumpled up tickets in the corner, commenced batting practice.

Danny explained, "The broker told her he wasn't sure if he could open the account, since Compliance might kick it back."

Thwack! Peter hit a paper ball across the room, striking the wall just above Danny's head. Danny glanced at the ball where it came to rest on the floor beside him and then continued, "But she was going on vacation and really wanted to get into copper. She thought it was going to go through the roof the next day because of some big telecommunications order from China."

"Copper in telephone lines?"

"Maybe they haven't heard of fiber optics over in China, yet."

Thwack! Peter sent a line drive into one of the windows.

"But the broker—" Danny continued.

"Who?"

"The Doctor."

"A stand up guy."

"None more upstanding. He took the order to buy five copper contracts on the condition the account was approved. Of course, it wasn't."

"She wasn't an acceptable client. With a fixed income from disability, she couldn't afford to lose the money. We did the right thing."

"Anybody got the bathroom key?" Frank asked when he reappeared at the doorway looking worried as he shifted his weight from foot to foot.

No one did.

"Aren't there two keys?" Maas asked.

"One went missing the first day," Danny said. "A broker probably took it."

A few weeks before, the building's management, tired of the janitors having to clean up paper towels and other debris scattered around the 14th-floor men's room, had issued two keys to El Dorado and two to the law firm that occupied the rest of the floor. Maas had wondered how the management thought the issuance of keys to El Dorado would end the mess in the men's room if, as the management had suggested none too subtly to Nickel, the brokers were responsible for the mess.

"You could go to another floor and use their john," Al suggested.

"No can do," Peter reported. "I tried yesterday. They're all locked."

"Great. What do we do if we have to take a leak?" Frank asked, grave concern in his voice.

"Wait outside the men's room for one of the lawyers to appear with the key and follow him in," Peter suggested. "And try to look manly."

"I gotta find a bathroom," Frank announced and scurried from the room.

"Try the women's!" Danny called. "They didn't lock theirs!"

Thwack! A paper ball sailed over Maas's shoulder into a cabinet door.

"Anyway," Danny said, "copper shot up the next day. The client—who wasn't a client—said we didn't open her account because we had already bought her copper contracts and we were keeping the profit."

Thwack!

"How much profit?" Maas asked Danny.

"None." Frustration showed in Danny's perpetually calm voice. "We didn't buy the contracts because the account was rejected."

"Okay, but how much would she have made?"

"She claims $60,000, but copper only went up $800 a contract. So with five contracts, it was only four grand."

"Maybe her disability is an inability to add," Peter suggested between pitches.

"Nickel and Vinny are going to risk a million-dollar company to rip some woman off for four grand?" Maas asked, shaking his head, then ducking to avoid an errant line drive. "Did you win?"

"No, we settled. She got $2,500."

"Settled?! She had no case."

"Women always win arbitration. They get before the panel and say the broker sweet talked them. They claim they didn't know what was going on."

"Foreigners are the same," Al added, having stopped pitching to return to his Torah. "They go before the arbitration panel and claim they didn't understand the agreement because they don't speak English, and they win."

"Then it turns out they're ninth-generation Americans," Peter said. "Their ancestor was the navigator on the *Mayflower*."

"Women are the worst, though," Danny said. "Women always win."

Chapter 14

Two days later Vinny walked over to Maas and handed him an account booklet.

"Good work, Mouse," the owner said, his low, gravelly voice barely audible above the cacophony of 40 brokers' voices in the bullpen.

"You sure it's mine?" Maas asked as he checked that it had his broker number on it. It did.

"If you don't want it, I know 40 guys who'd spot me a fine dinner and an old bottle of Grand Cru for it."

"I'll keep it," Maas quickly responded even as he read the client's name in the booklet and realized it was from one of the two people he had sent account paperwork to a few days before.

"I spoke with Nickel," Vinny said. "You can keep the desk another couple of weeks."

Maas was relieved and shocked. Clients almost never opened an account after only one phone call, let alone by taking the initiative themselves. At least four or five calls were usually required. Brokers always had to call and call and call to cajole, coax and promise the contents of Fort Knox in six weeks for a $10 initial investment before anyone opened an account. But here was some guy who owned a hot tub company in Alaska of all places who was just bursting to get into the wheat market. A one-call close and Maas had not even known it at the time; akin to sleeping through the best sex you ever had.

"Got any Alaska leads?" Leadless Joe asked as he leaned over the chest-high partition between the rows of desks.

"A few," Maas said, checking the new account paperwork to ensure that Compliance wouldn't kick it back. He always checked, but there was always an error: a missing area code, a signature on the wrong line or a box unchecked. Always something. Easy to fix with a phone call, but every call to a client before putting him in the market risked a change of mind, and a change of mind was always a change to deciding not to invest in commodities.

"Can I have 'em?" Leadless asked, eyeing the salmon-colored Alaska leads on Maas's desk.

"I want 'em."

"You always say all leads are the same. I have a bunch of North Dakota leads," Leadless Joe pleaded, offering a stack of yellow lead cards.

"There can't be more than a hundred people in both the Dakotas worth enough to invest in commodities."

"Are you kidding? All those rich farmers out there: five grand's nothing to them."

"Go away."

"The Dakotas are like black gold."

"Then you mine 'em. Go away."

"My style doesn't work well with farmers."

"Your style doesn't work well with humans. Go away."

Leadless Joe sighed. "Do you know who that is?" He pointed at a new, young broker across the room huddled over a phone delivering a pitch.

"Go away."

Leadless moved on to the new broker.

Danny strolled over and said, "Hey, Mouse, did you take the last account book from the cabinet when you sent out that paperwork a few days ago?"

Danny was quick to catch errors on tickets, saving brokers, including Maas, thousands of dollars, so Maas leaned back and considered the question. "No. There was a whole stack, because I remember thinking, 'If I could open every one of these, I could give them all to Old Man Winter to churn and burn; I'd make a couple of million on my half of the commissions alone.'"

Danny laughed. "You'd never have to work again."

"What's up?"

"Somebody stole the rest of them."

"Why would somebody steal a bunch of blank account booklets?"

"For kindling?" Danny suggested, shrugging as he wandered back to the trading room. Maas returned to his paperwork, hoping this client would live long and send in plenty of big checks. It was not to be.

The next day the Alaskan hot tub mogul called before they had made even a single trade to close his account.

"What changed since yesterday?" Maas asked, desperate to save his new account and his desk.

"My wife found out about it."

"When was the last time she asked you which type of bread to buy?"

"Huh?"

"Does she consult you on everything she buys?"

"No, but—"

"When this wheat returns a nice profit, she's going to be very, very happy with you. Think of the nice things you can get her: jewelry, a trip, maybe a new car. All you have to do is trust your initial judgment and go ahead with this investment."

Silence reigned on the other end of the line.

Maas tapped his shoe on the carpet to give his mind something to concentrate on other than the account that hung in the balance. He must not say a word. He could not sound desperate or the hot tub king was lost. He had to open this account.

"I just don't know," the Alaskan said.

Maas had won. The Alaskan was asking for him to support his desire to buy the wheat, to take the chance, to roll the dice. Even as Maas opened his mouth to provide just the support the Alaskan craved, Maas heard a woman's voice in the background, "Harold, just tell him you don't want to do it. Tell them to send your check back, today!"

"Are you are at home, Harry?" Maas asked, desperately hoping against all evidence to the contrary.

"Yeah," the Alaskan admitted, defeat in his voice.

"We can do this. You and I can make a bundle on wheat. I'm

buying wheat with both hands for all of my clients, even the one's whose wives are reluctant."

"I can't."

It was over. They talked for another 10 minutes, but Maas knew it was over. Wives always trumped brokers, especially if the wife was in the same room as the client. Brokers couldn't withhold sex from their clients; wive's could, besides being able to nag every second of every day.

Maas angrily tossed the Alaskan's account paperwork in the bottom drawer of his desk. Maas would call him back in six months and maybe then, if they could avoid the wife, he could open the hot-tub Czar and make some money. For now, Maas had no new account. Soon, he would have no desk, no income and no life.

Chapter 15

"How do, Mouse?" a familiar voice from above asked as Maas sat slumped in his chair.

Maas looked up, startled. Coop loomed above him.

"Just wanted to express my sympathy at your recent loss," the loan shark said, smiling in his loathsome way.

"Thanks, Coop."

"Lindhe suggested, and I concurred, that we give you a break for a week on your vig."

Maas's shock deepened. "That's really kind of you, Coop."

"We'll just tack the interest payment on to what you owe me."

"Thanks, Coop," Maas said, trying to keep the sarcasm out of his voice. "Thanks a lot."

"Besides that, I just wanted to check in. Mary was kind enough to let me into the inner sanctum. I have business relationships with many of the fine brokers in here. A very nice lady. Lindhe's out there talking with her about some art exhibit his wife dragged him to last night."

Maas just stared up at Coop.

"Ah, one other piece of news." Coop stared down at Maas. "I hear you may be losing your position here at El Dorado."

"I won't."

"You better not," Coop said with a smile that had menace behind every yellowed tooth. "I'll hear from you Friday?"

Maas managed a nod. It was only when Coop was walking away that Maas noticed Lindhe had arrived, dapper in a charcoal suit, as always.

"How do you sleep at night working with the likes of him?" Maas asked. As soon as he said it, he feared he had gone too far. Luckily, Cooper didn't overhear his impertinent question.

"I sleep rather well. Thank you for asking." Lindhe took two steps down the row of desks, then stopped, turned and asked, "Do you know why?"

Maas shook his head, not really caring why but deciding politeness might be crucial to his continued health. Cooper might not take kindly to anyone being rude to his accountant.

"I earned an MBA from Stanford and couldn't find a job. The last place I interviewed was with a credit card company. They charged 22 percent interest per annum. Cooper charges 10 percent a week, but it's the same principle. People borrow money. They pay interest based on their level of risk. Cooper lends to some rather unreliable people—no offense—hence the high rates. It's a basic business principal. Bank of America, Chase Manhattan, Citibank; all the big financial institutions follow the same principal. Call them and ask. They'll agree with me."

"They don't break anyone's ribs."

"No, they don't, but Cooper doesn't force anyone into bankruptcy. He'll never take your house, your car and everything you have. Which is worse, Mr. Maas, losing your house and everything you've worked for or a broken rib as an incentive to meet your financial obligations? Cooper believes in you, and all his clients. He believes you can make your payments, if you apply yourself. The big banks don't have faith in anyone. They just take everything you have and write off the loss. Cooper always gives you a chance. He never writes off a loss; never."

Lindhe turned, his smooth, precise motion reminding Maas of a Marine guard, and called over his shoulder, "See you Friday, Mr. Maas. Good day and the best of luck to you in all your endeavors."

Maas rested his head in his hands. How did his life get so bad, so fast?

"Did you get my message?" Genius asked. Even without looking, Maas could sense Genius shifting his weight from foot to foot like a second-grader recently arrived in the principal's office.

Genius worked in customer service, making a mockery of the name for anyone unfortunate enough to reach him.

"What message?" Maas asked, not lifting his head to bother to look up at the customer service clerk. Genius's voice was grating enough without having to look at his face, which reminded Maas of an ill-bred weasel.

"I asked the Doctor to give you a message."

"He didn't mention anything," Maas said, his voice flat as he finally looked up at Genius.

"Well," Genius said, glancing back at the Doctor who was working the phone, "I guess he didn't hear me."

"Maybe you should make sure people hear you when you give them a message."

"I didn't want to disturb him."

"Then you should have waited and given him the message when he wasn't busy."

Genius nodded and turned to walk away, digesting this bit of advice as if it was the first step on the path to complete knowledge of all things.

"Genius," Maas called, wondering how the clerk could be so stupid, yet still manage to breath. "Didn't you have something to tell me?"

"No, I told the Doctor."

"I know, but he didn't tell me," Maas explained slowly, fighting to control his temper. "What was the message?"

Genius looked over at the Doctor and then back at Maas. "I couldn't read the zip code on your new account, so I was supposed to ask you for it."

"The Alaskan?"

"Yeah."

"Don't worry about it. The account's DOA." Maas bent over his desk to get back to work. Better to get back up on the horse as soon as possible before the pain of the loss sank in and immobilized him, robbing him of his selling voice. He had to open another account today or he wouldn't have a desk.

Genius said, "That's too bad. I got the zip code, so the account's all ready, and she seemed like such a nice lady."

"Who was a nice lady?" Maas demanded, his head flicking up to eye Genius with suspicion.

"Well," Genius stammered, sensing the tension in Maas's body, "since you were cold calling and the Doctor was making a trade, I just called the client and his wife gave me their zip code." Genius grinned, waiting for his expected thank you for taking the trouble to actually call a client himself.

"You talked to my Alaskan's wife?" Maas asked, his voice like ice.

"Yes, she was very nice. She asked all sorts of questions about the firm, about commodities and about you."

"How nice." Maas carefully and slowly set a lead card back down on his desk and, standing, looked up into the dim eyes of Genius. His voice a low whisper, Maas said, "If you ever call, contact, meet, email, fax, conduct an ESP conversation with or, in any way, manner or form contact any of my clients, past, present or future, their wives, parents, children, siblings, pets, aunts, uncles, grandparents, friends or cousins, I will rip your right arm off and beat you to death with it. Understood?"

"But Ron in Compliance asked me to get the zip code," Genius said, eyes wide as he backed away from the furious Maas.

"Never, ever contact any of my clients. Understood?"

"But sometimes—"

"Never! Ever! Understood?!"

Genius swallowed, looked around for support, only to see brokers grinning at the brow beating he was receiving from the normally quiet and reserved Mouse. "Yes, I understand," Genius whimpered and rushed back to his desk in terror.

Chapter 16

"Fire Genius," Maas demanded as he strode into Nickel's office moments later.

Without looking up from his computer screen or changing his expression, Nickel asked, "What happened?"

"He deep sixed my Alaska account. He talked to the wife."

Nickel shook his head as he scribbled something he had seen on the screen onto a yellow pad. "I'm getting ready for the show." He gave a weekly commodities talk on the local business television channel. It led to a healthy telephone response in leads that translated into a few new accounts that easily covered the fee the station charged for Nickel to make his thinly disguised sales pitch on the air.

"He's done this before," Maas said. "He screwed Ford. He screwed Goldstein and he blew Eddie out of two accounts. One client called up and Genius actually told him Eddie was at the track."

"Eddie shouldn't have been at the track." Nickel looked up from his pad and took in Maas's furious demeanor. "I'll look into it, okay?" He stared back at the wheat chart on his computer.

"What's there to look into? He's a moron."

"He does a good job in customer service."

"He's a disaster waiting to happen. He's a disaster that's already happened—a dozen times."

Nickel stopped what he was doing and looked up at Maas across the barren top of his polished oak desk. "Mouse, we need someone to sit in customer service and take calls. Genius will sit there and answer calls. Anyone smarter and they get bored and wander around, missing calls or they quit or want a raise every other month until they're making twice as much as you."

"He costs us money."

"Brokers cost me money. I just settled for $2,500 with some woman the Doctor didn't even open. You cost me money not opening accounts."

"Genius just cost us an account."

"Probably would have blown out on verification anyway. I'm not going to fire him and risk getting someone worse."

"I doubt that's possible."

"I'll let you interview the next batch of illiterate know-it-alls who apply for our next opening. After that, you'll think Genius is a genius." Pointing at Maas, Nickel said with severe intensity, "Look. You focus on opening accounts and let me worry about the staff. You open five, 10 accounts, then I'll let you come in here and bitch about Genius. Until then, get the hell out there and pound the phone or you won't have a phone to pound."

Chapter 17

"My daughter wants to be a social worker," Detective Kovic told Leadless Joe as Maas stalked past them on his way back to his desk.

"Oh, God no," Leadless Joe exclaimed. "Everyone has enough problems of their own. You'd have to be nuts to want to deal with anyone else's problems."

"She likes people."

"She's a kid. How well can she know people? Once you get to know them, you realize 99 percent of people drive you nuts after 10 seconds' worth of conversation."

"What do you suggest?"

"Tell her to get a job that never deals with people." Leadless Joe leaned back, stared at the ceiling a moment and said, "Study rocks; that would be a nice, quiet job. Just rocks. No people; no headaches."

As he reached his desk, anger surged through Maas's body. Looking over at Nickel sitting in his high-backed leather chair, Maas realized that he loathed the man, even though they had got along well for so many years. Maas fought against the anger because he knew he had to get into a new mind-set. He had to sound confident on the phone. Then he would be able to sell, open accounts, make money, and keep his desk. But he had tried to do that for months and had failed. He just could not concentrate and sell with worries about debts and Cooper hanging over his head every second of every day, now compounded by the threat of losing his desk and the pall cast by the loss of his mother and worries about his father. He needed a breathing space, a chance to recover and start brokering anew or maybe somewhere else, far from Nickel and his ungrateful, loathsome company.

Maas sat back in his chair. His eyes fell on a yellowed photograph taped to the wall beside his phone. It showed a young Tony Maas, 18 years old, beside a metal sculpture. The uncle of a fellow student had bought Maas's sculpture. Sharon had arranged the sale, negotiating the price like a pro. She was a born salesman. The amount had shocked Maas. Someone was actually willing to pay for his art and not just a pittance: $2,500. New wonderful possibilities had opened up. He would become an artist, marry Sharon and he would sculpt while she sold his work. It would be like a dream. But with college the following year, it turned out to be just a dream and his first—and last—sale.

Life had turned out far different than he had ever thought it could, let alone would. He wanted to be a sculptor; he was a broker. He had wanted to tour Europe; he went to university. He had wanted to marry Sharon; he married Maria. He had never wanted kids; he had three. If he had a child, he had preferred a son; he had three girls. He loved his wife and his girls, but....but maybe Sharon was right; maybe he should return to sculpting. Maybe he still had the gift. He glanced down at his hands, wondering if he could still mold clay, shape metal and chisel marble into beautiful creations. He did not know; no one did.

Life was full of choices and every choice had its trade-offs. Unfortunately, you never had enough information about the choices, their costs and benefits. You never even knew what the choices and options really were most of the time. Life was like playing poker blindfolded: you didn't know what cards you held or what was in the pot, let alone what cards the other players held. Maas's eyes strayed back to the photograph of his younger self and his sculpture. Choices....

"Hey, Doctor, should I pitch corn?" a new broker asked.

"Maybe," the Doctor replied. "It should move up, but God only knows when."

Maas closed his eyes, remembering the camping trip, the sleeping bag, the first time, and the sale of his sculpture, and then his talk with Sharon on the porch in Vancouver. It had been as if they had never been apart; as if they were still in high school. She had taken him right back to his dreams.

He tried to remember what Sharon had said. She offered to try to sell his sculptures. Had she offered more? He thought so, but he could not be certain. What had she said? He remembered a word here, a phrase there, but mostly just the sensations of a happy time and a familiar, comfortable warmth between them that verged on being something much more. It had all been in stark contrast to the gloom of that day.

As he daydreamed, he imagined life with her: enlivening conversations; trips to Europe to tour art galleries; and long evenings in bed having great fun. She was still so beautiful, filling him with passion and lust. He would love to spend a lifetime with her, starting with several weeks in bed together, although that would just be the beginning.

"Do you have the rest room key?" Frank asked, his voice low and desperate.

Jarred out of his reverie, Maas replied, "Nope."

Frank sighed and hurried on to the next broker.

"Somebody would steal the big board if they could get it out the door," Detective Kovic observed.

"They could turn it sideways," Eddie suggested, tilting his head to better scope out the possibilities.

"Don't get much for big boards on the black market any more," O'Reilly née Goldstein said, firing a used lead card in a graceful arc over three rows of desks toward a garbage can in the front corner of the room. The card fluttered to the carpet inches short of its target. "Everyone just uses computers these days; less dramatic than the big board but more efficient, especially for short-sighted brokers in the back row."

"Much more re-sale value in leads," Leadless Joe said. "I know I'd pay top dollar for some decent leads. I never get any that are worth a damn florin."

"I'd take the computers," the Doctor said.

"Please don't give the thief any ideas," Danny pleaded as he crossed from the trading room toward Nickel's office. "We've lost enough lead cards, blank tickets and account booklets to open accounts for half of Missouri. I don't want to start losing computers."

"A thief in our midst," the Bond Lady called from the back of the room, covering her phone's mouthpiece so her client wouldn't hear her. "A case for Mrs. Marple!"

"Marple?" Eddie yelled back, contempt in his voice. "We need Sid Halley."

"Who?"

"One of Dick Francis' detective jockeys."

"Or Sam Spade," the Doctor suggested.

"Mickey Spillane would solve it," someone yelled. "With his fists."

Turning from thoughts of fictional detectives and real thieves, Maas knew that he did not want to leave Maria and the girls, yet he did not want to stay in the life he had now. He was stuck. He was in a rut so deep he could see no way to change course, let alone to climb out. He should have married Sharon all those years ago, yet if he had, he would have missed out on the many good years with Maria and would never have had his girls. Worse, if he had married Sharon, would the passion have faded just as it had with Maria? He feared so, yet he had felt the same old passion fluttering on the fringes of their talk in Vancouver.

If he started a new life with Sharon, it would have just as many bills as the old one and he would have no job, especially if he took up sculpting. Unless she managed to sell his pieces, how would they pay their bills? Maybe he could get a brokerage job in Victoria, but then he would be right back where he was now. Every life needed money, whether he was a broker or sculptor, stayed with Maria or pursued a life with Sharon. As Nickel was fond of quoting, "Money is coined liberty." Without money, you might as well be in chains. Maas had no idea where Nickel had picked up the quote from Dostoevsky, maybe from Hero or a temp clerk working on a doctorate in Russian literature, but Maas agreed wholeheartedly with the Russian master.

Maria had been his wife for so long they seemed natural together, but natural didn't produce much spark, let alone heat any more. The lively and sometimes contentious conversations about politics, life and the world they had when they were dating had tapered off over the years. Now they knew almost everything the other believed, thought or felt. Finding new things to talk about was getting more difficult with each passing year.

And then there were the girls. Maas loved them dearly, but knew he had been drifting into his own world as his work deteriorated and his money worries mounted. If things continued as they were, the girls would notice they had an unhappy father, if they hadn't noticed already. Was it better to have an absent, happy father or a present, unhappy father?

"The problem is, you can't take it back if you're wrong," Hero told Chisel Chest as they sauntered past Maas's row of desks.

"Can you take back the murder they committed to get the death penalty?" Chisel Chest asked as they continued their long-running argument.

"Not much in life you can take back," Hero lamented.

"And if you can take it back, you always need a damn receipt, which you threw out weeks before."

"No such thing as a receipt for a man's life."

Turning back to his own troubles, Maas snorted at novels and movies that offered such clear choices; the beautiful, ambitious, young mistress and the old, staid wife who was such a nagging witch you wondered why the couple got married in the first place. Or the couple who were fighting so much it made the choice of whether to leave and start a new life with the other woman or man as easy as the choice of whether to leave a burning building. Fiction never dealt with the reality of a couple with a pretty good life, a decent relationship and nice children, but with the husband or wife just wanting more—or at least a chance at something a little better. That was the tough choice and the far more common dilemma.

Maas loved Maria. He would hate to hurt her, but he just was not getting much out of their relationship anymore. He feared that she felt the same, but how could he ever raise the issue? If he was wrong, it would devastate her. They had not drifted apart, just drifted to a point where they were going through life together without any passion for their jobs, their lives or for each other. He wanted that passion back, at least for something. He had felt that passion for the first time in a long time when Sharon stepped out onto the porch. It had not just been lust; it had been far more than that. When he talked with Sharon, everything was exciting and interesting. A talk on a porch with Maria would have been boring, not only for him but for Maria, too. He wanted, needed to feel passion again.

Maas stared at the phone. Could a phone call hurt? Just one call? Just to see what Sharon had been thinking about when they talked on the porch? Had she been thinking what he had been thinking? Felt what he had felt? He thought she had, but he wanted to know, to be certain. Was she still thinking about their talk, about them, as he was?

He did not plan to leave Maria, run away to Victoria and join Sharon in her art gallery, but it would be nice at least for a brief time to consider. He would set down the load of responsibilities on his shoulders to take a little time to contemplate a dream. He had not dreamed in a long time and, as he thought about sculpting and Sharon, he liked dreaming again—he loved dreaming again.

He picked up the phone. He paused. Choices. He hit the buttons to call Sharon.

What was he doing? Did he really want to devote his life to sculpting? Was he any good? He had only sold one piece in his life, decades ago. What about Maria? What about Robyn, Coralea and Malena? What would his father think? What was he doing? Would Sharon think he was nuts for calling to talk about—

"Hello?" Sharon's voice had taken on a husky edge over the years, hinting at experience with an intensely sensual element.

"Sharon," Maas blurted out. He had to relax. He was just calling an old friend. That was all; just a phone call to an old friend.

"Tony?"

"Yeah, it's me."

"I'm so glad you called. How are you?"

"I'm getting by, and you?"

"Good."

There was an awkward pause. What did he want to say? To ask? He should have thought this through before he called.

"How was your flight home?"

"Good."

"How's your dad?"

"At war with the woman I hired to help him cook and clean, but I think they might both survive."

"Your family?"

"Fine, thanks."

The silence descended again. What was he doing?

"Are you going to come up and see my gallery?"

"I'd love to," Maas replied, then quickly added, "but I don't know if I can get away anytime soon."

"It's only a few hours on the plane, and I'd love to spend more time with you, Tony."

"That would be great, Sharon," Maas said, his gaze resting on the photo of his younger self. He may as well ask. He might never talk to, let alone see her again. What did he have to lose? "By the way, speaking of your gallery, I just wanted to ask...not that it's a big deal but, and I won't be offended if you say no, but...were you serious when you....well....when you said you thought you could sell my sculptures?"

"Of course. Do you have any completed pieces?"

"Well, no, not right at the moment."

"I'd love to see what you're working on."

"Truth be told, I'm not really working on anything right now. It'd take me a while to even get started on something. It's been so long and I don't know if I have the time. I have to work pretty hard to keep the bill collectors away and now I need to help my dad out some."

"Paul said he was laid off?"

"They closed his plant, gave him a year's salary and padlocked the gates. It wasn't nearly enough to retire on and at his age he wasn't able to find another job, other than minimum-wage stuff. Then he had a heart operation and lost the minimum-wage job he had at a big-box store."

"Money's always necessary, but the amount you have is never sufficient."

"True." Sharon had always had a way with words; short and succinct, but often subtly complex and laden with insight.

Silence again. He liked just having her on the phone. He absentmindedly flicked through a stack of lead cards on his desk, his mind racing through a thousand possibilities. "How's the art gallery business?"

"Not bad. Same problem; not enough money to pay all the bills. Other than that, I had some trouble with a supplier from Greece who thought he could shortchange me. The chauvinistic porker thought because I was a woman he could take me for a ride, but a morning in court showed him the error of his ways."

"You were in court?"

"Just small claims. The judge took a liking to me."

"I can't blame him."

"It helped being a woman who occasionally attracts some male attention, but I had the case won before we even went in there. It was as clear as glass. This guy sold me a..."

Maas did not hear the rest of her story because it hit him; the solution. It was far better than trying to make money cold calling, given his current long, deep slump and it was far better than trying to make money sculpting, given the odds of becoming an overnight sculpting sensation. If it worked, he could do whatever he wanted for the first time in his life.

"Are you interested in making some money, Sharon?" Maas asked, interrupting the story of her case against the porcine Greek art exporter. "No, not some money," Maas added before she could answer, "a lot of money. Enough for you to take a dozen buying trips to Europe every year and make your gallery the toast of the west coast, and for me to quit brokering, pay off my debts and sculpt full time."

Chapter 18

That evening Maria let the oversized T-shirt she slept in drop down over her body, Maas came up behind her, reached down and gently massaged her legs.

"Ahhhhhhhh," she said, letting the sound out in a long pent-up sigh. "That feels heavenly."

He worked his way up, slowly, until he was massaging her thighs, then her cheeks, and finally, working his hands under the T-shirt, her back.

"I don't know what I've been doing, but my back has really been sore," she said, hanging her head forward, eyes closed, as she revelled in the massage. "That feels wonderful."

"Anytime."

"Did you talk to your dad today?"

"Yeah. He says Anne—the lady who comes in—undercooks his chicken."

"Your father is of the carbonated school of cooking; it isn't cooked unless it's the color of carbon."

"Maybe she'll open up whole new culinary vistas for him."

"I found the hundred you put in my purse for the week, thanks. Any word on your desk?"

"Genius blew out my new account, so I'm not sure if the extension Vinny told me about is still in effect."

"I wouldn't ask; might remind Nickel about his deadline."

Maas nodded. He kissed her neck and moved closer to her, feeling her warmth through his clothes. He did not want to think about work, his dad or anything—save one thing.

"Would you like to spend the evening together?" He was supposed to call Sharon, but maybe he should forget about the whole thing.

"Ah, that's a very tempting offer, but I'm pretty beat. How about tomorrow night?"

He managed to smile as she spun around and hugged him.

"Sure," he said. He was used to delay in their love life. To Maria, tomorrow was always better than tonight. She liked to plan her lovemaking in advance. The odds, he knew, were that she would stay up reading for hours, even though she claimed exhaustion. He knew from long experience there was no way to change her mind, so he said with a forced smile, "I have a quick call to make anyway."

"Who to?" she asked, half interested as she released him from her hug and headed for the bathroom.

"A client on the edge I want to try and keep from falling off my run sheet."

"Oh, I just remembered, could you drop off some clothes at the cleaners tomorrow?"

"Sure."

Maas kissed her on the neck from behind in the bathroom as she prepared to brush her teeth and then walked down the hall to his office. He closed the door and sat down at his cluttered desk. He glanced at the bill pile, picked up a recent addition from Robyn for new shoes—didn't she already have 25 pairs?—put the bill back and picked up the phone.

He hesitated. Did he want to do this? He had not explained his idea to Sharon at work for fear of being overheard, so he had promised to call her tonight. But now, after an afternoon's consideration, he wondered if he was out of his mind. Was his life so bad that he was even contemplating what he was about to propose to Sharon?

He sighed. After a moment's reflection, he concluded that it wouldn't hurt to see what Sharon thought of his idea. He had always valued her judgment. If she rejected it, then it was a stupid idea and he would drop it. She probably would.

After she answered, Sharon said, "I hardly got any work done this afternoon wondering about your scheme. I'd love to be able to pay off some bills and recruit some new artists."

There was a pause as Maas sorted out how best to explain his idea. He had gone over the details repeatedly that afternoon as he halfheartedly cold called. His idea was simple yet foolproof, or at least he thought—prayed—it was. If it wasn't, he had no business involving Sharon.

"First, you need to open an account with my firm."

"A commodities account?" Sharon asked, her interest in the scheme vanishing. "Commodities are risky, aren't they?"

"There's an old joke: how do you make a million dollars in commodities?"

"How?"

"Start with five million."

Sharon laughed but then, serious again, said, "I don't have five million to start with, let alone to lose. Business has been a little slower than I let on."

"I'm sorry to hear that. I hope it's not too bad."

"If it gets much worse, I'll be looking for another line of work."

"I didn't know it was that bad, but maybe we can make some money together."

"I hope so. I need to raise some money so I can wine and dine some popular artists and convince them to exhibit at my gallery."

"I thought there were a million artists looking for exhibit space."

"There are, but only a very few can actually sell anything and keep a gallery afloat. The demand for those few artists is as intense as the bidding for a newly discovered Monet."

"With my plan, a lot depends on how much money we can raise."

"I might be able to contribute some money, but I can't afford to lose any."

"That's the beauty of it; there's almost no chance we can lose. I have about $60,000 I can take out of my IRA."

"There are penalties if you do that, aren't there? Are you sure you want to do that?"

"Certain. The way things are going I'll never be able to retire anyway. I'll also see about a second mortgage, which should get us another $40,000 or so. That's about $100,000 total."

"You're really serious about this."

"Absolutely."

"What are we going to do with the money?"

"Buy S&P contracts."

"S&P?"

"Standard and Poor's; the stock market index. I want you to open an account and buy S&P futures contracts. The margin for each contract is about $30,000, so with my money we can afford three. How much money can you raise?"

"I don't know, maybe $100,000, maybe a little more, $110,000, but why don't you just open an account?"

"That'd give us about $210,000, seven contracts. We should be able to clear maybe $600,000."

"Three-hundred thousand would keep my gallery afloat for a long time."

"With a bit of luck, there won't be any risk at all."

"And if we're unlucky?"

"We get our money back and try again."

"Since when do they give you your money back if you lose in the commodities market?"

"They do if you play it my way."

"What's your way?"

"You open the account."

"You're the commodities expert. I don't know a thing about commodities."

"But if you open the account, if we lose, we get our money back."

"What difference does it make who opens the account?"

"Because you're a woman."

"Thanks for noticing, but I still don't see—"

"My firm, like every other commodity brokerage, lives in constant fear of going to arbitration with a female client."

"Why?"

"Women always win."

"Always?"

"Always." Maybe not always, but he was selling the scheme, not testifying before the NFA. "Women appear before the arbitration panel and, eyes wet with tears, plead that the big, bad, mean broker led them down the garden path with sweet words and the promise of a vault full of gold at the end."

"Are you leading me down the garden path?"

"Of course not," Maas said, straightening in his chair. "You know me, Sharon."

"I knew you, Tony."

"You still know me. If we didn't know each other so well, I wouldn't be telling you about this."

"So we pool our money and I open an account with your firm. Then what?"

"You buy seven S&P contracts a few days before the Fed is set to make an interest rate announcement. Then the S&P will either blip up, in which case we sell and make a tidy profit and try it again, or it goes down and you lodge a complaint."

"A complaint about what?"

"You claim you didn't place an order to buy the S&P contracts. You say you placed an order to sell them."

"I don't have any contracts to sell."

"You can buy or sell futures contracts. If you sell them, you want the S&P to go down. Then you buy the contracts at a lower price to cover the contracts you sold earlier at the higher price. You pocket the difference in price as profit. It's just reversing the buying and selling process; you sell, then buy."

"If the market goes against us, what do I complain about? I can't blame a broker for the big, bad, mean market."

"You claim the trading room clerk took your order wrong."

"Don't you sign your order or something?"

"No, they tape it."

"The tape will show I said to buy the contracts."

"Not if I unplug the machine just before you place your order."

"I'll still lose at arbitration. I'm no actress."

"You won't."

"Why?"

"Because you're a woman and the firm is supposed to tape all orders. The panel will not look kindly upon El Dorado if they can't produce the tape. The arbitration panel will assume they're hiding the tape because they screwed up. They'll settle even before it reaches arbitration."

"I still think I'll lose."

"When you're opening the account and being taped you just

need to sound flustered. You make little gaffs and sound as if you don't know what you're doing. Then, if we lose, you complain. Any arbitration panel will give you the benefit of the doubt, especially since you're female."

"They let you place your own orders right away?"

"If you have experience."

"I don't have any experience with commodities."

"Your $210,000 is going to convince them to bend the rules. That'll work in our favor at arbitration, even though firms don't have written rules for their internal workings."

"Why not?"

"So they can never be shown to have broken their own rules."

"How can they bend rules that don't exist?"

"They exist; they just aren't written down. El Dorado requires trading experience to open an account if you want to trade without a broker."

"But I don't have any experience."

"You say you have some. At arbitration you say your ex-husband traded commodities. He handled it all, but you thought that counted."

"I don't have any records to support that claim."

"You say it was years ago, you don't have any records, and since your husband handled it all, you can't even remember the firm's name."

"Sounds like you have this all worked out."

"I've been thinking about it for a lot of years."

"That's a strange way to spend your time."

"I daydream about different ways someone might rip off a brokerage firm. It helps me be on the lookout for anyone trying to rip me off as a broker."

"Is this illegal, Tony?"

"If we place winning trades it isn't."

"If we place losing trades and complain?"

"If you claim your order was taken wrong, who's to say it wasn't?"

"You and I will know it wasn't."

"I'm not going to tell anyone, are you?"

"We could go to jail for this."

"I've thought it through from every angle and I can't see any way we can get caught. We might, in the worst case, suffer a loss, but it will be impossible to prove we've done anything wrong." Maas sounded more confident than he had sounded cold calling in months. He had to sell his scheme. He had not realized until now how important it was to him. He had to make some money to get a breathing space free from financial pressure to think about Maria and the girls, sculpting, Sharon, and his life. This had to work, and to work, he needed Sharon. Taking a deep breath, he asked, "What do you think?"

Chapter 19

"I don't know, Tony. It sounds shaky and criminal and…."

"If we buy the S&P and it goes up, it'll be a legal trade."

"And if it goes down, whose money are we stealing?"

"El Dorado."

"Which means who?"

"The company."

"Who owns the company?"

"My bosses."

"So we'll be stealing from them."

"Neither owner will miss it much. Nickel has a palatial place in Pacific Palisades and Vinny has a house down in Manhattan Beach and a penthouse on Maui. They'll write off the loss as a business expense, cajole the brokers into working a little harder, and make it all back in a month; a week if the markets are moving."

They fell silent.

"Look, Sharon, I work in a firm that has a million a month running through it, like storm water down a drainpipe. I used to make a pile of money, but I can't anymore. I don't have it in me anymore, whatever 'it' is. I want more of my share. I helped build El Dorado."

"No one earns what they think they should."

"I've made Nickel and Vinny ten times what we might take from them."

"It's still not right."

"What they're doing to me isn't right."

"They're running a small business. They have to keep costs down."

"They're doing more than just keeping costs down."

"What are they doing to you? They gave you a job and allowed you to make a nice living for years."

"They're taking my desk."

Sharon paused, shocked. "You just lost your mother and they're firing you?"

"I don't make enough money for them anymore," Maas said, and thought, 'or for me.' He closed his eyes, rubbing them with his hand. He had an ache directly behind his eyes. "Nickel and Vinny sit in their offices raking in money. For every dollar the brokers write in commission, the company takes 60 percent. Not bad for two guys who 10 years ago were furniture salesmen. If Nickel hadn't been fired for getting into a fight with a Persian rug salesman, they'd still be selling furniture."

"A Persian who sold rugs or a guy who sold Persian rugs?"

"I never found out. Either way, now they have 40 brokers pounding phones for them 30 hours a week and they're both making a fortune."

"I'm sure they worked hard to build their business."

"I worked hard, too. Years arriving at 5 a.m. Years cold calling. Years shoveling commissions through the company while Nickel and Vinny took their 60 percent cut from every shovelful. I made them a sizable chunk of their fortunes and now Nickel's going to toss me out in favor of some young broker who's never made the firm a penny. Does hard work count for nothing?"

"I've worked 80-hour weeks to build my art gallery and now I'm barely able to afford even my part-time assistant. Soon I'll have to let her go and if I'm not at the gallery, it won't be open, which means no sales. So no weekends off for me, ever, let alone any vacations."

"My grandfather would be appalled at the state of the world today. He lived through the Great Depression, digging trenches for pipelines by hand for Imperial Oil. Each man had a number on their back and the site boss stood above them along the trench. If anyone straightened up to stretch or stopped digging for even a second, the boss called out the number pinned to the back of that man's shirt. The man climbed out of the trench, collected his pay calculated down to the minute and the next man in the long line of men waiting outside the gate to work had a number pinned to his back. He slid down into the trench to dig until he stopped to wipe the sweat from his brow."

"Sounds like slavery, not capitalism."

"My grandfather prided himself on being able to dig for 12 hours a day. He kept his job through the worst of the Depression until he was promoted to pipe fitter and eventually saved enough to buy a farm and start a side business building houses."

"Not the most humane system if the weak starve."

"My grandfather supported a free market, but he also supported Tommy Douglas."

"Who?"

"Premier of Saskatchewan. He started universal health care, unemployment insurance, pensions, and aid to the poor."

"Probably on the backs of small business owners, like me."

"No, he kept taxes low and maintained a balanced provincial budget. Douglas realized that if society was to survive, the working man had to be given a better deal. His ideas spread around the world."

"They spread a little too well. My taxes hit 43 percent my best year to pay for all the social programs; almost didn't pay to stay open."

"That's too much, but we do need a safety net. Anyone can get sick, lose a job or have some disaster."

"Politicians have a habit of expanding the safety net until it encourages people to fail."

"Not any more. Now most of the safety net is gone and most people don't even seem to care. Big business has convinced people it's a good thing if they manage their own retirement and health care, as if it's a basic freedom. The reality is business has shifted the majority of the cost of pensions and medical care onto the backs of the workers. Companies cut pension benefits to retirees and employees, breaking contracts, and nothing happens. If the workers suddenly started working only seven hours a day instead of eight there would be hell to pay, but companies can do whatever they want, changing deals they made with workers years before.

They have the lawyers and the government in their pocket."

"My pockets aren't big enough to hold anyone, let alone the government, but if my competition cuts costs, I better cut or I'm going to go broke."

"If it's a capitalist economy, poorly run companies should go broke. If I can't pay my mortgage or credit card balances, I can't just tell the banks I'm unilaterally changing the terms because otherwise I'll go broke."

"I can't change the terms of my business loans, and if I don't raise some money soon, my gallery will be one of the businesses going broke. I've worked hard to make it a success; I'm sure just as hard as you did at the brokerage firm."

Maas fell silent. "I don't want your gallery to go broke. I'm just tired...tired of big companies rigging things in their favor."

"My gallery is far from being a big company. I run my gallery well, it's just that the city increased the business tax, the Feds raised the minimum wage and the city council approved a new mall on the other side of town. Cut our foot traffic in half. Running a business is hard, Tony, and a lot of the things that affect your future are beyond your control."

"That's why you need the social safety net, whether you're a worker or a business owner."

"I just wish my taxes were a little lower to provide that safety net."

"If companies shared more of the profits with their employees, there'd be less need for a safety net. It's in the owner's best interest to keep workers happy or the system won't last."

"I'm good to my employee."

"I'm sure you are, but some owners aren't. CEOs take millions in pay while their companies lose money and they lay off employees. It has to change."

"I doubt it will anytime soon."

"It's changed before. We went from robber barons in the 1800s to the 1930s New Deal and the 1960s Great Society. Then we had too much protection for workers. The economy stagnated in the 1970s and everyone suffered, so regulations and protections for workers were cut back to allow more growth in the 1980s and 1990s."

"Sounds like you're for both sides: workers and business."

"Depends on the times."

"Trouble is the times are always changing."

"That's why it's crucial that in a democracy no one stays in power too long. If we have a president heading one way, he can't ruin the country too much before he's replaced by someone who wants to go in another direction."

"But if we have a great leader, we lose out." She fell silent. "I don't think any of this talk is going to help keep my gallery afloat."

"Let alone allow me time to sculpt."

"I just don't know if this scheme of yours is the thing to do."

"I've tried everything else I can think of."

"So have I." Sharon paused. "Why do you need money?"

"My father needs help, my girls spend money like there's a limitless supply, and I have a pile of debts."

"I have debts stretching from here to Europe and back. Why do you need the money so much? Why now?"

Maas paused and rubbed his eyes, trying to ease the ache behind them. "My mom just died in her garden doing what she loved and I haven't done what I love in 20 years."

"What do you love, Tony?"

"Sculpting."

"Then sculpt. You don't need much money to do that."

"It's not....I need..."

"Why do you need the money, Tony?"

"Because they're kicking me out."

"You could find another job."

"At my age? I'd be lucky to find a job paying half what I make now."

"You didn't look old to me."

"Neither did you." Maas stopped rubbing his eyes.

"Why do you need the money, Tony?"

Maas sat thinking.

"Why, Tony? Why now?"

Maas sighed. "Because I met you again."

Chapter 20

At 9 a.m. Monday morning Maas stretched after three hours of cold calling. Sharon had not given him an answer yet, leaving him in suspense, although it hadn't been a bad morning. He had reached a couple of semi-interested potential clients—hope sprang eternal.

"You asked me for a hot tip," Eddie whispered as he crouched beside Maas's desk. Eddie glanced around to make sure no one was eavesdropping. "*Low Budget Thrill* in the third at Santa Anita this afternoon."

"Odds?"

"Ten to one. Not phenomenal, but a nice return on your investment dollar."

"Put me down for C-note."

"Will do."

Maas called to check on his dad, who had settled into an apparently workable, if simmering hostility with his cook/cleaner, and then started cold calling again. He got off one good pitch and even sent out account paperwork to the interested party before Nickel announced their weekly meeting would start in five minutes. Doggedly soldiering on, Maas kept calling, but got 26 almost instantaneous hang ups, answering machines or wrong numbers before Nickel emerged from his office.

"Hey, Mouse, want in the basketball pool?" Mac asked. The tanned, ex-baseball pitcher crouched next to Maas. Even crouched,

Mac's head was still six inches above Maas's head.

"No thanks."

"Two hundred in the pot; should hit five bills easy."

"Basketball's a crap shoot. They may as well just play the last two minutes."

"You always play the football pool."

"Every second counts in football."

Mac shook his head and slid along the row of desks to pitch his pool to the Doctor.

"Come on, Mac, I'm trying to hold a meeting here," Nickel yelled.

Under Nickel's baleful gaze, Mac scurried along the rows of desks, distributing his pool forms to each broker before retreating to his desk in the back corner.

Maas barely listened to the meeting. He'd heard it all before: Nickel analyzed the markets, chided the brokers to make more calls and then read the numbers. The top brokers topped $20,000 in commissions for the month, while Maas struggled at a measly $1,900 in the realm of the just-licensed, the terminally lazy and the otherwise interested. Nickel reiterated his standard pitch that it was a great time to be in commodities and finished with, "Now, let's get to work!" Several brokers, including the low-performing Ford, Goldstein and Weinstein, immediately headed outside for a cancer stick.

"Whoever has the bathroom keys, return them now!" Nickel barked over the intercom from his office. "You're not the only one who has to take a leak."

Maas sat at his desk thinking about $1,900. With the company's 60 percent cut, it meant a little less than $800 in his pocket for two week's work. He had made that much in one hour back when he started. Now he was down with horse-racing addicted Eddie; Goldstein, who spent most of his time managing rock bands; and Ford, who God only knew where he went after every pay day. The larger Ford's pay check, the more AWOL days he had post pay day. Once Ford had opened a whale who had run up $19,000 in commissions in two weeks, giving Ford the largest check of his life, almost $8,000. He vanished for two months. Nickel gave the whale to Old Man Winter to churn and burn. When Ford reappeared, Nickel screamed at him and threatened to fire him, but didn't, praying his prodigal broker would luck out and open another whale.

Maas overheard Chisel Chest, in a break from his death penalty debate with Hero, tell a client, "I think soybeans could go up or they could go down, but it's a great time to buy 'em with both hands." B.S. worked for some brokers. If you had the gift, you had the gift and clients would open if you said as little as 'hello.'

Maas sighed and prayed Sharon would agree to his scheme, as he slid a pile of white lead cards across his desk. Hunched over them, he started to pound the phone. After several dozen rejections and one good pitch that resulted in Maas faxing a wheat chart to a potential client, Danny appeared at his elbow.

"What's up?" Maas asked, throwing himself back in his chair and resting a shoe on the edge of his desk.

"Got you your rest room key." Danny handed Maas a key.

"Didn't know I rated my own key."

"Both keys went missing, so I had a key made for everyone in the office."

"If both keys are missing, how'd you make copies?"

"Slipped a secretary at the law firm 20 bucks and she borrowed her boss's key."

"Hope it was the company's 20 bucks."

"It wasn't mine."

"Always the font of wisdom and practicality," Maas said, slipping the key onto his key chain. "Too bad you didn't get the key to the women's rest room. Now that would have been interesting with this crowd of degenerates."

"I have to keep the brokers out of jail or I'll be out of a job," Danny said. Dropping his voice, he said, "Sorry to hear Nickel wants your desk. I could tell Genius and Kathy on the QT to transfer the most promising leads from Nickel's show to you."

Maas smiled, touched by Danny's attempt to help. "Thanks, but Nickel dropped me from the television call-in list months ago. I'll get hot again. I just need some time and some luck."

Danny nodded, said, "Good luck, then," and leaned against the partition behind Maas's desk. After a moment's reflection, he said, "Wish I could figure out who's stealing our supplies. It could be anyone; a broker, staff, the cleaning crew, anyone."

"Speaking of mysteries, have you seen my bird dog, Mouse?" Old Man Winter asked as he leaned over the partition in front of

Maas's desk.

"Isn't that him?" Maas asked, nodding toward a young man bent over a phone at the desk next to Winter's making call after call.

"That's one of 'em," Winter said, his fingers tapping on the partition's glass top as he scanned the bullpen for his quarry. "The other one's slipped his leash." He sighed and, shaking his head, added, "Have to call out the bloodhounds, I'm afraid."

"You lose another one?" the Doctor asked, feigning heartfelt disbelief.

"Yeah, couldn't stand the frigid temperatures with Old Man Winter," Maas said with mock sadness.

"Few can," Leadless Joe called from Ford's desk where he was taking the opportunity of Ford's absence to search through the stacks of lead cards on Ford's desk for what he hoped would be some prime leads. How he could tell a good lead from a bad lead without calling the number on the card was beyond Maas's comprehension.

"My bird dog said he was going to lunch and he never came back," Winter explained. "I should have guessed something was up when he took his briefcase and the photograph of his girlfriend with him."

"It wasn't his girlfriend," Detective Kovic said between cold calls. "It was his sister."

"A framed 8 by 10 glossy of his sister?" Winter asked, screwing up his face in horror. "Freaky. Maybe it's good he left, probably an ax murderer or, worse, an NFA auditor." The NFA, National Futures Association, oversees and regulates commodities trading in the United States.

Winter sat back at his desk, nearest the trading room. Being within spitting distance of the trading room meant he could run his tickets in to Frank faster than anyone else, taking less time away from cold calling. It made him that much more efficient and helped make him consistently one of the firm's top earners. Maas watched Winter return to work. Winter had taken his 30-second break to relax, but now once again he was all business. He worked from 6 a.m. until 1:30 p.m. with dedicated and unbroken regularity. Hard work sometimes did pay.

"I want my fill!" Martinez's voice roared from the trading room. "I'm entitled!"

"No, you're not!" Al's voice roared back. Apparently Al was taking a break from studying Torah.

"It went through my limit!"

"No, it didn't!"

"It did! Look at the fucking chart!"

Sam, from his office across the way, and Danny, from the rear of the bullpen where he had just completed his bathroom key distribution, raced for the trading room. Fights were not uncommon at El Dorado and the police had been summoned for one particularly violent scuffle, although they had not arrested anyone. When the attacking broker explained what the other broker had said about his wife, the officer said he would have attacked the son-of-a-bitch himself. Emotions ran high when money was at stake and money was always at stake at El Dorado.

The shouting in the trading room diminished to a low, emotion-filled rumble as Maas heard Sam and Danny attempt to calm the high-strung Martinez and the even-tempered Al. Maas marveled at Martinez as Sam escorted the fiery broker back to his desk. Maas and Maria had invited Martinez and his wife over for dinner once. Martinez was an actor and, contrary to his intense and volatile persona at the firm, was quiet and soft-spoken at the dinner. It was then that Maas realized that at work Martinez played a part; the hard-driving broker. He played it well, to the tune of a six-figure income.

The scuffle over, Maas returned to dialing. He had a possible client interested from the previous week and wanted to call him back to try to close the deal. He had to pay his father's cook, Coop, the credit card companies, and the mortgage. Maybe his luck would turn, especially if Sharon agreed to his proposal. Then maybe he would get a chance to sculpt, if he could remember how.

Chapter 21

"I closed a new account," Maas announced in triumph late one morning to Nickel.

"Great," Nickel said, without looking up from the chart he was analyzing.

Maas wanted to savor proving to the ungrateful owner that he could still open accounts, but Nickel wasn't playing his part in Maas's imagined scene at all. He was barely paying attention. As Maas debated what to say or do, Nickel said, "You can keep your desk for another month."

Maas thought Nickel just might be starting to value him again. Then the owner added, "The new guy's opened four accounts using the phone in the storage room. You may as well stay where you are until the next batch of new brokers wannabes comes through."

As he walked back to his desk, Maas felt the pressure ease, although in a life in which the days seemed to pass with an appalling sameness, he knew a month could pass with alarming speed.

The next morning Maas transferred the client to Frank, grabbed the ticket he had scribbled and ran down the aisle into the trading room, handing the ticket to Frank amidst his piles of newspapers. The clerk taped the client's confirmation of the order, time stamped the ticket and handed it to Peter, who placed the order at the CBOT—Chicago Board of Trade.

"A trade? Congrats," Danny said, leaning back to stretch.

"And a new client to boot," Maas said.

"Fantastic. We knew you could do it."

"Thanks. Where's Al?"

"He quit."

"Quit?" Maas asked, incredulous.

"Gone with the wind," Frank said.

"He said Martinez yelled at him once too often," Danny explained.

"How could Nickel let him go?"

"He told Nickel he wanted another three bucks an hour or he was out of here," Danny said.

"He was worth twice that," Maas said. "He could handle four phones at once and he never made errors."

"No way was Nickel going to give him that much of a raise. He isn't named Nickel for nothing."

"Should have been named Penny," Maas agreed. "He wouldn't part with a penny, let alone a nickel to save his own mother."

"You can't exactly be free spending to found a business and grow it into a company this size," Peter said as he handed Maas his yellow copy and slipped the rest of the ticket into a rack beside him. The rack was divided into two columns, futures and options, and subdivided into energies, grains, meats, financials, metals, and softs (coffee, sugar, cocoa, cotton, and orange juice). When the fill came back, Peter would grab the ticket from the appropriate slot, check the order number to ensure it was the right ticket, and then write the fill on it.

Maas asked, "Are they going to hire someone else to place orders?"

"Peter can handle it," Winter said as he came in to hand a trade to Frank, who started to verify it with the client on the phone. "This is nothing compared to advanced nonlinear astro-calculus."

Peter had a doctorate in mathematics but had been unable to find a teaching position, so he ended up as a temp at the firm and accepted when they offered to hire him full time.

"Unless it gets busy," Danny said. "You should come back and work here, Mouse. You can backup Peter."

Maas had started in the trading room when he had been studying for his Series 3. He had been a member of a large class and with more bird dogs than there were free desks, Nickel stuck

Maas in the trading room to help out. Maas enjoyed it, especially the camaraderie with the clerks and their long, absurd conversations about everything from the cruising altitude of flies to the best way to embezzle money, as well as challenging games of paper-ball baseball and attempts to devise practical jokes on each other or on brokers who caused them extra work by making errors.

"That might not be a bad idea," Maas said, trying not to sound overeager. It would be perfect for his scheme with Sharon. He would take her order himself. "It'd keep Nickel off my back about not producing enough." Then after what he hoped appeared to be a thoughtful pause, he added, "but I'd really miss brokering."

"You could work in the trading room in the morning and cold call and manage your accounts in the afternoon," Danny suggested, talking fast as the idea took hold. "Lot of places to call on the West Coast late in the day."

Moments later Maas tried to relax as he walked toward Nickel's office. He had to strike just the right note to convince the owner to hire him for the trading room. Before he reached Nickel's office, Eddie intercepted him.

"Good news, my friend," Eddie said, grinning so wide his cheeks were red. "*Low Budget Thrill* romped home with a good three lengths of open track behind his beautiful tail." Eddie handed Maas a wad of bills. "Even better, he went from 10 to 20-to-1 by post time; some heavy betting on a couple of speed-impaired nags. Here's your winnings, minus my percentage, of course."

"Of course," Maas said. "Thanks for the tip. You're a prince among gamblers." He folded the $1,825 and stuffed it in his pocket. That would keep Coop and the credit card jackals at bay for a while, as well as ensure his father could keep complaining about his cook's underdone chicken for a few more weeks. Maybe his luck was changing: a new account, a long-shot winner at the track, and a possible new job that would make his scheme a little more of a sure thing, not to mention coming with a steady, if modest paycheck. If things kept looking up, maybe he would somehow even get some free time to sculpt.

Nickel sat in his office comparing rates from companies from which to buy business directories. Brokers used the directories to call small businesses to pitch the owners.

"Got a minute?" Maas asked. Even as he stood at the doorway, he flashed back to the meeting when Nickel had wanted to take his desk. Maas set his face in a neutral, even friendly countenance as he buried his anger deep inside.

Nickel waved Maas in, but kept peering at the price lists on his desk.

"I heard Al quit," Maas said, sitting in one of the two padded, leather chairs at Nickel's expansive desk.

"You heard right."

"You think Peter will be able to handle all the tickets?"

"If I were you, I'd worry more about hanging onto your desk than about the trading room. That's my problem. Besides, if Winter or Martinez get hot, Danny will back up Peter."

"Danny's pretty busy already."

"Then Frank can help out."

"He'll be busy verifying trades if Peter's swamped entering them."

Nickel looked across at Maas, his eyes narrow. "Given the crappy state of your run sheet, you can't be worried about whether your trades are going to be placed as fast as they were with Al."

"I'm not."

"Then stop busting my balls and get the hell back to work."

"As you said, my business has been down recently," Maas said, glancing at the carpet and then forcing his gaze up to meet Nickel's stare as he played the supplicant. "I just thought I could use a little steadier income for a while, at least until I get over my mom and...." Maas's voice trailed off.

"And you thought you could take Al's place."

"Just until you find someone new," Maas said quickly. "I just need a little time; a steady income for a while."

"You, Mouse?"

Maas nodded.

Nickel leaned back in his high-backed leather chair and, threading his fingers behind his neck, tilted his head to the side. "It'll take time away from cold calling. You'll lose your desk."

"I'll work in the morning in the trading room and in the afternoon hit the phones. I can call the Mid-West in the early afternoon and the West Coast in the late afternoon."

"Focus on opening accounts. You can do it. You just opened one. What's the problem?"

Maas shook his head. "I don't know. I just can't seem to open accounts anymore."

"That's your problem right there."

Maas looked up, longing to grasp the hope Nickel offered, even as his hatred for the owner seeped around the edges of his hope. Did Nickel know the secret to rescue him from his slump?

"The easiest lay-down in the country wouldn't open with you if you believe you can't open any accounts. Everyone is going to hear that lack of confidence in your voice from the second you say, 'hello.'"

Maas nodded, but felt a monumental let down. He had heard it all before. You had to dress confident, sound confident, be confident to open accounts. The slightest hint of doubt in your voice translated into so many hang ups it would drive a veteran broker to tears.

"If I can just get some steady money coming in, take a bit of time off from cold calling, I can get my mind back in the game."

"Might be a big mistake. You take time off, you lose the edge and it might be gone forever and your desk with it."

"I've already lost my edge, Nickel."

"I know my brokers, Mouse, and you have it. You had it when I hired you and you have it now. I thought a deadline would give you the kick in the ass you needed."

"I just really need a break." Despite their earlier clash, Maas found it hard to dislike the brokerage owner. It was hard to hate someone who believed in you, but the thought of Nickel kicking him out the door after so many productive years loomed dark in the back of Maas's mind, inflaming his hatred for the man.

Nickel frowned and, glancing out the window and then back at Maas, asked, "How long?"

"A few weeks, a month."

"I'll have to give your desk to someone else."

"A new guy can use it until the markets close, while I'm in the trading room, but then I want it back."

Nickel pursed his lips, pondering the suggestion.

"Almost nobody stays after the markets close anyway."

Nickel leaned forward, picking up a wood Mt. Blanc pen with gold accents. He tapped it on his desk's leather blotter. "You certain? Back room clerks are as common as dimes; good brokers are as rare as a winning SuperLotto number."

"I'm sure."

Nickel sighed and said, "Alright. How much?"

"Twenty-five an hour?" Maas suggested, but even with this opening bid his lack of confidence seeped into his voice.

Nickel laughed. "I wouldn't even pay Al that much."

Maas was surprised. He thought the back room clerks were well paid, but every dime the firm paid the clerks, was one less dime in the owners' pockets.

"Twenty?" Maas asked.

"Ten."

"Bird dogs make ten."

"Eleven."

"My nephew makes twelve as a temp."

"Thirteen and you work six to 1 every day."

"Done."

Chapter 22

As Maas drove home, he smiled. His plan was taking shape. Nickel wanted him out; well, to hell with him. Maas would leave, but with a golden parachute of his own making. He had earned Nickel and Vinny a fortune over the years. He had been the top broker for at least a dozen months over the years. Now he would reclaim a little of the profit he had earned them. Now all he had to do was wait for Sharon to call—and say yes. If she said no....

He dreaded the prospect of returning to work the next morning. It seemed even harder to cold call now. His hopes, raised by the new account, the win at the track and the new job in the trading room just seemed like Band-aids on a six-inch bleeding wound. His worries about the future were still there, just as large and painful. Hovering in the background were images of sculptures he longed to create.

Pushing through his depression when he arrived home, Maas took out the garbage, dug the sleeping bags out of the garage for a sleep over Coralea was hosting, and checked the timer on the sprinkler system, which appeared intent on flooding the front yard, while creating a mini-Mojave desert in the backyard.

"Danny was complaining about his silver client again," Maas said during dinner between mouthfuls of Maria's wonderful fajitas, homemade salsa and refried beans.

"The one who won't sell?" Maria asked.

"Yeah. He's Danny's only client and sticks with Danny because even he says Danny is right most of the time, but the client just buys and buys."

"Stupid. I'd listen to Danny."

"Few clients listen to their broker when they recommend selling."

"I would. You always say Danny is the best technical analyst in the country."

After helping clean up after dinner, Maas retreated to his office since he expected the screaming girlish hordes to descend at any moment for Coralea's sleepover.

Deciding that Sharon had passed on his scheme, Maas fought his looming depression by trying to think of someone else who might participate in his scheme. As he leaned back in his swivel chair, resting his feet on the bottom desk drawer, he thought it ironic that he shared a house with four females, yet desperately needed another—one who was unrelated to him. No arbitration panel in the world would award a penny to a broker's wife if she claimed to be unfamiliar with commodities. When he tried to think of another woman, he came up blank. The brokerage business had few females in it and he had spent his adult life in the business. He knew few women.

In Vancouver, Sharon had come as a lust-reviving surprise. He had thought that his capacity to notice, let alone lust after another woman had seriously diminished over the years. Sure, he looked at beautiful women on the street, but he was content with Maria. She was pretty, attentive and, apart from her free spending ways, a good wife.

The phone rang just as Maas heard the front door open and Coralea welcome her invading hordes with squeals of excitement.

"I got it!" Maas reached over with his foot to push the door closed as he answered the phone.

"It's me."

"Sharon," Maas blurted out, surprised.

"I've decided to join you in your little scheme." Her voice was even, calm and, still after so many years, reminded him of the girl who had whispered lustful thoughts in his ear at movie theaters when they were in high school.

"That's great."

"One question."

"Shoot."

"After we make a few hundred grand, are we going to split it 50/50 or....well....we sorta talked about it, but not really, so I just need to ask. It doesn't really matter. I mean it does, but...." After a pause, her words tumbled out in a torrent. "I need the money in any case. I've wracked my brain to think of another way to keep my gallery, but there's no other way, but I have to know—are you going to come up here?"

The question hung on the line awaiting an answer. Maas heard Coralea and her friends yelling, screaming and tramping around the great room, the stereo on even as it competed for noise dominance with the television and computer. He felt as if his whole life had telescoped down to this one question.

"Tony?"

His mind full of a jumble of conflicting thoughts and emotions, Maas said, "I want to sculpt."

"Here or there?"

Maas glanced at the door. The initial rumble of the slumber party was dying down to a distant, even thunder as the girls settled into their various activities. "It would be hard to do any sculpting here."

"I see," Sharon said, her voice even and professional—all business or at least trying to be.

"But I have three kids." And a pretty good life, but he wanted better. He had been raised to always try to do better, to aim higher, to reach for the stars and then to reach for still higher stars. Was his life—brokering, running the girls to school and a dozen activities, and trying to be a good husband—the best he could do? He did not, could not, know....unless he tried something new. But would he lose too much if he did try something new? Would he get as much from sculpting as he got from raising three girls and being with Maria? Would Sharon be as good a wife as Maria? Better? Or would Sharon, somehow, be worse?

Interrupting Maas's thoughts, Sharon said, "I just want to know what I'm getting out of this deal before I get into it."

Maas stared at the floor, pondering the future. The line did not even buzz to fill the silence.

"Tony?"

"Yeah?"

"What's your answer?"

Maas sighed, then, his anger and frustration boiling over, said, his words a torrent, "I'm buried by bills. My girls put so many demands on my time I don't have any time for myself to do much of anything, let alone sculpt. Every vacation we take is to see relatives or go to some volleyball tournament for Robyn or a swim meet for Malena. I'm helping out my father, which takes every last dollar we have and a pile we don't. I don't have any real friends and my wife thinks I'm a commodity broker, period. I have a million chores around the house. I could take two years off and not fix everything that's broken around here. I'm tired, bored and on the verge of giving up. I desperately want to do something I want to do, something that's important to me. I want a point in my life, a goal. I want to ditch it all and sculpt." His anger spent, he sighed. But I love my wife and girls. He did not say it, though. Half of him wanted to leave, but half wanted to stay and try to improve the life he had. It was a special kind of hell to desire two lives, yet only have one life to live.

After a long pause, as Maas attempted to sort through the conflicting emotions locked in tumultuous battle in his head, Sharon said, "Maybe it's just a passing phase."

"I doubt it. It's been building for years. I've just turned into someone I never intended to be."

"Not a sculptor?"

Maas laughed. "Not even close. I seem to be living someone else's life, as if I'm a spectator without any control over what's happening."

"If we pull this scheme off, you'll have control."

"Maybe it'll put my life back on track."

"Does that track lead to sculpting and...to me?"

"I think so."

"Not exactly a ringing endorsement."

"No, but...I don't know about you, but when we met again, I felt something I hadn't felt in decades."

"So did I. We certainly had something in high school."

"When you asked me about sculpting at my mom's funeral, it was the first time someone had asked me about something that was truly important to me in years. It was as if you saw the real me."

After a long pause, she asked, her voice soft and tentative, "What about your kids?"

"They're everything to me. I live my life for them."

"I don't think you should spend your life living for others, even for your children."

"Commitments sneak up on you like a fog over the years, a wisp here, a tendril there until you're enveloped in them. Responsibilities mount and before you know it, you don't have any life of your own left. I was raised to do the right thing, to do my job and to support my wife and family. I did it for Maria and the girls and they're happy, but it didn't leave me with much of a life."

"Maybe we can get your life back."

Maas sighed and, glancing at the photograph of his wife and girls on his desk, said, "If we can pull this thing off, I'd love to give sculpting a try."

"And you and me?"

Maas stared at the photograph. As the din of the slumber party mounted, cresting over the television and stereo, he thought he could do better. At the least, he had to try to do better somehow.

"And me and you," he agreed, but even as he said it, he wondered.

Chapter 23

"Why do I have to learn all this?" Sharon asked one night as she was having trouble keeping straight the difference between initial and maintenance margins. For several weeks Maas had let his household chores languish as he spent time on the phone each night briefing Sharon on the finer points of the S&P market, margins, placing trades, and the various types of orders. "I hate learning this."

"To place trades without a broker, you have to prove that you know how to place orders by yourself," Maas said, staring at the floor between his socked feet as he sat in his home office with the door closed.

"Why don't you just be my broker?"

"If I'm your broker and we go to arbitration and the company loses, guess who pays half the settlement?"

"Why don't we just use another broker, someone you hate?"

"Then the broker and the trading room clerk will check your order."

"No one checks it if I place my own order?"

"That's why it's called a self-directed account. The clerk is supposed to make sure he takes and places the order correctly, but if I unplug the machine and then take the order, it will be your word against the firm's about whether you placed a buy or a sell order."

"So the firm will charge some poor clerk for my 'wrong'

order?"

"Some companies do have a pool at the start of the year. If the errors for the year totals more than the pool, then the clerks get nothing. If the errors are less, then the clerks split the remaining money in the pool at the end of the year."

"And El Dorado?"

"No pool, and no charge to the clerks if they make an error."

"Sounds like your bosses are lenient."

"They might fire a clerk who makes a bunch of mistakes, but most clerks don't make enough to pay for a big error anyway."

"Well, I better call it a night," Sharon announced with a yawn.

"Me, too. I have to be up at 5."

"It's almost 11."

"I don't need much sleep."

"Take care of yourself, Tony," Sharon said, concern clear in her voice even from a thousand miles away. "I like talking with you like this."

"Me, too. I missed you."

"All those years?"

"All those years."

"Why didn't you ever call?"

"I didn't realize I could do better."

Chapter 24

"Who were you talking to?" Maria asked as she put down her novel, *The Pearl*. She was snuggled up in bed, a comforter tight around her.

"I called the cell-phone company about our bill," Maas said, closing the bedroom door and pulling off his T-shirt. "They're open 24 hours. Probably talked to some guy in India. He spoke English so precisely he couldn't have been an American. They knocked 50 bucks off our bill."

"Why?"

"They double billed us for something or other. They haven't got our bill right yet." Maas took off his jeans and slid into bed. Maria's hand reached out under the covers to search for his hand and then held it. She dropped her novel on the floor and snuggled over to him. She pushed the covers down and rested her head on his bare chest. He could smell the shampoo in her hair and felt her warmth as she pressed against him. Maas said, "I also called the gardener. He still hasn't fixed the sprinkler system."

"I asked him to."

"You have to stand over him to make sure he does stuff or it doesn't get done."

"I didn't know that."

"It's no big deal. I tried to call Coralea's piano teacher about the recital, but he was out."

"Thanks for doing all that. I called about getting tickets to see my sister in May, but the wait was so long to get through to the airline I gave up."

"I'll call tomorrow. Their lines aren't as busy during the day."

Her hands massaged his thighs under the covers, then explored further as she pressed herself against him. He ran his hands through her long hair and then massaged her back.

She sat up and leaned over him. They kissed, then he held her tight and kissed her again.

A while later she was on top of him. Then he was inside her and he felt as if they were the only ones in the world. Her head was nestled by his chin, her chest against his, thighs pressed tight against his. He wished they could stay that way forever.

Chapter 25

Maas stood under the big board just behind where Genius and Kathy sat in Customer Service and saw a new, young broker cold calling from his desk. It hurt. He felt old, useless and out of place—and angry. He wanted to haul the young bastard out of his chair and toss him out the window. Or better yet, treat Nickel to a one-way trip to the pavement 13 stories below.

Pushing his anger deep inside, Maas glanced at his watch: 7:55 a.m. The night before he and Sharon had decided they were ready. She would call at 8 a.m.

"Good morning, Mouse," a voice behind him said, even as a heavy hand clamped down on his shoulder like a vice.

Maas turned. Cooper smiled up at him. The loan shark always seemed to be smiling. His accountant, Lindhe, stood behind him, ramrod erect, but somehow at ease.

"Glad to see you at work bright and early," Coop said. "I was a tad concerned over some recent news."

"What news was that, Coop?" Maas asked, feeling more confident facing the loan shark in his own office with plenty of witnesses than he had alone on his front step.

"The news that you're working in the trading room."

"I needed a steady income and a chance to recharge my batteries. Then I can get back to brokering full time and make some real money," Maas explained, leaving out that he might soon lose his desk.

"Well, take my advice, Mouse, don't recharge too long. You know what happens if you recharge a battery too long?"

"Can't say I was ever of an electrical bent."

"It burns out, if you get my meaning. No longer of any use to anyone; useless. You just have to toss it on the trash heap."

Maas nodded, feeling far less secure than he had a moment before.

"That said, we'll bid you good day and hope you get recharged right soon," Cooper said, turning and leading his pilot fish up the hall and out of El Dorado.

Maas watched them go with relief, then turned back to look out over the bullpen. He was absentmindedly rubbing his ribs when a phone in customer service rang. After wiping a layer of nervous sweat from his hands onto his pants, Genius picked it up on the fifth ring. Talking on the phone made Genius nervous: far from the perfect trait for a broker, which is what he dreamed of becoming, if he could ever pass the Series 3 test the Feds required of all would-be brokers.

"El Dorado Trading."

Maas stepped forward, then back. He did not want to appear interested. He was on a break, just hanging out.

"Have you traded commodities before?" Genius asked. After a nervous pause, he circled 'yes' under 'Trading Experience' on the yellow pad of lead sheets on his desk. "How did you hear about us?" He barked the question with such emphasis on the word 'how' that it sounded like a KGB interrogator dealing with a suspected CIA double-agent. Genius continued his interrogation and elicited the caller's name, phone number and address. Then he ordered the hapless caller to "Hold on."

"You could say, 'Please hold while I transfer you to one of our brokers,'" Maas suggested as Genius looked around, his head jerking left and right like a ferret on speed.

Genius scowled for an instant as he tried, apparently, to think. Then he asked Maas with evident confusion, "I have someone who says they've traded before."

"Transfer them to Peter and he'll check to see if they can trade discount." Even Maas knew Genius' job better than Genius did.

"But it's a woman," Genius wailed as if the four horseman of the apocalypse were bearing down on him at a full gallop.

"We take women."

"No, we don't."

"Yes, we do," Maas said patiently. "Most of the brokers don't, except for the Doctor and the Bond Lady, but for self directed accounts, we do."

"Oh." Genius sat, his hand poised over the phone keyboard as he held the receiver at arm's length, as if it was a snake intent on sinking its fangs into him.

"Shouldn't you tell the caller that you're transferring her?"

"Yeah, yeah, right."

Maas strolled back toward the trading room and waited just outside the door. He did not want to take the call; it must be Sharon.

Peter was placing a trade. Frank was reading *The Reno Gazette-Journal*. Danny was hunched over his part of the counter that ran around the room, trying to make the numbers for El Dorado match their clearing company's numbers. If they didn't, it meant they disagreed about a trade or trades. Errors had to be fixed as soon as possible, since the cost of fixing an error usually increased as a market moved over time.

The phone rang beside Peter. Maas waited. It rang again. Peter was still on another line and Danny had not even looked up. Frank did not answer the trading phone since he had to be ready to handle clients brokers transferred in to place trades. Maas thought he should have gone to the bathroom to avoid the possibility of someone seeing him and telling him to get the phone, but he was transfixed as he watched the scene unfold, his future in the balance.

The phone rang again, the volume up as usual so it could be heard in Sam's office in case he was needed to reinforce the clerks if trading got heavy enough to require another body. Danny looked over at Peter.

The phone rang again and Peter, glancing back at Danny, called, "Can you get that? Mouse is on break and I'm waiting for a fill on Martinez's 10 lot of corn. I don't want him bellowing at me like he did Al."

"Certainly," Danny said, mimicking Curly of the Three Stooges. He strolled over to the other end of the room and grabbed the phone. "Trading," he said. "Okay, transfer her in.....Hello, this is Daniel Molina, I understand you would like to open a discount trading account?"

Maas stepped into the room.

"That's great. We like to make sure you have the experience to place trades for that type of account since you won't be working with a broker," Danny explained as he sat in Maas's chair. "We don't want you to make any mistakes from lack of knowledge."

Maas walked in and sat on the counter beside Danny as Peter got Martinez's fill and tore off one of the copies. Peter handed it to Frank, who ran it out to Martinez with three other fills that had been sitting on the counter waiting to be returned to brokers.

"How would you place a grain order to buy, let's say, corn?" Danny asked. "Oh, you just want to trade the S&P? Okay, then how would you place an order to buy an S&P?"

Maas swallowed. He prayed Sharon would get it right. From the amount of time they had spent on the telephone she had to have learned it well enough to pass the Series 3 exam. In fact, she had learned it faster than most people did.

"Okay, that's very good. Do you know how to work with limits?" Danny asked, his voice the epitome of pleasantness.

Maas waited as Danny politely grilled Sharon for a few minutes. Would their plan fall apart even before it began? Could she pull it off? Maas waited, his anxiety hidden behind a bored face. Finally, Danny said, "You sound very knowledgeable. I'll transfer you back to customer service and they'll send you the paperwork to open a discount account. Welcome aboard and good luck with your trades." Danny pushed the button to transfer the call and then added *sotto voce*, "You're gonna need it."

Maas breathed again. The first stage of his plan was complete.

Chapter 26

"It's okay to open an account from Canada?" Sharon asked Maas on his cell as he waited in his car at Robyn's school that afternoon. Robyn was at volleyball practice. Maas had already shuttled Malena to an acting class and Coralea to a friend's for a play date. Maria was at work in the afternoon, so after the markets closed Maas drew the brunt of the after-school ferrying of the girls to their various activities.

"Sure," Maas said. "The firm will take accounts from North Korea, Cuba, Iran, anywhere, as long as someone sends in money."

"Are you going to send me your share of the money now?"

Maas hesitated. He had arranged a second mortgage a week ago and withdrew the money from his IRA two days ago. Since he handled the finances, doing it all without Maria's knowledge had been simple. He just told her he was refinancing their mortgage at a lower rate. They had done it before, so Maria asked few questions and signed the paperwork. Getting the money had been easy. Sending someone $100,000 was much harder.

"Tony?"

"I have the money; that was no problem."

"I have my share, too, $110,000."

"It would look better if the money came in two checks," Maas said, delaying.

"Why?"

"If we do go to arbitration, it'll make it appear as if you had to draw on several sources for the money. You won't look rich. The money is supposed to be money you can lose without adversely affecting your lifestyle, so it always goes better with arbitration panels if they think the company let you risk your last dollar."

"You said women always win arbitration."

"A little insurance never hurts."

"Maybe I should send in some of the money from my personal checking account and some from my gallery's account."

"Even better, but make sure you send a copy of your gallery's incorporation papers to show that you're the sole owner and can legally write checks on that account."

"Is this going to work, Tony? We're risking a lot of money."

"It'll work. Trust me." He winced at the irony of his situation. He could not open new accounts to save his job, yet he could convince his first love to commit potential fraud.

"If I lose this money—"

"We won't."

"I took a loan out against my car, my house and the inventory in my gallery to raise the hundred and ten thousand. If this doesn't work, I'll lose everything. I'm too old to start over."

"Are you sure you want to do this?"

"Are you?"

"Yes, but I don't want to drag you into something you don't want to do."

There was a long silence. Sharon said, "I'm certain, but I'm still scared."

Chapter 27

"I've got an account for Ken Scott in Alexandria, Virginia," Vinny announced over the intercom system above the cacophonous din of the bullpen the next day. "Whoever forgot to write their broker number on it will lose it to Old Man Winter unless they claim it now."

"Why does Vinny open all the new account envelopes?" a bird dog asked Maas as he walked back to the trading room from a visit to the rest room, having just used his personal key.

"He opens all the mail."

"Why?"

"The NFA doesn't want clients sending bribes to brokers in exchange for better fills."

"How would you do that?" the new broker asked, frowning as he tried to figure it out.

Maas peered at the young man; was he asking out of curiosity or to learn how? Deciding the former, Maas replied, "A broker can place orders for two clients and give the better fill to the client who kicks a little something back to him. By opening the mail, Vinny helps prevent kickbacks."

"Couldn't a client just mail the kickback to a broker's house?"

"Sure."

"Then why bother?"

"Makes it appear legit," the Doctor said, looking sadly at the naïve young broker from his desk one row back. "This is America;

fake tits, leased BMWs and living large on credit. Appearances are all that matter."

Just after Maas returned to the trading room, Genius strolled into the trading room with a note and stuck it on the bulletin board beside the printed list of discount clients in front of Maas. Maas filled in a ticket, having just received a palladium fill from the NYMEX, the New York Metals Exchange. He leaned forward and read Genius' block-printed note. It looked as if it had been printed by a mental defective wearing a hockey glove.

Maas whistled. "Sharon Calloway, one hundred and ten thousand smackers," he read off the note, enunciating each word slowly as if he was counting each and every dollar.

"A big one," Genius agreed. "And she sounds hot."

"She does, does she, Genius?"

"Yeah," Genius said, then, under Maas's stare, added in a mumble, "At least I thought so."

"What about Peter?"

"I don't know if he thought she was hot. He hasn't talked to her yet, has he?"

"No, I mean, why don't you have a note for him?"

Genius looked confused, his head jerking from side to side as he looked to Peter, Frank and then Danny for support, or at least an explanation. Genius was often out of his depth; his depth being that of a puddle in a parking lot.

Maas said, "Without a note, Peter isn't going to know who Ms. Calloway is if she calls to invest her one hundred and ten thousand simoleons or even how many simoleons she has to invest."

"He can just look over at your note."

"That takes too much time, especially if it gets busy, and what have Sam and Danny told you about giving us both info on new clients?" Maas asked sweetly, like a caring and loving teacher with a favorite, if glacially slow, pupil.

Genius snuck a quick look over at Danny, who had leaned back from his work balancing the numbers to watch the show. Genius pursed his lips and, deciding he couldn't lie with Danny right there, admitted, "I'm supposed to give you both the information."

Maas nodded. Genius snatched Maas's note and turned to stalk back to his desk, but not before he shot back over his shoulder, "It's not like you couldn't copy it yourselves."

The clerks broke out laughing as Genius stormed out of the room.

When his stint in the trading room was done, Maas headed to the ATM across the street.

"It lowers the crime rate," Chisel Chest said.

"There's no proof the death penalty lowers the crime rate," Hero stated, emphasizing each word with a jab of his cigarette as Maas passed the bickering duo in front of the building.

"The murderers and rapists who are executed sure as hell don't commit any more crimes," Chisel Chest said, "unless it's in Hell."

Maas jaywalked across Century Park East, withdrew $100 from the ATM for Maria and then stepped into the bank. He used $100,000 from their checking account—recently transferred from his IRA and extracted as a second mortgage against their house—to buy a cashier's check made out to Sharon Calloway. He already had an envelope addressed to Sharon and, placing the cashiers check in it, sealed the envelope and walked over to the mail box on the corner of Constellation Avenue. Once he dropped the envelope inside, there would be no going back. He was giving $100,000 to his high school love, who he hadn't seen in more than 20 years.

Maas rocked back on his heels as cars rushed past on Century Park East through the canyons formed by the towers that housed LA's financial district. There was more wealth within five miles of where he stood than almost any other place on earth and all he needed was a minuscule percentage of it to get out of debt, quit his job and sculpt. Since his run sheet, cold calling and car roulette had all but dried up and shriveled away, he had only one idea of how to get a lot of money fast before he lost his desk and his world collapsed. He opened the mailbox and stared into the darkness within. Could he trust her?

He thought he knew Sharon, but a sliver of doubt sliced into his confidence. He hated that sliver, but it made him wonder whether she would just take his $100,000, close her account and walk away having doubled her money. It was why he had stalled sending her the money. He had considered getting a legal agreement stating that the account was really joint, but leaving a paper trail would be foolish if their scheme ever unraveled. He had considered making the cashier's check out for deposit directly into Sharon's brokerage account, but a cashier's check coming from a Century City bank for a client in Canada would arouse suspicion. He could have wired the money into the brokerage account, but the electronic trail would have pointed right back to his account. He had to trust her. There was absolutely nothing to stop her from taking his money—except their past.

He pursed his lips and thought of her long blonde hair, high cheekbones, large round eyes, and full lips, not to mention her lovely, curvy hips. He smiled at his silliness; such attributes were hardly information from which to decide whether to trust someone—or maybe they were. How do you decide whom to trust?

If he lost the $100,000 he held in his hand he would be working as a broker, assuming he kept his desk, until he was too old to lift a phone. His debt would be greater, owing not only Coop and the credit card companies but also the second mortgage, and with no IRA. He would be hard pressed to keep anyone on to cook and clean for his father. Even so, he could probably scrape by, just as he had been for years, but unable to save even a dime for the future.

However, even with the $100,000, he would be working forever with no salvation in sight. He could use it to pay off Coop and the credit cards, but he would then have to pay the second mortgage for 30 years, would have no IRA and would still be facing the cost of taking care of his father, the girls' college funds and dozens of other bills every month. Either way, with or without the $100,000, he would be working the rest of his life with little, if any chance to sculpt, whether he stayed with Maria or ran away into Sharon's arms. If his future looked bleak with the $100,000, it was merely a darker shade of black without it.

His scheme was his only hope. If he could clear a few hundred grand, he could repay the second mortgage, refund his IRA, pay off Coop and the credit cards, have money for his father and the college funds, and a breathing space to consider his future: Brokering or sculpting? Maria or Sharon? It would buy him that most precious of commodities: time.

He stared into the mailbox, the darkness winking at him as light slipped in through cracks in the welding on one side. The breeze through the man-made canyons of Century City ruffled his short hair. A car honked. A seagull swooped past overhead, its shadow flitting across his face.

Maas dropped the envelope inside.

Chapter 28

"Genius, Kathy," Maas said, forcing himself to sound relaxed and at ease early Thursday morning as he talked with the customer service pair. "That new account, Sharon Calloway...."

"Yeah," Genius said, as Kathy nodded, unfolding a paper napkin on her desk containing her blueberry muffin breakfast.

"Peter doesn't like trading women, so if she calls and wants to trade or has any questions about her account—any questions or anything at all—transfer her to me, alright?"

"Sure," Genius said, glad to transfer potential work to someone else.

"Always on the lookout for a new lady, eh, Mouse?" Kathy said with a comically exaggerated leer. Tough as a brothel madam, Kathy had the extroverted personality required to survive in the male-dominated world of commodities.

"Always," Maas said. With a Mae West figure that left many men panting with desire, Kathy could make most men feel like little boys coming face to face with an extremely experienced woman, but Maas had always got along famously with her. "That is, unless you give me a shot, beautiful."

"Just say the word, handsome."

"I'm just afraid you'd be too much woman for me."

"But what a way to go."

Maas laughed and started back toward the trading room. Then, remembering Genius and enough instances of his complete lack of brilliance to script a 10-season sitcom, turned back and said, "Please remember, Genius. It's important." As soon as he said it, he feared he had said too much, but Genius nodded and had already returned to his business newspaper, which he tried to read cover to cover each day, his lips slowly mouthing every word.

Maas returned to the trading room and slumped into his chair. He strongly, ardently, even vehemently believed that Sharon would not double-cross him and take his money, but the sliver he did not like, even abhorred, kept warning him, pestering him with the grave worry that maybe, just maybe Sharon had changed. Maybe she had no feelings left for him or, even if she did, maybe she valued $100,000 more than she valued him. He tried to banish those thoughts, but they kept creeping around the edges of his consciousness, fighting to take center stage.

At least now if Sharon decided not to send in his $100,000 and called to close her account she would be transferred to him. He could plead with her and remind her of all the good times they had enjoyed to try to convince her not to take his money.

The phone rang. A discount client wanted to buy five Japanese yen put contracts. A call option increased in value if the underlying commodity rose in price, while a put option increased in value if the underlying commodity fell in price. There was a bet for everyone in commodities. Maas placed the order.

It turned out to be a long day since Maas did not trust Genius. Maas didn't think it would happen, but his mind kept sliding back toward those dark thoughts of being double-crossed by his former love. Luckily, it was a slow day. Maas wandered past customer service 12 times the first hour, 15 times the second and then a steady 20 times every hour the rest of the day hoping that if Sharon called, he would overhear the call before Genius could screw-up and transfer her to someone else. Kathy must have thought he had a crush on her, since by the end of the day she was smiling and winking at him as he leaned against the wall behind customer service during the last of his multitude of breaks.

"Mouse, seen this?" Kathy asked. She pulled up a game of solitaire on her computer, but it only lasted a moment before a bright yellow screen appeared with 72-point bold black text, "Kathy, aren't you supposed to be working? Sam."

Maas chuckled. The manager, Sam, was into computers and also into making sure all of El Dorado's employees worked hard.

After the markets closed, Maas was picking up his jacket and mustering his courage to return to his desk to cold call for a few hours when his phone rang. The markets had closed 20 minutes before and Peter had already left. Maas picked it up. "Trading."

"Tony?"

It was Sharon. Maas closed his eyes. His shoulders slumped. His stomach churned. His skin was clammy. He felt nauseous. She was calling to close her account. She was stealing his money. She did not love him. She had no feelings at all for him.

"Ms. Calloway," he managed to say, his voice faltering. The line was taped. The last thing he wanted was anyone to ever know, regardless of how it turned out, that he knew Sharon, although it did not look like there would be anything questionable going on now, save for his appalling judgment in sending an old flame $100,000.

"You can call me Sharon," she said in the smoky voice that had always brought him to life. Now it just increased his mounting misery at what he knew she was about to do. "Customer service said I should talk to you about getting my correct account number."

Feeling as if his world had collapsed, Maas leaned against the counter. He felt faint. He waited for Sharon's next brutal words: 'I need the account number so I can close my account. Please send me my money back.' And my money with it, he thought, devastated.

"I wanted to make sure I had the right account number."

"Pardon me?" Maas managed to say through the choking sensation in his throat.

"When the man at customer service gave me my account information, he said my account number was 717-796-142. That's my Canadian Social Insurance Number. I put it in the account forms since I don't have an American Social Security Number. I think he got mixed up and I wanted to make certain I had the right number for when I make some S&P trades Monday."

Maas collapsed into his chair. She wasn't calling to close her account. She wasn't taking his money. She wasn't abandoning him. He hadn't been mistaken. In Vancouver there *had* been a spark between them. Maybe she did still love him.

Chapter 29

On the crucial Monday, Maas arrived at work at a quarter to six. He came in the side door, since Mary was not at her desk yet and the front door was still locked. Sam always unlocked the side door to admit the morning trading room crew. Maas walked down the carpeted hall past the lunchroom. He neither saw nor heard anyone. None of the brokers would show up for at least 15 minutes, with most drifting in between 7:30 and 9. Crucially, Maas had noted that the new broker who was using the phone in the storage room never arrived before 8:30.

With no one in sight, Maas slipped into the storage room just past the conference room. Black filing cabinets full of client account files lined two walls. On the third wall stood a gray metal cabinet containing office supplies, locked to reduce broker thefts. Brokers were supposed to provide their own office supplies, although few did even with the cabinet supposedly always locked.

A closet on the storage room's fourth wall held a mass of telephone lines in multi-colored jumbles that rivaled the Gordian knot. Next to the telephone closet sat a black computer that served as a taping machine. It recorded every call into and out of the trading room. It also recorded the phone number and duration of every call made to and from each of the brokers' phones, which allowed Nickel to track the number of calls each broker made each week.

His heart racing and his skin damp, Maas glanced back at the open door. There was still no one in sight. He heard no one. Anyone coming down the hall would have to enter through the side door, which Maas would hear close, giving him a crucial few seconds to escape from the room. However, if Sam, Peter, Frank or Danny had already arrived and decided to go to the john or grab some coffee, they might walk along the carpeted hall from the back right past the storage room without Maas hearing a sound. It was a risk he had to take. If he closed the door, someone might notice, since the door was never shut during business hours.

Swallowing, Maas reached down to the power cord for the taping machine. With an ever-watchful eye on the bottom line, Nickel and Vinny had bought a basic model, which in screen-saver mode displayed a black screen. Maas pulled the plug. The screen flickered and went black. It looked the same as it had when it had been plugged in. Unless someone tried to retrieve a recording, no one would notice that the machine was no longer taping every trading room call. When Sharon called there would be no record of her order to prove whether she said to buy—go long—or to sell—go short—the S&P.

Maas licked his parched lips as he rushed out of the room. He had taken only two steps down the hall when he heard a door close behind him. Maas turned and saw Frank hurrying toward him, his over-the-shoulder bag stuffed full of the newspaper clippings he habitually collected from his wide-ranging readings.

"Morning, Mouse," Frank called with a grin as he caught up to Maas and they hurried into the trading room together. Frank, Maas thought with great relief, hadn't seen anything.

Peter and Danny were already in the trading room. Sam was in his office across the hall, running off the brokers' run sheets for the day, which showed each client's cash left in their account, as well as the value of all of their positions—futures and options—at yesterday's close. The two run sheets for the trading room, each nicknamed the Bible, were already printed and held together with black, one-and-a-half inch binder clips. One Bible sat between Peter and Maas, and another in front of Frank, who checked it when brokers transferred clients for a trade to make sure they were selling positions they owned or, in the case of futures, they had enough margin to cover the trade.

A horrible thought struck Maas. Sharon could keep the $100,000 he had sent her and just not send it in to her account. Maas slid the Bible over and flipped to the discount accounts at the back. Clients who did not use a broker paid a discounted $9 per trade compared to clients who used a broker, who paid anywhere from a flat $150 to a high of 35 percent of the value of a contract. Such a fee could run to thousands of dollars depending on the commodity, strike price and expiration date of the option. Even so, 35 percent was far from the highest commission charged in the industry. Some firms charged 45 percent, which meant an option had to increase 45 percent for a client just to break even.

Maas searched for Sharon's account. Would his money be there? He found the account. Cash: $210,000.

He let the pages fall back into place. She had wired his money into her account. He had been right to trust her. All he had to do now was await her call, which they had agreed she would make at 7 a.m. Soon they would have enough to make both their dreams come true.

"I'm going to the storage room to pull some tapes," Danny announced, the words cutting into Maas's dreams like a scalpel.

Maas froze. As soon as he tried to retrieve a record, Danny would realize the machine was unplugged. "What for?" Maas blurted out.

It was 6:53. Maas had to keep Danny away from the tape machine for seven minutes until Sharon called. Seven minutes? An eternity.

"The Kennedy case," Danny replied, standing, a thick file in one hand. "I want to get it done before we get busy."

"If we get busy," Peter said. "The markets have been comatose."

"Kennedy?" Maas asked, turning in his chair. Seven minutes. "What happened?"

The phone behind Maas rang. Peter had just taken a fill and handed one copy to Bill, who was running it out to one of the rare early-bird brokers.

Danny said, "Kennedy opened an account and then died."

The phone rang again and Maas hoped Peter would answer it.

"I remember," Maas said, appearing interested. "He's the guy who trusted us enough to send us $12,000 but wouldn't trust us with the name of his next of kin on the account papers."

"He was right; they probably knocked him off. Trading," Peter said, as he grabbed the phone.

6:54.

"Isn't he the one who sent us the signed blank check?" Frank asked as he returned to the trading room from his ticket errand.

"That was some other guy," Danny said. "Kennedy's heirs think there are still open positions in the account. They want to sell them." Danny stepped toward the door.

"Hold on," Maas said, as he reached for the phone, which was ringing again. "I want to hear all about it."

He picked up the phone. "Trading."

It was a fill. He searched through the rack of tickets, found the right ticket but passed over it. "Where the hell is that ticket," he mumbled for his audience as he kept faux looking.

Danny, welcoming a chance to tell a story, sat back down and stared out the window toward the mansions of Beverly Hills.

6:55.

"Found it," Maas told the clerk in Chicago.

Maas glanced back. Danny was still in the room.

"Three Christmas corn at three four zero," the clerk in Chicago said as Maas scribbled the fill onto the ticket.

"Three Dec corn at 3.40," Maas repeated. "Got it, thanks."

There was a deep clang from the time clock as Maas time stamped the ticket, tore off the bottom yellow copy and handed it to Frank, who ran it out to the broker's desk. Maas put the completed ticket in a stack of filled orders for later entry into the computer system.

"All of Kennedy's positions expired worthless, so there's nothing to sell," Danny continued as if they had not been interrupted. "Apparently Mr. Kennedy didn't tell his wife or family his investment in the commodity markets didn't quite turn out the way he hoped."

The others laughed as Danny stood, the Kennedy file in hand ready to go to the storage room and the tape machine.

6:56.

Maas watched, filling with dread as Danny stepped toward the door.

"How many tapes do you have to pull?" Maas asked. Sweat trickled down his back. His mouth was dry. His stomach felt as if it was in one of those machines that shakes paint at the hardware store, and the machine was on full speed.

"I have to find every one of his trades to verify what he bought to prove that all of his positions have expired worthless." Then, flipping open the file, Danny added, "Luckily, he only had nine positions. I shall return."

He strode out of the room.

"Danny!" Maas called, his stomach churning. He needed more time. He could not risk even a part of Sharon's call being taped.

"Yeah?" Danny's head poked back through the open doorway.

"Did you get a chance to run those wheat charts?"

"I was buried up to my eyebrows yesterday, so I didn't get to it. The numbers didn't balance; bunch of puts that should have been calls, and a bunch of sells that should have been buys—a mess. I should be able to get to the charts for you this afternoon, unless Bell makes more errors today." Bell was El Dorado's clearing firm.

"That'd be great. I have some clients in wheat."

6:57.

Maas asked, "Do you think I should still buy wheat?"

"I'll take a closer look at it, but I think it's done."

"What would you buy?"

"Corn looks excellent right now, but you'd have to hold it a couple of months or so."

"Anything else?"

"Maybe the Canuck buck."

"Up or down?"

"I think it's starting a long-term trend up. The Canucks have a bunch of natural resources, oil and gas, and it's been down for years, so the fundamentals and the technicals look great for the next few months, even years. I think the Canuck buck trend is up, definitely."

"I'll see if I can convince my clients to buy in. Let me know about the wheat."

"Sure." Danny headed for the storage room, the tape machine and its errant plug.

6:58.

Maas stared at the phone. 'Ring, damn it, ring,' he urged, his teeth grinding, his jaw taut.

It didn't ring.

Maas waited an agonizing few seconds. This could not be happening. Sharon had to call, now.

Maas rose to rush to intercept Danny before he reached the tape machine. Maas took two steps toward the door. The phone rang. Peter reached for his phone. Maas spun around, snatched his receiver from the cradle and got the call first from the common line.

"Trading," he barked.

"Hello, this is Sharon Calloway."

6:59. Thank God, she had called a minute early.

"How can I help you?" Maas asked as he grabbed a blank ticket, eager to place the trade before Danny discovered the unplugged tape machine.

"I, I think I'd like to make a trade." She sounded hesitant and confused; perfect. If anyone ever asked him how she had sounded, he could just tell the truth.

"What's your account number, please?"

"That would be, ah....65000-31456."

"Thanks," Maas scribbled her account number on the top of the ticket. "Order?" he asked, rushing, even as he expected any second to hear a yell from Danny that he had discovered that the tape machine was unplugged.

"I would like to buy seven Standard and Poors futures contracts."

"Sam!" Maas heard Danny yell from the storage room.

"Okay," Maas said, steeling his nerves and keeping his voice steady, "for account 31456 we're buying seven S&Ps."

"Yes."

"Thanks. Hold for the fill." Maas put Sharon on hold and, hitting the speed dial for their clearing firm, waited as the call went through to Chicago. Should he place the order? Had Danny plugged in the machine? Had the machine taped Sharon's order?

Even as Maas waited in an agony of indecision for the call to go through, Danny stalked back into the trading room.

"Bell," the clerk in Chicago answered.

Maas looked back at Danny.

"Hello?" the Chicago clerk barked, as always in a hurry.

Danny tossed the Kennedy file on the portion of the counter that served as his desk.

"Hello? Do you have an order?" the Chicago clerk demanded, his anger mounting at the delay.

"What's wrong?" Maas asked Danny, before telling the clerk in Chicago, "Hold on."

"The tape machine's not working. Use the tape recorders for now," Danny called as he turned on his heel and disappeared out the door.

Maas and Peter reached for the tape recorders that had been gathering dust on their desks for more than a year since the firm purchased the computerized taping system.

Peter popped open his machine and announced, "No tape."

"Nada," Maas said, holding up his empty recorder.

"We need tapes!" Peter bellowed after Danny, as Maas allowed himself a smile of relief and continued with the order.

"This is El Dorado, buy seven S&Ps," he told the Chicago clerk.

"For El Dorado, we're buying seven, that's seven S&P."

"Right." As soon as Maas agreed with the clerk's read-back of the order, it was done. Whoever spoke last took responsibility for the order.

"Hold on," the clerk said as the order went to the floor via a computer system. A floor broker would grab the printout of the order and make the trade in the pit. Less then 20 seconds later, the clerk reported the fill to Maas. "Seven at 1173.80."

"Seven at 73.80. Thanks," Maas said, not bothering to repeat the first two digits of the price since they rarely changed in a day of trading. He scribbled the fill on the ticket and hung up on Chicago. He got Sharon back on the line and reported the fill.

Danny strode in. "The plug from the tape machine fell out. The wall outlet's a little loose. Sam's going to call an electrician to replace it. How many trades have you done since the open?"

"All the trades I put in on the open from last night," Peter said. "Ten or 12."

"A few," Maas said.

"Hopefully nothing goes wrong with them. We don't have tapes for any of them." Danny flipped through the stacks of orders in the rack between Peter and Maas. He stopped and stared at a ticket on the top of the stack in the financials section. "An S&P seven lot?"

"Yeah, that new woman, Calloway," Maas said, keeping his voice calm, even as his nerves drew taut.

"Does she have enough margin?"

"Yep, $210,000."

"Wow. Guess she's hoping the Fed cuts interest rates tomorrow and it blips up. Let's pray it goes up and she makes money," Danny said. "That way, if there's anything wrong with her order we won't get screwed for not having a tape."

The S&P meandered up and down the rest of the trading day, eventually closing up two at 1175.80. Sharon called at 1:20, just after the markets closed.

"I wanted to double check how I stand," Sharon told Maas. "Is each point $2,500?" She talked fast, her voice betraying her excitement.

"No, Ms. Calloway," Maas explained patiently on the now-taped line. Sharon was doing well. She sounded almost completely incompetent to trade on her own. "Each point is $250. The S&P closed at 1175.80, a two-point move, so it's $500 per contract from where you entered the market."

"That's $3,500 for the seven contracts?"

"Correct." Maas could have screamed for joy that she did not say whether she was up or down. If they had to go to arbitration, there would be no record of whether she thought she had bought or sold the S&P.

Then she said, not quite making it a question, "I could sell on the overnight."

"Yes, you could."

"Oh, well, I guess I'll hold on. Maybe I'll have some luck tomorrow. What do you think?"

"I can't really advise you, since you're a discount client, but waiting and seeing what the Fed does sounds logical to me. It hasn't moved much yet, so there may be a big move tomorrow."

"Good. I'll talk with you tomorrow then."

"Good-bye," Maas said and wished her good luck, praying for a blip up with the fervency of a saint.

Chapter 30

Maas drove home, his mind racing. Sharon had placed the trades and the order had not been taped. If the S&P shot up Tuesday, they would make a tidy profit. If the S&P plunged, she could claim she placed an order to sell seven S&P contracts. By selling, she would have profited when the S&P fell because she could have bought the seven contracts she had sold Monday at the lower Tuesday price, reaping the difference in price as profit. Without a tape, El Dorado had no way to prove she had not placed an order to sell. Maas smiled. Sculpting looked like it had moved a giant stride closer to his outstretched fingers.

He drove into his driveway, narrowly avoiding Robyn's new bike. As he walked to the front door, he noticed a flat bed truck parked at the curb. Two Latino workmen were unloading 2 by 4s. One glanced at him and nodded. Maas nodded back before entering his house. Maria would not be home from work until 6 and the kids were at school for another hour. Getting home early was one of the benefits of working in a brokerage firm and, given that Maas expected to reap a windfall from his S&P scheme, he had not stayed to cold call after working his shift in the trading room ever since Sharon agreed to his plan. Maybe he should have in case someone noticed a correlation between Sharon opening an account and Maas's cold calling behavior, but he just couldn't bring himself to cold call anymore. Besides, anyone who knew anything about brokering would conclude that he, like almost every other human who ever tried it, had given up cold calling out of frustration.

Maas dropped his briefcase on the sofa and walked through the silent house to the kitchen in the back. He poured himself a cold glass of water and, standing at the rear sliding doors, took a long drink—then choked on it. Three workmen had dug up the back corner of his yard and were constructing a foundation.

Hurriedly setting his glass on the counter, Maas flung open the sliding door with a rattling bang and stalked across the yard to the three men. The two younger men kept working after a glance at the irate Maas, but the older man stood as Maas approached.

"Mr. Maas?" the older workman asked, smiling as he extended a tanned hand.

"Who are you?" Maas demanded, eyeing his destroyed yard. "What are you doing?"

"Wolfgang Merrem," the man said, his hand still outstretched.

Maas stared at him, searching and failing to find the name in his memory.

"Of Merrem Construction," the man added, as if that explained everything.

Maas frowned. The young workmen hammered together another piece of a wood frame for a foundation into which concrete would be poured.

"Stop. Please," Maas told the young men. They glanced at their boss, who nodded. The men stopped hammering. "What are you doing here? Who sent you?"

"Oh, no," Merrem said. He closed his dark eyes and, as a look of great pain swept across his face, said, "You're wife said we were supposed to be out of here by 2." He glanced at his watch. It was 2:30.

"My wife?"

"Maria Maas."

"Yes, I know my wife's name. What does she have to do with this?" He swept his hand over his ruined yard.

"She, well, maybe it would be better if she told you. It was supposed to be a surprise."

"It definitely is. Don't move." Maas stalked back into the house and called Maria at work.

"Calm down, dear. It's just a little studio. Don't tell me Merrem's still there?"

"A studio?" Maas demanded. "Why do we need a studio? None of the girls even likes art class."

"It's not for them. It's for you."

Maas's anger was transformed into confusion by one of the greatest shocks of his life.

"When we were first married, you used to drag me to every art exhibit within 100 miles, and you often said you wanted to be a sculptor. You always said it with such feeling that I thought for our anniversary I'd build you your own studio."

"But...what? Why? I don't...."

"I wanted to balance things out a little. The girls and I buy what we want—a lot of little things—and then you see the bills and decide you can't afford to buy what you want. I wanted to get you something big that you wanted. I knew you'd never build a studio for yourself, so I thought I'd better do it as a surprise."

Maas slumped into a kitchen chair.

"Are you alright, Anthony?"

"Yes, yes." Maas looked out the sliding door at the three men, now sitting on the foundation frame.

"You're going to love it. It'll have a nice big work area with space for whatever type of sculpting you want to try. It should be finished by our anniversary, but I wanted to surprise you with it tonight, or at least the start of it. Are the workmen still there?"

"They are."

"I told Merrem I wanted him out of there before you got home."

"I think I would have noticed half the yard torn up."

"He was supposed to hide whatever he had done today behind some lawn chairs until I told you about it tonight."

"How much is all this costing?" Maas closed his eyes and waited for the devastating figure.

"I'm paying for it," Maria said, pride in her voice.

"You? Me? What's the difference? We're married."

"There's a huge difference."

Maas was perplexed. "You don't have any money."

"Dad gave me some at our wedding."

"Just a grand; you were supposed to spend it on something you really wanted."

"I invested it for a rainy day instead."

"A thousand isn't going to cover the cost of a studio."

"Of course not. You know the $100 a week for groceries you've been giving me since we got married?"

"What's that got to do with—"

"At first I spent it on food, but after a while every store started to accept credit cards and, after Donna was mugged—you remember, about 20 years ago—I didn't like to carry around that much money, so I used credit cards for everything. Didn't you ever wonder why groceries for four still cost the same $100 you'd been giving me 20 years ago for two of us?"

"No, I was just thankful they did. There were always plenty of credit card bills from the supermarket, but I thought they were for extras or something."

"No, they were for our food. I invested the $100 a week."

Maas rapidly did the math: $100 a week is $5,200 a year, so over 20 years that would be a little more than $100,000. Could it be that much? "So you saved enough to pay for the studio?" he asked, brightening somewhat. At least their debt was not going to suddenly increase.

"Yes, and then some."

"You'll have a few grand left over?" Maas asked as he stood, realizing they had narrowly avoided financial disaster and might even come out a few dollars ahead.

"More than a few grand. I invested in a conservative stock index fund in the eighties and added to it every week."

Maas froze, trying not to get too excited before he knew the results of Maria's investing.

"Twenty-four percent was my best year, but I made 12 percent several years."

"That's fantastic." Maas's excitement grew.

"But I only made 7 percent one year."

"There are always down years, but that's great. You were smart to stick with an indexed stock fund; low fees and all."

"Then in the late nineties I began to agree with the chairman."

"Who?"

"The Chairman of the Federal Reserve, Mr. Greenspan."

Maas would have bet heavily against Maria ever having even

heard of the Federal Reserve, let alone of its chairman.

"I began to agree with him about the 'irrational exuberance' in the market, so I pulled out with a tidy profit."

"How much money do you have?" Maas asked, fearing the answer—any good news couldn't be true—yet desperate to know the truth and end the suspense.

"A little more than $250,000."

Maas stood like a statue, shocked. "Why didn't you tell me?"

Maria fell silent.

"Maria?"

"I was afraid you'd take the money away from me."

"What? It's all our money. We're married. What difference does it make?"

"I know, but you run all our finances. I didn't want you to take over my little investments. You were busy with the bulk of our money anyway, with bigger and better things."

"Maria, you were the one doing bigger and better things. With me running the finances, we owe about $80,000 on credit cards and it's growing at double digit percentages every year." Maas didn't mention Coop and his loan shark interest rates.

"We're in debt $80,000?" It was Maria's turn to be shocked.

"Besides the mortgage, yes."

"My God, why didn't you tell me?"

"I mentioned it a long time ago but it didn't seem to make much of an impression. After a while, I just stopped mentioning it."

"You mentioned a few times that we should cut back, but I thought it was just until you had another big month as a broker. I thought we owed a few thousand."

"With Dad's surgery, Mom's time off with her hip, and helping them out, as well as my slump brokering, we've been slipping deeper and deeper into debt for years."

"I'm glad you told me now. We can use my money to pay off the debt, but I better cut back on my spending and the girls will need to cut back. I'll have a talk with them. They've been wondering why you've seemed touchy and distant recently, shutting yourself in your office every night."

Maas felt a great weight shift off his shoulders as if Atlas had reassumed his load.

"I can get at most of the money," Maria said, "but I have some invested in something that will have to wait to mature for a few months."

"Can you get $80,000 to pay off the credit cards?" Then, looking out at the studio in the making, Maas added, "And pay for the studio?"

"Sure."

The day was suddenly brighter and the sky bluer. Maas heard bird songs through the open sliding glass door. He said, "I didn't even know you knew that I still dreamed about sculpting."

"After 20 years, I know you pretty well. I'm glad you like the studio."

"Thank you."

"You're welcome, Anthony. For all you've done for me and for the girls, you're more than welcome. You deserve it."

After telling Merrem to resume construction, Maas returned to the kitchen. He was halfway through a celebratory beer when it hit him; he didn't need his scheme with Sharon any more. He was going to have a studio, enough money to pay off their credit card debt and Coop and, if he could get his $100,000 back from Sharon, he could repay the second mortgage and refund his IRA. He would even have enough to cover his dad's help for a while. Relieved of his money worries, he could refocus on brokering. He wouldn't sound desperate on the phone any more. He would be able to open accounts and keep his desk. He might even be able to make some time to sculpt. In a rush, he called her.

"Sharon, we have to call it off."

"We aren't going to take just a $3,500 profit, are we?"

"Yes, well, no," Maas stammered. "Wherever the S&P is tomorrow we need to get out on the open or, even better, you can call now and get out on the overnight."

"Why?"

"I don't need the money anymore."

Maas explained about Maria's investments.

"I thought you were going to come up here," Sharon said, every word edged with frost.

"I was, I can, but I don't need the money from this scheme to do it anymore. Maria's investments will pay off our credit card debt. I couldn't leave her with so much debt. Now she, and you and

I can all start with a clean slate."

The line fell silent.

"Sharon?"

"Yes."

"We need to close the account. If I leave Maria, we'll be able to start fresh; free and clear."

"If?"

The word hung in the air like a guillotine, waiting to fall.

"I meant, when."

Another long pause.

"Sharon?"

"No."

"No?"

"No. I need to make a big profit off this or I'll lose my gallery and my house and my car. I told you I'd borrowed against everything I own for your scheme. There's no way we're pulling out now."

"Sharon, it's not going to work."

"You certainly thought it was going to work when you wanted to do it."

"I know, but so much can go wrong. It's against the law. If anyone discovers that we know each other, game over."

"No one will."

"They might."

"Then make sure no one does, because I'm not quitting now."

"Sharon, please."

"No." It was the same 'no' she had used the first time he had attempted to seduce her in the back seat of his Honda Civic in high school. He figured his chances of changing it into a yes were far worse now than they had been then, and it had taken three months to change her mind then. The commodities market wouldn't give him anywhere near three months to convince her now.

"If I mean anything to you," Maas said, "please let's get out of the positions."

"If I meant anything to you, you wouldn't ask me to."

"At least let me take out my share of the money."

"No."

"It's my money."

"You aren't going to abandon me again like you did in college."

"I didn't abandon you in college."

"Yes, you did."

"No, I didn't. We just drifted apart."

"We didn't drift, you did. You changed. I was the same."

"I didn't change."

"You quit sculpting and went off to take business classes," she said, the word business loaded with loathing. "When I came back from Europe you weren't the same person any more."

"You weren't the same person either."

They fell silent. Maas tried to remember what had really happened so long ago.

"Don't you want to sculpt?" Shannon asked, breaking into Maas's memories.

"I do."

"Then you need money. Just paying off your debt isn't enough. You'll just run up new debt. All that stuff about the artist starving in a garret is just so much bunk. Poverty and deprivation don't breed great art; all they breed is anger, worry and depression."

"Maybe I can sell some works."

"It'll take time to make, let alone sell any pieces, so we need some money to tide us over until you get up and running as a sculptor. If we don't, I'll lose my gallery."

"I know."

"Don't leave me again, Tony."

"I won't." Maas had no choice, but it was also the right thing to do—or was it? He sighed. "I never should have left you the first time."

"Then why did you?"

"I didn't realize what I was losing."

Chapter 31

The next morning, Maas sat at the portion of the counter in the trading room that served as his desk, staring at the computer screen that displayed the S&P in bright green numbers: 1170.20. Down more than $750 per contract. If Sharon hadn't wanted to sell the night before when they were up, she certainly wouldn't want to sell now when they were down.

Maas closed his eyes and wished he had just plugged away at being a broker. He could have done it. He just hadn't tried hard enough. But how could he have ever known that Maria was salting away money like a chipmunk storing nuts for a long, hard winter? He might just as well have staked their financial future on Robyn becoming an Olympic gold medalist in volleyball, Malena a business mogul or Coralea the next Hollywood child star.

The phone rang. Maas took a fill from Chicago and passed it along to Frank to run back to a broker.

"Did you see this ticket?" Danny asked, leaning over Maas, whose mind was still engulfed in his own nightmare.

Peering at the eight-by-five inch ticket, Maas said, "Looks like CC, cocoa."

"Old Man Winter says he wrote crude, CL."

"No way," Peter said, leaning over after placing a Euro order to pass judgment on the scribbled abbreviation. "It's CC. Winter writes like an inebriated doctor."

"You should know, doctor," Danny said with a laugh. Peter had a doctorate in math.

Maas asked, "He didn't notice the fill was way off for crude?"

"He says he didn't get the ticket back until this morning," Danny said.

"Frank, did you give Winter this ticket yesterday?" Peter asked, grabbing the ticket from Danny and showing it to Frank.

"Yeah," Frank said. "I think so. We did a lot of tickets back yesterday, though."

"You placed it as cocoa?" Danny asked Peter and Maas, since he didn't know which clerk had placed it.

"Don't recall," Maas said.

Peter shrugged.

"I'll have to check the tape," Danny said. "I sold it out and bought Winter his crude, but we got hit for a $1,756 loss. Cocoa was down this morning and crude was up. At least I'm sure we have a tape for it. It's time stamped after I plugged the machine back in."

"That's good, especially since the NFA is coming today," Peter said.

Maas froze. "What?"

"The NFA called Sam first thing this morning to tell him they're coming today on a surprise audit."

The last thing Maas wanted was federal auditors snooping around.

Genius rushed into the trading room, panting, and fumbled with his time card as he jammed it into the time clock. Sweat glistened on his forehead.

"Little late there, old Genius," Peter called, theatrically peering at his watch and then looking over at Genius with a put-on disapproving glare.

"I had a little trouble getting here," Genius said, twitching as he stuffed his card back into the metal rack beside the time clock.

"Accident? Alarm clock malfunction? Shaving catastrophe?" Peter asked, sprawled back in his chair, enjoying a brief period of silence; no phones were ringing.

"Sort of," Genius said, turning to leave.

"What happened?" Peter asked.

Maas picked up the phone to call Sharon, but stopped.

"I had some trouble with the elevators," Genius said, an

undercurrent of anger and frustration in his voice.

"You got stuck in the elevator?" Frank asked, turning from reading one of his stack of newspapers, the Toronto *Globe and Mail*.

"Not *in* the elevator."

Maas debated whether to call Sharon. He had to consider all the angles. He had to think. Why couldn't they all just shut up for a minute?

Genius said, "I couldn't get up in the elevator. I had to take the stairs."

"What?" Peter asked, frowning.

"I tried three elevators, but none of them came up to the 14th floor. They kept only going to the 9th floor."

"Genius!" Sam yelled. "Where the hell are you?"

Genius cursed and rushed out to customer service, where Maas could hear phones ringing.

Peter laughed.

"What?" Frank asked.

"There are two banks of elevators in the building," Peter explained. "One bank for floors one through nine, the other for 10 and up, right?"

"Right."

"Genius must have got into the wrong set of elevators and didn't realize there are two banks," Peter said, laughing.

"How long has he worked here?" Frank asked, incredulous.

"Two years," Peter said, shaking his head. "What a moron."

Maas considered. If he called Sharon and told her the NFA was at El Dorado, she would ask if there was anything illegal for them to find. There wasn't. She and Maas had done nothing wrong yet, other than using his money in her account. Brokers were not allowed to trade their own money unless they notified the NFA. The NFA would then monitor the broker's personal account to make sure the broker was not hedging by taking the opposite positions he advised his client's to take or, worse, bucketing trades by placing simultaneous orders and taking the better fills for his own account. Maas had done neither. He could be fined or might even lose his license if the NFA learned that he had given money to Sharon to trade with, but that would be all. The serious crime would only occur if they lost a trade and she had to lie to an arbitration panel about whether her order had been to buy or sell. It would be perjury, fraud and conspiracy. But he didn't see how anyone could prove even the perjury, since with no tape, no one could prove what Sharon had said: buy or sell. Maybe the S&P would blip up after the Fed announcement and all would be well.

Maas decided not to call her. Even so, the next hour and a half until the Fed announcement was torture. Maas did his job, phoning in orders, taking fills and working out the math on tickets. For each filled ticket he calculated the cost of the contract based on the fill and the commission for that type of account. He then determined the break-even; the price at which the client would make back the cost of the contract plus the commission and fees. He also scribbled in the expiration date, which was when an option contract expired, usually the month before the month on the contract: September wheat, for example, expired in August. Luckily he could do the calculations in his sleep since his mind was engulfed by his worries about the S&P. The stock index meandered up a tad, down a smidgen and then rambled around within a two-point range as if stuck in a deep rut. Everyone was waiting for the Fed announcement.

As he leaned back in his chair, forcing himself to relax but with little success, Maas overheard Chisel Chest and Hero arguing in the hall.

"It's right and just," Chisel Chest asserted. "An eye for an eye and a tooth for a tooth."

"It's more like vengeance," Hero countered.

"Revenge has a place in the courts," Chisel Chest said. "What would you do if your wife was killed in some hideous way by some bastard? You'd want to kill him. If the court just gives murderers a slap on the wrist, people will take the law into their own hands. Then we'd have anarchy. To avoid that, there has to be some element of revenge in sentencing."

"Vengeance is reserved for God."

"God often has a pretty damn weird sense of vengeance, let alone of justice. The good suffer right along with the evil in this world."

"Did you straighten out my crude fill?" Old Man Winter asked, rambling in and sorting rapidly through a stack of fills by the window, which Frank had yet to run out to the bullpen.

"You mean your cocoa?" Peter asked.

"My crude," Winter said, emphasizing the second word as he turned with mock severity on Peter. "Can't you read?"

"Can't you write?" Peter asked with a smirk.

"Danny's sorting it out," Frank said, looking up from his copy of the Fredericton *News-Record.* With most of the markets slow recently, he had begun to catch up on some of the smaller market newspapers in his stack of reading materials.

"If anyone can fix it, our man Danny can," Winter said, holding three fills he had found.

"How's the wife and kids?" Peter asked. It was a slow day and for some reason he did not have a math article with him to work on.

"In Mexico on vacation. It's costing me a fortune but, boy, it's worth every peso. I have the house to myself; peace and quiet." Winter beamed at the thought of his own private Shangri La.

Maas tapped his fingers on the counter top as he watched the S&P, wishing time would accelerate and the Fed would make its announcement. He did not like the thought of the NFA being at El Dorado, but they would be checking trades over the past year. There was no reason to believe they would focus on yesterday's tape machine 'malfunction.' For one reason or another the firm had missed taping trades before. Why would yesterday's malfunction attract any special notice? Maas took several long, deep breaths. Everything was going to be fine.

"The NFA wants tapes from all our trades yesterday," Danny announced as he stalked in and tossed a note-covered legal pad on his desk.

"What?" Maas asked. He suddenly felt ill; sweating, shaky and nauseous. Why had hell descended on him?

"They wanted to do a representative day, so they figured yesterday would be easy for us to dig up," Danny explained. "They said we wouldn't have to go down to the storage room and beat off the rats to unearth the old tapes."

"The machine was unplugged part of yesterday," Peter said, voicing the thought that was foremost in Maas's mind.

"I'll have to ask Sam and Nickel how they want to handle it," Danny said. "Probably just tell the NFA we had a malfunction. Of course, then they'll want to see all the tickets from yesterday and inspect every single one with a magnifying glass on loan from

Sherlock Holmes."

"Doesn't the NFA use monocles?" Winter asked. He stood ramrod straight and, adopting a German accent, said, "Ve vill find oot vhat you 'ave bin hiding! There are no secrets from the NFA. *Seig heil der* NFA!" He goose-stepped out of the room with his fills, his right arm outstretched in a Nazi salute.

Maas turned back to his computer terminal as Danny headed off to consult Nickel and Vinny. Maas told himself there was nothing wrong with Sharon's order. They had done nothing wrong. Watching the S&P meander up and down on his screen, Maas prayed it would never come to an arbitration case. He wanted to get out, even if it meant losing some money.

Maas watched as the hands of the clock on the wall crawled toward 10 a.m. He read the twenty-third story he'd found on the newswire on his computer about the Fed. The consensus of the 23 stories was that the Fed would cut rates a quarter-point. Maas closed his eyes and prayed the Fed would cut rates at least a quarter of a point. If the Fed did, the market, having already factored in such a cut, would probably blip up. Most importantly, it would not plummet. Then maybe Sharon would sell.

"Danny said somebody stole a bunch of tapes from the supply cabinet," Frank reported as he returned from the rest room having used his own key.

Peter said, "Must be a music lover in our midst; wanted to tape some songs."

"Maybe they wanted to tape trades," Frank suggested with a grin. "Wanted to relive the excitement of trading in the comfort of their very own home."

Maas watched the corner of his computer screen where the S&P was displayed; high, low, last, and change for the day. It was down .30 for the day. The clock changed to 9:55 a.m. God, time crawled.

"Did you hear Donner wanted to copyright his pitch?" Peter asked as he finished filling out the commission on a ticket.

"You're kidding," Frank said.

"He moved up to the Frisco office and after a couple of days realized some of the other brokers were using his corn pitch to open accounts," Peter explained.

"So?" Frank asked, as Maas stared at his screen. "Everyone

uses everyone else's pitches. It's the salesman who makes the sale, not the pitch."

"I know, but Donner got all upset. He stormed into Marty's office and demanded a royalty on his pitch."

"What'd he want, a dime a pitch?" Warming to the idea, Frank said, "It could be quite profitable, just writing pitches. Each broker makes hundreds of pitches a day. Maybe I should write a few."

"Brokers should only pay when the pitch results in an account though," Peter suggested. "Why pay for failure?"

"Studios pay stars even when their movies bomb."

"Maybe $100 per successful pitch, or a sliding scale: the bigger the account, the bigger the royalty."

Maas wished they would shut up. He was in hell and they were talking nonsense. The seconds ticked off with an infuriating slowness.

"It really doesn't matter, though," Peter said. "Marty fired Donner for not showing up half the time and took his run sheet." Marty was a broker, but he also managed the San Francisco office.

Frank said, "That's how Marty gets half his accounts, firing brokers and taking their clients."

It was 10 a.m. Maas watched the screen. In Washington, the Fed chairman would be making his announcement.

Leadless Joe wandered in, looking for a fill.

"How's it going, Leadless?" Peter asked.

Leadless Joe moaned. "If corn doesn't go up soon, my whole run sheet's going down the crapper."

"Danny thinks all the grains are due for a run up," Peter said.

"God bless him, then," Leadless Joe said, managing a hopeful smile. It did not last and, having picked up his fill, he slunk back to the bullpen.

The S&P shot up.

"Fed cuts rates half a point," Frank announced as he read the news off his screen.

"Half?!" Maas exclaimed, not believing his luck even as he verified the news on his own screen.

The S&P was up five, then seven and quickly hit 1202.30. In two minutes it was up almost 30 points from where Sharon had bought it. They were in profit to the tune of about $25,000 for the seven contracts. It wasn't anywhere near as large as he had hoped, but it was time to get out. It wasn't going to go up much more, if any, today. Sharon could have all of the profit. He did not need it nearly as much as she did.

Why didn't she call? He could not call her. Order room clerks did not call self-directed clients to suggest, let alone to tell clients to sell. If he did, it would be taped. Maas fought the urge to call her. He had told her to watch the S&P closely, warning her that it was a market that could move rapidly, especially after a Fed announcement. She had to be watching, but she didn't call. Since he could not risk anyone overhearing him telling Sharon to sell, he would have to leave El Dorado to call her on his cell. If he left, he feared he'd miss her call to the trading room. There were 25,000 reasons for him to call her and only one not to—but the one stayed his hand. That one reason could land them both in jail. Why didn't she call?

Chapter 32

In agony, Maas watched the S&P hit a high of 1203.40 and then retreat. His agony increased with each tick down.

Sharon called at 10:12. The S&P was at 1187.20.

"Why's it falling so fast?" she asked. "I watched it go up, then it fell a bit and I was wondering whether I should call, but then it started down so quickly."

"Day traders taking their profits off the table from the blip up," Maas explained, fighting to control his anger and frustration. "Do you want to get out?" Even as he said it the S&P fell another half point. He desperately wished the line was not taped so he could tell her to get out, now.

"I don't know. It's moved so little."

"Sometimes moves are small. You can always try again on the next Fed announcement."

"I was hoping for a really big move. Where will it bottom out?"

"If I knew that, I wouldn't be working in a trading room."

"Let's wait and see. I'd really like a nice big profit."

Maas winced, tapping his foot hard on the floor. He resisted the urge to scream at her to sell before it was too late. Did she want to go to arbitration?

The S&P fell fast. With each point down, Maas felt another piece of his world shatter into ever smaller pieces. How was he ever going to tell Maria that, whereas she had put together a $250,000 nest egg, he had squandered $60,000 from his IRA and $40,000 from equity in their home? He had also convinced Sharon to put all her money into this scheme and now she would lose her gallery. He would not be surprised if Maria divorced him and Sharon never wanted to speak to him again.

He kept Sharon on the line, reading off the quotes as they appeared on his screen.

"Eleven sixty-six even. Do you want to place an order?"

"No."

"Sixty-five, ninety. Now?"

"No."

"Eighty."

"No."

"Seventy."

"No."

The S&P bottomed out at 1165 even, before climbing back a few points. By noon, as Sharon announced she had to return to work, it was at 1172.80, a point below where they had bought it Monday.

"Maybe you should get out," Maas suggested, weary and discouraged.

"Why?"

"If you were playing the S&P to make a big move after the Fed announcement, you missed it."

"I run an art gallery and I was selling a piece," she said. "I was only a minute or two late checking the market after the Fed announcement. When I checked, it was up, so I thought I would see how far it would go. It didn't reach a target a friend had mentioned, so I waited. It started down and before I knew it, it was plummeting. I couldn't believe how fast it moved."

"The S&P—well any commodity market—can lose you a fortune in five minutes."

"Or make a fortune, someone told me. I think I'll see what happens tomorrow."

Maas suppressed the urge to scream. She was acting like every other investor in commodities. Why had he ever agreed to work with an amateur? Then he thought of her blonde hair, big eyes and curves that drove him to distraction at 17 and still held his attention at 42. The emotions he felt at the sight of her made him feel young again. They had a strong connection, old and unbroken.

"I would really recommend closing out your position," Maas said. Then, remembering the line was taped, added, "I'm not supposed to make recommendations to discount clients, but since this is your first trade with us, that is my strong recommendation."

"I see. I'll keep it in mind, but let's see what happens tomorrow."

Maas said goodbye, hung up and leaned back. He felt as if he had just fought a war single-handed. He was spent, drained emotionally and physically. His brain felt like tepid tapioca.

"Have you talked to this Calloway woman?" Danny asked, striding in holding an account booklet.

"Yeah," Maas grunted, waiting for the other shoe to drop. Nothing in the way of bad news would surprise him today.

"The NFA is looking at her trade yesterday since we don't have it on tape. A seven lot of S&P, right?"

"Right."

"She close it out today?"

"Nope."

"No?" Danny glanced at Peter's screen, which displayed the chart for the recent S&P blip up and its rapid decline. "Why not? It posted a nice run up; a thirty or forty grand profit."

"It moved too fast for her."

"Gotta be faster than the Road Runner to trade the S&P. Anyway, I need the ticket from yesterday. The NFA wants to make sure it's time stamped correctly."

Struggling to keep the worry out of his voice, Maas asked, "Nothing else?"

"Not that I know of," Danny said, heading across to his desk to leaf through yesterday's tickets to find Sharon's fateful order.

Chapter 33

That afternoon, Maas sat at his kitchen table sipping a soda and watching the workmen construct his studio. His studio—the words had such a pleasing sound, if he could manage to keep it. The doorbell rang.

Maas was not expecting anyone, but given the amount of grunt work he had every week, he had no doubt he could have forgotten an appointment. Workmen rarely appeared when they promised anyway.

He opened the door.

"Peter," Maas said, surprised

"Mouse," the clerk said with a nervous smile, glancing past Maas into the house. "Got a minute?"

"Sure. I have to pick up my girls in a bit, but come on back to the kitchen."

Peter stepped inside. He jingled keys in his pocket as he walked through the living room and into the kitchen, where he sat at the spruce table.

"Want something to drink?"

"No….Thanks….Well, sure; some water would be great."

After dropping his empty soda can in the recycling bin, Maas poured two glasses of water as Peter looked out the sliding doors.

"Building an addition?" Peter asked before he gulped down some ice water.

"A studio."

"Wife an artist or something?"

"Something like that," Maas said, feeling old as he sat across from the twenty-something Peter. "What's on your mind?"

"I have a…well a….I guess it's a proposal for you." Peter gulped his water and ran the tip of his tongue along his lips. "The thing is, this has to be confidential. I mean, whether you run, pass or punt, this has to remain between us."

"We've known each other a few years. I think I can give you that."

Peter set his empty glass down on the table and held it between his hands. Sitting straighter and with a self-satisfied grin, he announced, "I'm leaving El Dorado to start my own firm."

"Good for you," Maas said and meant it. "I'm sure you'll do well and I wish you the best of luck. What are you going to call it? Dewey, Churnem and Howe?" It was an old joke, but Peter still chuckled.

"No, GRQ, Incorporated."

"GRQ?"

"Get Rich Quick."

"Might want to change that," Maas said with a grin.

"Maybe, but I thought GRQ, Inc. sounded big, stable and secure. I wasn't going to ever tell anyone what it stood for."

"You told me."

"I trust you."

"Still…"

Peter appeared to reflect on the name and then said, "You're a good broker."

"Nickel and most of my clients would disagree, but thanks."

"I want you to come with me to run my new company," Peter said in a rush as he leaned across the table. "I know back room operations. I'm good at math and can keep the books, but I need help to recruit brokers and teach new ones how to sell. You'd be great at the broker side of it. I've seen you help new brokers. Most of them do better than you do now."

"Thanks, I think."

"I didn't mean—"

Maas waved off Peter's attempt at an apology. "Why don't you ask Old Man Winter or Martinez?"

Peter shook his head. "They make so much money at El Dorado, they'd never leave."

"And I don't." It was a statement of fact, but it hurt.

"You could. You're a great teacher. Winter and Martinez never talk to the new guys except to steal their accounts by offering to trade them for half the commission. You always help the new guys. You could get the broker side of my new company up and running fast."

"It takes years to build a new firm."

"At first we wouldn't make much, but after a few years we should be comfortable and in 10 we should be making six figures a year." Peter paused and, looking Maas in the eye, said, "I'd make you a full partner."

"With a full share of the costs?"

"I've got those down to a minimum. I have an office picked out along the 405 freeway."

"Not the most desirable address."

"In Brentwood."

"A good return address to put on account paperwork."

"The rent's low but it looks posh for walk-ins, too," Peter said. Nickel and Vinny often stressed that people rarely give their investment dollars to a company that looks like it needs the money.

"What about the account booklets, tickets, phone system, desks, chairs, computers, and the million other things you need?"

"I've got most of what we need, and I got it cheap." Peter looked down at his empty glass.

Something clicked in Maas's mind and he blurted out, "You've been stealing from El Dorado."

Peter raised his gaze and, his hands still around his glass, met Maas's stare.

"They're going to figure out it was you the second you open your firm," Maas said, worried for the young clerk.

"I doubt it. Nothing I took is traceable. I'll order big stickers for the account booklet covers with my new company logo on them. They'll cover the El Dorado logo. The tapes are generic, the phone system—"

"The phone system?"

"The old one they put in the basement storage room a few years ago."

"You stole an entire phone system?" Maas asked, aghast at Peter's forthright discussion of his thievery.

"They haven't missed it yet. They never would have used it again. Who would want an out-of-date phone system?"

"Apparently, you."

"It still works and a new one costs a fortune."

Maas sipped his drink and chose his words carefully from the multitude of thoughts swirling around his mind. "Why didn't you just buy the stuff?"

"I don't have any money."

"You can borrow to start a business."

"Banks don't exactly rush to lend you money if you already owe more in student loans than you're going make in a decade."

"Why'd you get a Ph.D. then?"

"My parents stressed that education was the key to success."

"Doctors and lawyers don't do too bad."

"No, but don't get a doctorate in math or physics or, God forbid, English. You'll be lucky to make thirty grand a year. Even a friend of mine in computer science can't find a job because he choose the wrong sub-specialty. I couldn't even find a university teaching job, and I end up at a brokerage firm where guys with a BA from Podunk Community College make six figures just because they can talk other people into taking a long-shot gamble."

"My uncle always said, if you can sell, you'll always have a job."

"America is all about selling, and we'll hire guys who can sell to make us both a fortune."

"But stealing?"

"Nickel and Vinny have got a lot of work out of me, cheap. Did you hear they gave me a nickel raise last month? A nickel an hour, can you believe it?"

Maas nodded. He believed it.

"I know starting a new firm will be a lot of work, but I'm working hard now for peon's wages. I want my hard work to translate into something for me, and it could translate into something for you, too. How about it, Mouse? I can run the trading room and you can recruit and train brokers. Together we can make a nice living, and we work well together. You know that."

Maas considered the proposal. "You caught me at a bad time, Peter. I have some things going on right now that may change my future plans, so I can't really say yea or nay."

"Oh," Peter said, slumping back in his chair, spent.

"But I'll keep it in mind. It's a generous offer and I might be interested, but I still say it'd be better for you to find a more successful broker as a partner."

Peter glanced around Maas's house and said, "You're successful."

Maas pursed his lips. "Thanks, but in any case, I don't want to leave you hanging."

"So you're saying no?"

"I'm interested, but the timing just isn't right."

"But you might want to join me in…?"

"In a month I could see myself either not interested at all or very interested."

"What's going to change in a month?"

Chapter 34

After his question-plagued night—El Dorado or Peter's new firm? Brokering or sculpting? Maria or Sharon?—Maas gulped down the dregs of his third cup of coffee as he stumbled into work at 5:46 a.m. The sun was just cresting the horizon as he staggered into his chair in the trading room and set his empty coffee cup from home on the counter beside him. He missed the days of being a broker when he could arrive when he wished and did largely what he wanted. No one liked being told what to do. After all this was over, he promised himself, he would succeed as a broker again, reclaim his desk, a six-figure salary and his self respect—not to mention the right to come in late after a worry wracked night. Or maybe he would become a sculptor; sculptors set their own hours.

Peter took fills from the overnight desk as Maas inventoried his body. His head felt as if it was stuffed with wool and his eyes were itchy, as if there was a handful of fine sand grinding away in each socket. His stomach felt like a clothes dryer with jagged rocks tumbling around in it. His left shoulder ached, as did his lower back on the right side.

Peter found the last ticket, scribbled the fill on it and, bidding goodbye to Chicago, hung up. "Stick a fork in 'em, they're done," he announced, squaring up the wad of filled tickets before him. "Care to do a few, Mouse? Frank can do some, too."

Maas nodded, not trusting his fuzzy tongue to form words. He had a few minutes before the S&P opened. Peter handed him a wad of tickets from the overnight and Maas slid his calculator over to start filling out the price, commission, break even, and expiration date for each order.

"Want to trade calculators?" Frank asked Maas as Peter handed them each some tickets.

"Why?"

"Sam bawled me out for making some mistakes filling out tickets yesterday, but it's not my fault. This stupid calculator keeps making mistakes. It's funky."

"So you want me to use the funky calculator, make the mistakes and get reamed out by Sam?"

"Maybe you'll have better luck with it," Frank said with a hopeful grin as he held out the offending calculator like a questionable gift.

"Ah, hell, why not?" Maas traded calculators with Frank, who returned to his space at the counter happy. Maas liked Frank, even if he believed the errors had not been caused by the calculator, but by the calculatee.

Keeping one eye on the clock in the corner of his computer screen, Maas rapidly filled out his tickets. He finished his stack just after Peter completed his. They took a couple each off Frank's stack and finished them. By 6 a.m. they were ready to start the day's trading as the first, early bird brokers straggled in and the trading pits in Chicago and New York began to open at staggered intervals over the next couple of hours. Today Maas was only interested in one pit: the S&P. It opened down to a groan from the exhausted Maas.

Frank asked, "What's wrong?"

"S&P fell."

"So?"

"My IRA's heavily into an S&P fund."

"It'll be nice working with you until you're 96 then," Frank said with a grin as he patted Maas on the shoulder.

"More like 196."

"Better start eating right, then, and working out," Frank advised as he started reading an article on the recent Fed rate cut in one of his newspapers. "Says here the Fed Chairman doesn't have as much power as he used to."

"The market isn't buying that cutting rates will help the

economy," Danny said, having overheard Frank as he came in. Danny set his briefcase on the floor by his chair and sat down. "So the market keeps going down."

Peter said, "It isn't like the Fed sets interest rates, anyway."

Maas watched as the S&P fell: one point, two points, then five and, quickly, ten. Less than two minutes had passed since the open.

"What do you mean?" Genius asked as he arrived for work and began his daily search for his time card in the rack.

Maas swallowed. Should he call Sharon? Was she watching the S&P and, if she was, would she know to call? He had briefed her on what price they were hoping to sell at if the S&P went up, which, unfortunately, it had not hit the day before. If they got out now, with the S&P down, it would require acting on Sharon's part since she would have to place an order to buy her seven S&P back, as if she was short, not long. Unfortunately, they had not discussed the price at which they would get out of their feigned "short" positions if the market fell.

"The Fed just sets the overnight lending rate that banks charge each other, and a few other rates," Peter explained. "They don't set the interest rate for most things. They don't set mortgage rates, car loan rates or even rates for CDs or most bonds."

"But they are related," Frank said.

"Yeah, but it's not like the Fed can say tomorrow that mortgage rates will be 6 percent."

"No, but the government does have some effect."

Then the phones started ringing, terminating the budding debate. Frank verified a trade even as Peter called the floor to be ready to place the trade as quickly as possible.

The S&P fell through 1169 and then the bottom dropped out of the market. Maas had time and sales up on his computer, which showed all of the sale prices, as well as the offer and bid for S&P contracts. The numbers on the screen started flashing.

"Fast S&P market," Peter announced as he placed an order.

The clerks in Chicago entering the trades could no longer keep pace with the deluge of orders being run through the pit, so they entered as many of the tickets as they could. Therefore, time and sales, which appeared on traders' computer screens around the world now only showed a sampling of the trades that were occurring.

Just as they started flashing, Sharon called. "Where's the S&P?"

"S&P through the floor," Peter announced.

"1158 and dropping—fast market," Maas told Sharon. "Want to place a trade?"

"Anyone long the S&P?" Nickel asked as he stalked into the trading room.

"Just checking," Danny said, leafing through his copy of the Bible.

"Sharon Calloway is long seven," Maas called out, covering the phone's mouthpiece with his hand. "She's losing big, fast. I have her on the line."

"Long?!" Sharon yelled into the phone having overheard Maas's comment. "I'm *short* seven!" If she was short, the S&P going down would be good news for her.

"What?!" Maas exclaimed, overjoyed that Sharon had caught on to the con so well. Then again, he had not only lusted after her body in high school; her body housed a mind as sharp as a scalpel and a wit to match.

"I *sold* seven S&P contracts," she said.

"How much margin does she have?" Nickel demanded, striding over to Maas's computer to watch the S&P drop. He had not heard Sharon's taped performance.

Danny grabbed his calculator and in seconds announced, "Not enough."

"Where's her stop?" Nickel leaned over Maas to better see the screen.

"No stop," Maas said.

"Who the hell let her trade the S&P without a stop?"

Maas and Peter looked at each other.

"She says she sold short," Maas said.

"What the fuck's she talking about?" Nickel roared.

Maas watched as the S&P tumbled; 10 points, 15 points, 20 points, accelerating as it fell.

"Get her out, now!"

"I'll do it," Maas told Nickel. "I'm going to have to put you on hold," Maas told Sharon and then called the floor. "This is El Dorado. I want to sell seven S&P at the market." The order was read back to him and he agreed to it. Moments later he had their fill: 1075.80. Maas did the numbers in his head; $24,500 per contract, in all $171,500. He stared at the screen. He had seen worse losses before, but it had never been his money. It was like an execution. The guillotine had fallen.

"She out?" Nickel hissed in Maas's ear, his face a mask of barely controlled rage.

"She's out; down $172,000." What was $500 either way?

"She claims she was short, not long?"

Maas clicked back to Sharon's line. "Mrs. Calloway—"

"Give her to me." Nickel snatched the phone from Maas.

Maas prayed Sharon would play her part well. She stood between them and a $172,000 loss, which would mean the loss of her gallery and a crippling increase in Maas's debt, not to mention putting his ribs at risk of breakage by Coop and ending any chance of starting a new life with Sharon, let alone of ever having time to sculpt.

Maas slid his chair out of the way and listened. He tried to keep his breathing steady and even, even as his heart pounded. His stomach tightened as the jagged rocks he felt in it tumbled faster.

"Mrs. Calloway, we were just forced to liquidate your seven long positions in the S&P on a margin call," Nickel explained in his most calm and professional voice as he stood beside Maas. Sharon said something, but Maas could not make out the words.

"No, we had you long seven," Nickel said, as Danny handed him the page from the Bible. Danny had highlighted her account and circled her seven long S&P positions.

"No, long, not short," Nickel repeated. "I'm sorry, but—"

Maas could hear Sharon's voice through the phone, but still could not make out the words even as, growing angry, her voice increased in volume.

After almost a full minute of listening to Sharon make her case, Nickel nodded, his face grey and somber. He said, "Alright, Ms. Calloway, I'll have to look into it and see what happened. I'm sorry for the trouble, but I hope we can work this out to our mutual satisfaction." He sounded the soul of reasonableness. If it was the firm's error, he didn't want to lose a client who could open with $210,000. Her future commissions could help offset the loss. Even if it had been her error, she might still trade with El Dorado, but only if the firm was polite and professional.

Turning on Maas and Peter, Nickel displayed a scowl that

would have traumatized a 30-year Marine veteran for life. "What the hell happened?"

Peter and Maas glanced at each other, silent, a wrong word away from being fired.

"Why didn't she have a stop in?" Nickel's head swiveled between his clerks like a cobra, venom dripping from his tongue.

A stop order placed just below the market would have been triggered when the market fell to that point, thus limiting Sharon's loss to a predetermined small amount. Maas could not have had Sharon place a stop-loss order. A client short the S&P—wanting it to drop—might put a sell stop well below the market at a point where they would make a nice profit to avoid getting greedy, but never as close to the market as a stop-loss order would be placed to avoid losing too much on a long position. Someone holding a long position wanted the S&P to go up and would place a stop loss order just below the market.

"I don't believe you shit-heads," Nickel yelled, seething as his body shook with disbelief at his clerks' appalling lack of attention to such a crucial detail.

Older and more experienced than Peter, Maas felt he should say something, even if he would have preferred to remain silent. "I thought she was just day trading."

"That doesn't make a damn bit of difference," Nickel yelled. "She lost $172,000 in a lot less than a day. Danny, why the hell didn't you notice she didn't have a stop in?"

"I've been busy with the NFA," Danny shot back.

"Jesus Christ," Nickel said, running his hand through his tight, curly hair.

"I don't have time to check on everything, Nickel," Danny said.

"Everything?" Nickel stalked over and said, his voice calm and even, but clearly struggling to maintain that calm façade. "From now on, your number one job is making sure that at the end of the day every index trade in the rack has a protective stop, got it?"

"Yes."

"And you two," Nickel said, turning on Maas and Peter. "Make sure every order that comes in for the S&P or any other fast-moving markets has stops when it's placed. Got it?"

"Got it," Peter and Maas said in unison.

"I don't believe this crap," Nickel roared. "This is not happening again. Danny," he said, stalking over to loom over Danny and lowering his voice to a whisper, although Maas still easily overheard him. "Find the tape of her order. I want to clear this up fast before the NFA hears about it." Nickel turned and told Peter, Maas and Frank, "Not a word about this outside this room. Understood?"

All three nodded.

"Nickel," Danny said. He sounded hesitant and looked as if he was bracing himself to withstand a physical blow.

"What?" Nickel barked.

"We don't have her order on tape." It was clearly the last thing Danny wanted to tell Nickel and, Maas reflected, he would have waited at least a few minutes before giving Nickel that particular piece of information.

"What?!" Nickel exploded, the calm façade blown away by his anger.

"The tape machine plug fell out Monday morning. Her order was one of the trades we missed taping."

"The order and the fill?"

"It was an S&P." Such orders were filled right away; the order placed and the fill given back to the clerk during the same brief phone call while the client was on hold.

"Did the new broker in there screw with the machine?" Nickel demanded, searching for a target for his wrath.

"I don't think so. The outlet's just loose."

Nickel lowered his head. "Who took the order?"

"Mouse."

Nickel turned on Maas. "Did you place it right?"

Maas hesitated. "I think so—"

"Think so? My God, I thought we had a foolproof system here. Now I'm looking at eating a $172,000 loss, and God knows how much else if she starts bitching." Gritting his teeth, his body as tense as steel, Nickel stalked out of the room.

Maas leaned back and sighed as a tense calm enveloped the trading room. His scheme might work after all. Nickel sounded like a man ready to settle fast to get out of this potentially costly mess. Even if he didn't, Maas had repaid Nickel for threatening to take his desk. For a while, let Nickel worry about having his income threatened.

Chapter 35

"Why didn't you use one of the backup tape recorders in the trading room to tape her order?" Nickel demanded as he grilled Maas in his office later that morning. The owner leaned forward in his chair, taut, coiled and ready to pounce if Maas admitted making even the slightest hint of an error.

"Danny didn't tell us the tape machine was down until after her trade." Maas felt oddly calm, as if he was playing poker and held a Royal Flush. "When Danny told us, Peter's tape recorder didn't have a tape in it. Neither did mine."

"Why the hell not?"

"Genius was supposed to keep them loaded and ready for use." Maas managed to keep from smiling at the irony. If Nickel had fired Genius after the clerk scuttled Maas's Alaskan hot-tub king account, the recorders might have had tapes in them since it would have been someone else's job to ensure the machines were operational—someone competent.

"From now on, they're kept ready to go," Nickel ordered, jotting a note on a legal pad. "Did Calloway ever say she was short?"

"Not that I recall," Maas said, trying to remember if, in fact, she had.

"I'll have Danny pull the tapes from all her conversations with us. I hope to hell she says on tape that she's long. How many times have you talked to her?"

"After that first trade, maybe once or twice Tuesday, and then this morning before you spoke with her."

They both glanced at the door, where Genius had appeared. He looked at Maas and said, "Oh, there you are." Then he hurried back toward his desk. After frowning at each other over Genius' odd behavior, Maas and Nickel returned to the topic at hand.

"Did she ever say anything to suggest she knew she was long and not short?"

"I can't remember, but the tapes will show it." Then, glancing down at the carpet as if he was wracking his memory, Maas added, "She did act a little strange when the market was up yesterday after the Fed announcement."

"Strange how?" Nickel came halfway across the desk to reach for what might be a sliver of a chance to avoid losing $172,000—or $344,000 if he had to cover what Sharon would have made if she had been short.

"The market blipped up after the Fed announcement, so I suggested she might want to get out."

"What did she say?"

"She didn't have any interest in selling," Maas said, as if he was just thinking of it for the first time. He looked across the expanse of polished desk at Nickel. "It was almost as if...."

"As if what?"

"As if she thought she was short and didn't want to get out with a loss." Maas realized the irony in the fact that his attempt to get Sharon to end the con with a small profit of $25,000 yesterday, might now reinforce her case to win a $172,000 settlement against the firm today. Maybe his luck had finally turned.

Deflated, Nickel threw himself back in his chair, which emitted a complaining squeak. Owning a brokerage firm was a license to rake in money from those who wanted to participate in a form of legalized gambling, but you had to keep a keen eye on each and every trade. If a client went on margin call and could not meet it or if an employee made an error, the company was on the hook for the entire amount.

Nickel asked, "Did we send her any statements yet?"

If they had and she had not called to correct the incorrect trade, some, if not all of the onus for the error would be on Sharon. Maas shook his head. "She only opened her account last week."

"I can't believe you let her trade the S&P without a stop. How long have you been in this business?"

"My clients never trade the S&P; too much risk. You can take huge losses in the S&P before you even have time to pick up the phone," Maas said, then, noticing Nickel's glare, added, "As you know."

Chapter 36

After his grilling, Maas returned to the trading room to find Danny awash amidst a turbulent sea of client files.

"Mouse, where the hell were you?" Danny was always the picture of tranquility and calm amid any storm, yet he looked harried and frustrated.

"Nickel was interrogating me," Maas said as he slumped into his chair. Nickel's cross examination had taken it out of him, even if it seemed to go well and a part of him—the wicked, vengeful part—had enjoyed it. He only realized the tension he had been under when the grilling was over. He felt exhausted, as if he might pass out.

"Don't worry about Nickel," Danny said. He glanced at the doorway to make sure he was not overheard and whispered, "Even Nickel screws up. I just spent an hour looking through an account because the NFA wanted to know why we rebated a client $953. Turns out it was supposed to be $9.53 for some exchange fees we overcharged a client. You know what happened?"

Maas shook his head. He did not really care, but was too drained to do anything but sit and barely listen.

"Nickel wrote the decimal in the wrong place when he gave Sam the chit to cut the check."

"Maybe correcting that error will help cover a little of the $172,000 loss he's facing now."

"A very little," Danny agreed with a grin. "Anyway, I need your help. I sent Genius to find you, but he never returned."

"Genius looked in Nickel's office, saw me, said, 'Oh, there you are,' and scurried back to his desk."

Danny shook his head, looking at the floor with a pained expression as if the world was too much for him—or at least one Genius-sized part of it. "I told him to find you, but I guess I need to tell him to not only find you, but to tell you to come see me."

"It does pay to be precise with him." Maas dug into his reserves and, gathering his strength, asked, "What do you need?"

"Can you cover the desk? I asked Peter to make a copy of the conversations we did manage to tape between you and Calloway. I have to brave the rats in the basement storage room to find some tickets the NFA asked for from some other clients' trades over the past few months. Nickel's going to rupture something if we don't get him the tapes on that Calloway thing fast and the NFA doesn't like to be kept waiting either."

"No problem."

As he worked placing trades and taking fills, Maas overheard Hero and Chisel Chest lounging in the hall, probably sipping coffee as they debated.

"It's uncivilized, just like murder," Hero asserted.

"You're comparing capital punishment and a nice, swift, painless injection to the way some of those bastards murder people?" Chisel Chest asked, incredulous. "And what about rape?"

"Capital punishment just lowers us to the level of the murderers and rapists."

"States have always had the authority to kill people when they wage war. Fighting crime is just a domestic war."

Returning from the storage room, Peter sat at his part of the counter beside Maas as Maas scribbled the break-even for a palladium ticket at $762.50 per troy ounce before tearing off the yellow slip and handing it to Frank. Peter watched Frank leave on his way to the bullpen to return the ticket to the broker and then tapped a cassette tape on the counter as he stared at Maas.

"What?" Maas asked, noticing Peter's stare.

Peter said, shaking his head, "Didn't peg you for a hypocrite, Mouse."

Maas remained silent; baffled and vaguely worried, but silent.

Peter held up the tape as if it held profound significance.

"Danny will be back in a few minutes, so we don't have much time."

"Time for what?" Maas kept his voice calm, even as his guts churned and sweat broke out on his palms.

"The first conversation on this tape is between you and Ms. Calloway just after she opened her account."

"Yeah, after her first trade."

"No, the Friday before, just after she opened her account." The recordings were date and time coded. "You know what her first word was after you answered the phone?"

"Hello?" Maas guessed with a sarcastic smile.

"No, it was 'Tony.'" Peter let the fact sink in. "How'd she know your name, Mouse? It stuck out, since no one here ever calls you Tony."

"I don't know," Maas said. His head swam. His stomach churned. He was glad he was already seated for fear his legs might fail him. "Maybe I mentioned my name when I gave her the test before she opened her account to see if she could go discount."

"I thought of that, so I checked. Danny grilled her. Their conversation was recorded."

"Maybe I talked to her before."

"Why would you? She hadn't even opened an account yet."

"Maybe Genius mentioned my name to her."

"Genius hasn't mentioned anyone's name since Sam pointed out that if he didn't give anyone his name, they couldn't call and ask to speak to him. Makes it easy for him to avoid doing anything, the lazy bastard. Of course, he took the idea to the extreme and never mentions anyone's name now."

"Maybe he did this time."

They stared at each other until finally Maas, realizing he had lost the point, said, "What's the big deal? She knew my name, so what?"

Peter glanced back. Maas heard Frank hurrying back across the bullpen toward the trading room.

"The big deal is; you knew her. You two worked out this little con, didn't you? If the S&P goes up, you win big. If it goes down, she claims her order was placed wrong and she wins in arbitration by crying a brimming bucket full of tears. What is she, some broke actress wannabe you met? A hot bod wouldn't hurt in arbitration before a bunch of repressed, pencil-necked NFA accountants."

"How could anyone know what was going to happen in arbitration?"

"Just like Danny said, women always win arbitration, but as a little insurance you unplugged the tape machine the morning she placed her trade."

Maas looked at Peter as Frank hurried in, sat down and sank his nose into *The Hartford Courant.* After the flurry of calls when Maas had been ensconced with Nickel, the trading room was now quiet.

Maas whispered, "What are you going to do?"

"I know you have something on me," Peter whispered.

"I'd never tell anyone what you told me." Maas would keep Peter's thefts from El Dorado secret.

"Maybe, maybe not, but I just did you a big favor." Peter held up a second tape. "The first few words of that call aren't on this tape, which is the one I'll give Danny."

"Won't he notice?"

"It sounds fine; no gap."

Maas looked warily at his colleague. "So we're even?"

"That depends."

"On what?"

"I really want you to join my new firm."

"Partnership by blackmail?"

"You'll like it when the money starts rolling in. You could use some of the money from your scam to get the new firm up and running in style."

"We don't have a penny yet."

"You will after arbitration."

"What are you two whispering about?" Frank asked, peering over his newspaper at them.

"We're arranging a gay S&M tryst for this weekend," Peter shot back. "Want to make it a threesome, you handsome devil?"

Frank chuckled, shook his head and returned to his newspaper.

Furious, Maas tried to see a way out of Peter's blackmail. "How much?"

"I'll leave that to you. Consider it your share of the start-up costs."

Maas glared at Peter.

"The NFA is right down the hall. I'm sure they'd love to hear the start of this tape and my little hypothesis." He waved the first tape at Maas.

"Nickel's right down the hall, too, and he'd love to hear who's been ripping him off."

"So much for not telling, Mouse."

"The markets are a jungle, Peter."

"Mouse," a voice called from the trading room door.

Maas turned and beheld Cooper and Lindhe standing at the door. Maas cursed under his breath.

"Just stopped by to say hello," Cooper said, something between a greedy smile and a menacing sneer on his face. "How's business?"

"Good, and you?" Maas asked, wondering how many other ways his day could get worse.

"Fine, fine. Thanks for asking."

"Well, thanks for dropping by," Maas said, wishing the loan shark and his pilot fish would cruise away without delay. Didn't sharks have to keep moving or die?

"You're more than welcome," Cooper said. "We'll see you soon, Mouse. We're always in the neighborhood."

After Cooper and Lindhe left, Maas muttered, "I wish Mary wouldn't let that bastard in here."

"Coop knows quite a few of the brokers, doesn't he?" Frank asked.

"Yeah, the ones who aren't doing too well," Peter said, eyeing Maas.

If looks could kill, Maas's glare would have put Peter in his grave.

Peter whispered, "What proof would you have for old Nickel?"

"I'm sure the NFA has an application from you to open an IB with your name typed neatly in the appropriate box."

"An FCM, not an IB," Peter countered, offended that Maas would think he was only opening an Introducing Broker and not a more profitable, full service Futures Clearing Merchant. An FCM placed its trades directly with a clearing firm on the floors in Chicago and New York instead of—like an IB—placing them through another brokerage firm.

"I thought you were broke." Far more capital was required to start an FCM than an IB.

"I just stumbled into some money," Peter said with a sly grin.

"I think you better stick to opening an IB."

"An FCM would be so much better—for both of us."

The two men glared at each other. The phone rang; neither moved.

Peter said, "Looks like a stalemate."

"For now," Maas said, as he reached for the phone. "Don't do anything stupid and maybe we can both come out of this with what we want…within reason." He put the phone to his ear and barked, "Trading."

Chapter 37

Late that afternoon, Maas returned home after depositing the girls at their respective after-school activities for what he planned would be a half-hour rest before he had to collect them again. As he came in the front door, however, Maria stood by the telephone with a look that could have froze a flame.

"What's wrong?" Maas asked, fearing more devastating news, his mom's death fresh in his mind.

"I have a message for you," Maria said, her voice flat. "Sharon Calloway called."

Maas remained silent. A wrong word here could destroy his world, and their world.

Maria turned and picked up a pad. "She said to call her tonight." She turned back and, shaking the pad at Maas, added, "At the usual time."

"She's a client." It was the truth and in the present circumstances truth appeared to be the safest course, although every course seemed to entail grave peril.

"She has a 604 area code. Vancouver?"

"Victoria. You're home early," he said, praying the conversation would turn to other subjects before Maria's questions got any nearer the truth.

"A meeting ended early and the director is in Europe on vacation, so I left early." Maria put the pad down on the counter, stared at it a moment, and said, "That name sounds familiar."

Maas debated his policy on truth but truth was, once again, victorious. "I dated her in high school."

"Did you see her when you went up to Vancouver?" Maria asked, staring at him, daring him to lie—or maybe daring him to speak the truth.

"That's why she opened an account. She asked what I did and when I said commodities, she asked about opening an account."

Maria's shoulders lowered as some of the tension eased out of her, but far from all of it. "She sounded....nice."

Maas nodded, uncertain what to say.

"I better start dinner," Maria said, turning toward the kitchen.

"I'll go call Sharon back," Maas called to Maria and headed for his office.

"I forgot. I need to run to the store to get some tomatoes for dinner," Maria called. "I'll be back in 20 minutes."

Maas heard the front door close. Even though Sharon had asked him to call that night, Maas hoped she would be at her gallery. He could talk to her before Maria returned. Sharon answered on the first ring.

"How's it going?"

Maas said, "Well, the company's in a bad position trying to make you eat the error, since they didn't tape your order."

"Then they'll have to settle, right?"

"Probably. We should get most, if not all of our money back, but I doubt Nickel will go for giving you the $172,000 profit."

"Nickel?"

"My boss."

"His parents only thought he was worth five cents?"

Chuckling, Maas said, "It's his nickname; he's never parted with a nickel without a struggle."

"I hope he parts with a lot more than that. If I say that my order was taken wrong, what choice does he have but to pay the $172,000 I would have made if they took my order correctly? It could have been even more if he hadn't sold me out."

"It's still your word against his. At the minimum, we should get most of our money back."

"Why not all of it?"

"The company will argue that if there was an error, it was up to you to notice it when I reported the fill to you. The firm will argue that you should eat the entire loss."

"That's terrible."

"It's not that bad. Since you're a woman, they'll probably realize they're unlikely to get you to eat the entire loss if it goes to arbitration. You've been rock solid so far, so we should be able to get the firm to eat the loss."

"Then we'll just be back where we started."

"You can try again at another firm, if you want to."

"*I* can? What about you, Tony?"

"I thought I could do this, Sharon, but I'm not cut out for this type of thing. I did it to be able to sculpt, not to end up in prison."

"I thought we were in this together." Her voice was devoid of its former rich timbre. She sounded grieved, as if she had just lost a loved one.

"It's just not going the way I thought it would."

"It's going exactly as you said it would. We lost on the S&P and we're headed to arbitration, just as you planned."

"Except for Peter."

"Who's Peter?"

"A clerk in the trading room." Maas briefly explained Peter's discovery. "He wants me to quit El Dorado and start a new brokerage firm with him."

"Oh, no."

"It could be worse."

"How in the world could it be worse?"

"He could have turned us in. Joining his firm wouldn't be the end of the world."

"I thought you wanted to come up here and sculpt."

"Not if it means Peter ratting us out."

"You could always quit after the arbitration case is settled."

"We could still go to jail for fraud, even if he decides to talk years down the road."

"Destroy the tape."

"I'd have to erase the recording off the machine, too, and someone would notice the missing recording. It's a mess."

"Only Peter knows about it?"

"So far."

"I guess you'll have to go to work for him," Sharon said, her voice full of a bleak resignation. "Who knows, maybe you'll make a lot of money. At least he doesn't want any money."

"He does."

"Oh, God no. How much?"

"He left the amount up to me."

"He sounds like slime."

Maas closed his eyes and, slumping down in his office chair, opened his eyes to stare at the floor. "We're the ones defrauding the company. My God, I wish we had just got out when the S&P was up. We could have taken our $25,000 profit and we wouldn't even have broken the law."

"I'd have lost my gallery. Just make sure Peter keeps his mouth shut. If he talks, he won't get anything from us."

"He knows that."

They fell silent, each stewing in their own worries and fears.

"Tony…"

"Yes?"

"I hope you can arrange it to come up here, even if it's in a few months after you disentangle yourself from this Peter. I think we make a great team, and I still think about you…a lot."

"I would like to come up, too, but it's not that simple."

"It can be."

"But it isn't. There's Maria and the girls. There's the question of whether I can even sculpt anymore, and how would we support ourselves?"

"If this turns out well, I can get my gallery back on its feet and support us both for a while."

Maas fell silent, lost in his competing dreams of the future.

"I thought you wanted to sculpt."

"I do."

"Then what's the problem?"

"I want to sculpt, but I also love my girls."

"You love them more than sculpting?"

"I can't choose. I don't want to have to choose. I love sculpting. I love my daughters." And, he thought, 'I love Maria and I love you, too.'

"If you came up here you would still be able to see your daughters. You'd get visitation."

Visitation sounded like something the families of terminal

hospital patients were granted.

"You sculpt and I'll sell your work. I've been in a slump, just like you, but with some cash I can get some new artists—you the first among them—and make some sales. You'll see."

"I'm sure you will."

They fell silent as Maas tried to figure out what he wanted in life. Unfortunately, he could see no way to reconcile the different futures he so fervently desired: to sculpt; to be there for his daughters growing up; to see if he and Maria could improve their life together; to see if he and Sharon could make a life together. "I just don't know what to do."

"You better decide soon."

"I will." Even as he said it, Maas was far from certain he could.

"If you don't, someone else may make the decision for you."

After saying goodbye, Maas hung up and the door opened. Maria stood framed in the doorway, a cordless phone in her hand. Her face the picture of pain and betrayal, she asked, "What have you done?"

A nightmare invaded Maas's life.

"Are you leaving me?"

"Of course not."

"Then what were you talking with Sharon about?" Maria demanded. Then she broke down, sobbing.

Knives went through Maas's heart as he beheld his wife crying. He rose to take her in his arms, but she shoved him away.

"I never planned to—"

"Yes, you did," Maria spat out the words between sobs.

Maas struggled to think of something to say, something that would make it all better and right, but his mind was a swirling confusing storm of emotions.

"If you want to go off with Sharon, then go."

"I don't."

"You're damn well considering it, aren't you?"

Maas fell silent, refusing to lie to Maria. She sank to the floor, sobbing, dropping the phone to the carpet beside her.

"I met her in Vancouver, when I was up there, and..."

"And what?"

"She asked me about sculpting." Maas sat back at his desk, afraid to look at Maria. "No one had asked me about sculpting in

20 years."

"What are you talking about? We've talked about sculpting. We've been to art galleries, dozens of them. I don't understand you. What do you mean?"

"You and I talk about sculpting and art sometimes, but there's never any passion in it. When Sharon asked me about it, she sparked something in me. Reminded me of what I wanted to become."

"You're going to run off with her and become a great sculptor then?" Maria asked, contempt permeating every word. "What was stopping you from sculpting for the past 20 years?"

"You and the girls, and a million chores, and bills and work and—"

"You could have sculpted if you'd wanted to."

"I didn't have time. I didn't have the money to buy supplies. I didn't have a place to work."

"I'm building you a studio."

"I didn't know that until after I met Sharon again."

"We have money."

"I didn't know we had any money either. You didn't tell me. We were slipping farther and farther into debt, and I couldn't see any way out."

"You're a broker. You make a lot of money."

"Wake up, Maria, I haven't made a lot of money in years."

"You will again."

Maas shook his head at her naiveté, yet at some deep level he was touched at how much she believed in him. "Maria, they're taking my desk. Nickel's kicking me out the door. There are younger brokers who are raring to go, all piss and vinegar. Nickel likes them, and he doesn't like me anymore. Actually, liking doesn't have a damn thing to do with it. He thinks they'll make him more money than I will."

"I work."

"We've been living beyond our means for years."

"What about the money I invested?" Maria asked, having stopped crying. Even so, tears pooled around her eyes as she looked up at him from the floor, her back against the door frame.

"That changed everything."

"You'll stay with me if I have money, but run off with Sharon if I don't?" Maria demanded. Her face was a fierce mask, filled with hatred and the pain of betrayal, even as she fought to stem her tears, which started flowing again.

"No, of course not."

Maria inhaled, snuffled and, her arms crossed, said, "Tell me the truth or I'll take the girls and leave you. That will be the end of us."

Maas forced his mind to think through the swirl of emotions engulfing him before he spoke. There was a long pause, broken only by Maria's intermittent sobs.

"I could have gone," he said, weighing his words carefully. The wrong word here or the right word said with the wrong intonation could doom his marriage. He had to explain, clearly and precisely. Everything depended on it. The choice could not be made for him this way, not now. "Once I saw the chance, the opportunity to change my life, to leave you and the girls and brokering and everything we have, I realized I didn't want to. I didn't want to leave you. I love you and the girls too much. I hate all the errands, and the running around, the bills and the hassles, brokering and not being able to sculpt, but I love you, and the girls."

She looked up at him, their eyes meeting; his pleading, hers a solid wall of resolve.

"I should take the girls and go to my dad's house," Maria said, her voice low, filled with bitter emotion. "I should leave you," she said, shaking her head, her hair swishing back and forth, her mouth set in a thin, white line.

"Please don't. Please don't make the price of me almost making a monumental mistake losing you and the girls."

Maria wiped her eyes. She stared at Maas for what seemed like an eternity, as his fate—their future—hung in the balance.

"Did you sleep with her?"

"No."

"Not in Vancouver?"

"No."

"Never?"

"Not since college."

"Not even once?"

"No."

"Do you love her?"

Maas hesitated, then admitted, "I did, years and years ago."

"What about now?"

Maas paused again. His policy on truth had entered dire straits. "No."

"You must love her to think about leaving me and the girls."

"It was more….It was more that I was failing at work, we were falling deeper into debt and I couldn't see a way out. We were in a rut."

"I wasn't in a rut. I thought we were doing fine."

"I didn't think we were."

"She was going to help you out of this rut?" She spat out the last word as if it burned her lips.

"She reminded me of the dreams I had as a kid. I thought they looked wonderful, but they're just that, dreams, not reality."

After a long pause, Maria asked, "What's this thing with you and her and El Dorado?"

Maas explained his scheme, leaving nothing out.

Appalled, Maria asked, "Why'd you do it?"

"We needed the money. We're in debt and I wasn't making any money. I thought that if I could just get a breather, I could refocus, open new accounts, keep my desk—"

"And leave me and the girls to run off with Sharon and sculpt?"

"If I'd wanted to leave, I could have left weeks ago, before I even thought of this scheme," Maas said, realizing the truth of his words even as he said them. Why did he need the money? If he truly wanted to leave and live with Sharon, he could have worked out something financially with Maria and the girls. He and Sharon could have survived financially somehow. He could sculpt with little or no money. What had he been so desperate to buy?

Maria stood and stared at him.

"I should leave. I should take the girls and….." Maria took a deep breath, wiped her eyes and said, "If it wasn't for the girls, I'd be out the door, forever."

Maas nodded, silent, not trusting that he could say the right thing.

"I wish you weren't so unhappy," Maria said. "I don't know why you are. I thought we were happy. I thought we were doing okay. I wish life had turned out more like you thought, but this is the life you have, Anthony. You have no choice. You have three daughters and a wife. You swore to love, honor and cherish me and, even if you've forgotten that vow, your daughters deserve a lot better than you leaving them to pursue some dream you had as a kid that you weren't man enough to follow when you had the chance."

"I never felt like I had much of a choice at all."

"You had all the choice in the world," Maria yelled. "You can't go back and choose again if you don't like the outcome." She snuffled, considered a moment, and said, "Okay, then I'll give you what you say you want; a choice. Do you want to stay with me and the girls or leave?"

This was not how he wanted to decide, not like this. Yet again he had no choice. What could he say? "Stay with you and the girls."

"Then make it go away," Maria said, wiping her wet, red-rimmed eyes with the backs of her hands. "Get our money back, but I don't want a dime of profit from it. Talk to Sharon as much as you need to so you can make it go away and then never talk to her again. Understand, never again?"

Maas nodded.

Maria said, "You better go get the girls."

"Will you be here when I get back?"

"Of course; it's my house, too."

Chapter 38

Reeling from his confrontation with Maria, Maas's head throbbed from a sudden, sharp headache as he climbed into his car. He forced himself to think clearly as he backed out of the driveway. He had better make a stop before getting the girls.

"What are the flowers for?" Robyn asked as she and Malena scrambled into the car.

"Your mother," Maas said. "Be careful."

"There's no room back here," Robyn complained as she twisted and turned to wiggle into the back seat beside the enormous bouquet of flowers in a ceramic vase. Maas had wedged the vase into place with Coralea's books from her acting class. Malena sat in the front, having called shotgun. She read a book. Maas noticed she was near the end, hurrying to find out what happened in the hopefully dramatic final scenes.

Once wedged into her seat, Robyn reported, "I can't play volleyball and swim next semester."

"Why not?" Maas asked as they drove toward the elementary school, glad to think about something other than his own problems.

"Practices are at the same time."

"Which are you going to choose?"

"I really love volleyball, but coach said I might make the relay team this year in backstroke. I wish I could do both."

"So do I, but if they overlap, you can't."

"That sucks."

"Robyn, don't talk like that," Maas chided his daughter, glancing at her in the rearview mirror. "Maybe you can play volleyball in the fall and swim in the spring."

"Then I won't make the relay team because everyone else will have been swimming and getting better all year."

"It was easier when I was a kid. Each sport only ran for one season."

"If you want to be any good, you have to practice all year. Ugh," Robyn said, thumping her hands in frustration against her red backpack on her lap. "If I knew I'd make the relay team, I'd swim and just practice volleyball on my own. But if I'm not going to, I'd rather play volleyball and maybe they'll pick me for the rep team."

"That would be great."

After a moment's reflection, Robyn said, "Actually I do better swimming, but I like volleyball better. I wish I was better at volleyball."

"You certainly practice enough. I'm sure you'll get better at it."

"If my wrist ever heals."

"Lay off it for a while and it will."

"I have to practice," she said as if it was a commandment.

Robyn sank into deep thought, then, her agile mind turning to more immediate concerns, asked, "Where's Coralea going to sit?"

Maas did not face that problem for five minutes. When they arrived at the elementary school, Coralea was waiting amid a gaggle of her diminutive, giggling girlfriends.

"Wow," she exclaimed, as she saw the huge flower arrangement in the back seat. "Did someone else die?"

"No," Maas said. He hoped the flowers did not look like any of the arrangements for his mom's funeral and prayed Maria would not use them to mark the burial of their marriage. "Just get in."

"Where?" Coralea asked, eyeing the already filled-to-capacity back seat.

"Sit on Robyn's lap."

"No way," Robyn declared.

"It's just for a couple of minutes," Maas pleaded.

"No," Robyn reiterated. "It's dangerous."

Maas recalled his younger days of riding bikes without a helmet, kneeling on the front seat of his parents' car without wearing a seatbelt so he could see out, and swimming in the swirling waters of Lynn Canyon, which was now fenced off because of a single drowning over the past four decades. What had happened to kids today? No sense of adventure.

"Just get in," Maas told Coralea, his headache increasing with a brutal throbbing behind his eyes that threatened to rend his skull. "Sit on Robyn's or Malena's lap; you're choice."

Robyn said, "She's not sitting on my lap."

"She's not sitting on mine," Malena declared. "I've got to finish my book."

"Are you sure no one else died," Coralea asked, as she climbed onto the squirming Malena's lap in the front seat and pulled the seatbelt around both of them.

"No one else died," Maas reassured her, pulling out to head home.

"Is Granddad okay? You said he went to see the doctor last week," Malena said, having given up trying to finish her book with Coralea on her lap.

"It was just a routine checkup," Maas said.

"Johnny's grandmother went to see the doctor and she died," Coralea reported, concern etched on her young face.

"No one else died," Maas repeated, wishing they were already home so he could turn his daughters over to Maria's tender and more patient care.

His clear denial bought him two minutes of peace before Coralea asked, "What happens when you die, Daddy?"

Maas wished he had bought chocolates instead of flowers. "I don't know, Coralea. Ask your mother."

"How would she know if you don't?"

"She's a lot smarter than I am."

"You're better at math."

"I don't think your question has much to do with math."

"But how long you live is a number."

Maas stumbled on the doorsill as he lugged the flower arrangement inside behind his daughters, who rushed through the doorway, eager to pursue their various after school hobbies.

"Maria," he called, far from certain she would still be home.

"In the kitchen."

Relieved, he maneuvered the flower arrangement through the doorway. He stood with a hopeful tentative grin, facing his wife as she diced potatoes.

"You didn't need to do that," she said, using a Chinese chopper to cut the potatoes with aggressive swipes.

"I wanted to."

"Dad screwed up," Maas heard Robyn tell someone in the living room.

"Don't use that kind of language, Robyn," Maria called over the music that now screamed from the computer.

"Could you turn that down a tad, please?" Maas yelled, wishing he had his wife alone for even just five minutes.

Maria kept chopping as if she was splicing and dicing a sworn enemy.

"Where should I put them?"

Maria shrugged with cold indifference.

Maas sagged before her resolute defenses. He set the flowers on the kitchen table.

"We need room to eat dinner."

Maas nodded and lugged the arrangement into the living room. He put it on a side table and, admiring it for a moment, prayed that the temperature in the kitchen would rise. He was freezing and the mercury showed no sign of rising any time soon.

He stood in the doorway, watching Maria as she opened the oven door to check on dinner. "Smells good."

"Teriyaki chicken," she said, her voice frigid. "And rosemary potatoes."

"My favorite."

Maas saw daylight, but then Maria said, "I planned it last night." The frigid darkness closed in again like a shroud.

It was times like this that Maas just wanted to walk over, put his arms around Maria and hold her tight so she could feel how much she meant to him, banishing all the hurt and pain.

Maria said, "I called and told them to stop working on the studio."

"Why?"

"With all the errands and running around you have to do looking after me and the girls, I doubt you'd ever have time to do any sculpting. I assume that's why you wanted to leave and start a new life. We keep you too busy? You're family."

"I'm sorry. I screwed up." His words had no effect. "I felt overwhelmed. There was too much going on."

"You could have told me. You could have asked for my help."

"Then you would have got frustrated and depressed."

"I wouldn't have."

"Remember how depressed you got when we were just married and didn't have any money, or when I started brokering and worked such long hours, you never saw me and you had to do everything?"

"I'm not that fragile anymore." She stopped and stared at him. "I can do things. I can handle problems. I do every day at work."

"I know."

"No, I don't think you do. I lived alone for two years before I even met you. I can balance a check book, pay bills, run errands, and handle all three girls without anyone's help. I get them ready for school every morning while you're at work. I can do a lot. I *do* do a lot."

"I know," Maas said, glancing out the window at the studio that had been paid for by Maria doing a lot in the investing area.

"If you hate being so busy, why don't you let me do more?"

Maas shrugged.

"Why, Anthony?" she whispered as she stepped toward him. He felt her love and concern winning the battle against her sense of betrayal and anger, if just barely. "I'll be the first to admit that I'm a bit lazy. If you'll do things for me, I'll let you. Who wouldn't? But I can do more if it's making you miserable."

"I'm not miserable."

"You thought about leaving," Maria whispered, keeping her voice down, although it was filled with emotion.

Maas hesitated. "I considered it, but I've also considered buying a motorcycle, taking up scuba diving and trying mountain climbing. I've considered ditching it all to see if you and the girls wanted to run away to Italy so I can sculpt in the land of Michelangelo. I've considered going on a round-the-world cruise. I thought about moving to Belize and running a bar. I haven't done any of them, but I considered them all at one time or another."

"Maybe you should put more time into considering what you already have," Maria said. She put the chopped potatoes in a bowl, added olive oil, rosemary, ginger, salt, and pepper, and mixed it all until the potatoes were well coated. Then she dumped them onto a cookie tray and slid them into the oven beside the chicken. She turned back to Maas, took a deep breath and asked, "What are you going to do about this thing at El Dorado? You can't defraud the company. They've been good to you."

"Nickel was pushing me out the door the minute my numbers sagged a few grand. He thinks the younger brokers fresh out of Sam's class can post better numbers than I can. What crap. Nickel's a penny-pinching bastard and deserves what he gets."

"You might get caught."

"Shhhh," Maas warned, glancing back into the living room where Robyn and Malena were engrossed in music videos. "It's too late to come clean now," Maas whispered. "If I did, I'd go to prison for fraud, conspiracy and probably embezzlement."

"Prison?" Maria asked, her face betraying the fear she felt at even the prospect. "Could you really go to prison?"

"Probably not; Sharon should win arbitration, or Nickel will settle and that will be the end of it." He tried to sound confident even as he wondered what was going to happen to him, to Maria, and to Sharon.

Chapter 39

Maas straggled into work the next morning drained from his confrontation with Maria. After a sleepless night, he felt exhausted, battered, and found it a challenge just to walk. Luckily it was a quiet morning with few trades. He sat back in his chair, eyes closed, trying to imitate Rip Van Winkle and allow his body to recuperate from the tension and stress of the past few days. He realized he was no more cut out for a life of crime than a career criminal was cut out to be a 9-to-5 desk jockey. He should never have started the S&P scheme.

"You don't want to place the trade, Mr. Lawson?" Frank asked a client as he attempted to verify a trade. "Let me transfer you back to your broker.....Well, you really should let your broker know that you don't want to place the trade."

Maas opened his eyes. A brokerage firm was far from an ideal place to sleep.

Old Man Winter rushed in, ticket in hand. Frank put the client on hold and told Winter, "He doesn't want to do the trade and he never wants to talk to you again."

"What? Why?"

"Says you twist everything around and he can't think straight when he talks to you. I convinced him to let me transfer him back to you."

Old Man Winter blew back to his desk to calm his irate client.

Genius rushed in, a smile as broad as the Pacific on his bland face. He clocked in and sauntered over to the window between Peter and Frank, hands deep in his pockets. He clearly wanted someone to ask him what was up, but Peter, Frank, Maas, and Danny acted as if they were deeply involved in their various work-related or time-killing projects.

Frank's phone rang. "Verification...Him again? Okay....Mr. Lawson, this is Frank at the verification desk again." Winter rushed in with a ticket and handed it to Frank, who read it to the client. "I understand you want to buy two October 390 wheat calls at the market. Is that correct?....Okay, your broker will call you back with the fills.....Oh, okay. Thank you."

Frank hung up, laughing. He time stamped the ticket and handed it past the still loitering Genius to Peter to place.

"What's up?" Winter asked Frank.

Genius was about to answer, when Frank said, "He never wants to talk to any other broker but you, Winter."

"A second ago he never wanted to talk to Winter again," Maas said, incredulous, emerging from his attempted nap.

"Just a minor display of routine salesmanship," Winter said, lifting his nose high in the air as if he were the snootiest of Wall Street brokers as he strutted back to his desk.

"Amazing," Danny said, laughing. "Old Man Winter could sell pork bellies in Israel on the Sabbath."

Maas closed his eyes again as Frank returned to his paper and Danny checked the numbers from the previous day's trades. Peter placed Winter's trade and then returned to editing the math article he was writing about the diverging relationship between the paper and physical gold markets. Genius rocked back on his heels, sighed, looked around the room, and announced, "I've got some great news."

"Well, good for you Genius," Peter said. "Go tell Nickel."

"Nickel?"

"Yeah, he'd love some good news after losing two-hundred grand this week."

Maas glanced at Peter, who met his gaze and flashed a conspiratorial smile.

Genius, smiling like a five-year-old on Christmas morning, blurted out, "I won the lottery."

Maas realized at that moment that he believed in luck; how else can you explain the success of those you despise? Genius couldn't even find the right elevator to come to work; how could he win the lottery? Was there no justice in the universe?

"No way."

"Let's see the ticket."

They crowded around as Genius extracted a lottery ticket from his pocket. It was in a plastic Ziploc bag. "I wanted to keep it safe."

Frank dug through his stack of papers and pulled out the morning's *Los Angeles Times*. He found the lottery numbers from the night before and, laying it on the counter, they clustered around to compare the numbers.

"You didn't win," Peter announced.

"Yes, I did."

"No, you didn't," Maas said, relieved that there was some justice in the universe, although it would have been interesting to see whether Genius would have even made it through a single day without Old Man Winter, Martinez and the other top brokers convincing him to invest every dollar in commodities.

"Look," Genius said. "Seven here in the third row, 12 in the second, 23 and 32 in the first, 47 in the fourth row, and 48 in the bottom row."

"Those are five separate tickets," Peter said.

"No, they aren't."

"Yes, they are," Maas said.

"I bought the ticket," Genius said. "Cost me five dollars. All the numbers are there in black and white."

"You paid five bucks for five different tickets. Each row is one ticket," Danny explained. "You have to get all six numbers in one row."

"You can't mix and match," Maas said.

Genius stared down at his ticket struggling to understand this new way to look at a lottery ticket.

"Mouse, my office, now," Nickel barked from the door.

As he walked through the bullpen toward the owner's office fearful of what Nickel wanted to talk to him about, Maas passed Hero and Chisel Chest.

"It's cost effective," Chisel Chest said, just hanging up from his first failed cold call of the morning as he tossed a lead card into a trash can.

"What the hell are you talking about?" Hero asked, his feet up on his desk.

"Putting a crook in jail for 30 years costs a fortune," Chisel Chest explained, stretching and flexing his ample biceps. "Must be about 40 grand a year. Over 30 years that's more than a million dollars. How much does an execution cost?"

Maas followed Nickel into his office.

"I need a signed statement that you heard Calloway place an order to buy seven S&P contracts," Nickel ordered as Maas sat down. "And that she accepted the order as a buy when you reported it back to her."

"I'm not a hundred percent certain what she said."

Nickel stopped halfway down as he went to sit in his black leather chair. "If you aren't certain, then this error is yours and you can eat the $172,000."

"I guess I'm a hundred percent certain then." His statement would make little difference. With no tapes, neither side would admit making an error, and it would be a classic case of the firm said/she said.

"You better be sure, especially if this thing goes to arbitration," Nickel warned. "Have Kathy type something up for you, sign it and get it back to me by lunchtime. I'm going to call Calloway this afternoon and settle this nightmare today."

Maas nodded and then asked as if he was just idly curious, "What are you going to offer?"

Nickel's eyes narrowed as he looked up at Maas. "Fifty grand to eat the error and go away."

"Not much on a $172,000 error."

"A third. She could end up paying it all if we go to arbitration."

Maas nodded, hiding his disappointment. It was far from enough. They could not accept it. It would mean eating the remaining $121,500 loss. "What if she doesn't accept?"

"Arbitration Monday."

"That's fast."

"With the NFA here, I want to get it cleared up before they start digging around. We're spotless as a nun, but they can always find something the longer they stay."

After he left Nickel's office, Maas asked Peter to cover for him. Maas rode down in the elevator and walked outside into the smog-filtered LA sunshine. He avoided a gaggle of brokers who were already out for their third cancer stick of the morning and stood near the closed entrance to the Cellar, the building's pub. It would not open until 11 a.m. for the lunch crowd. Making sure no one was within earshot, he called Sharon. She was not yet at her gallery, but he reached her at home.

"We need to talk before Nickel calls you."

"What a stupid name," Sharon said.

"We all have nicknames at the firm; Boatin' Bob, he fishes; Scot E. Terrier, he's small and feisty; and—"

"What's your nickname?"

Maas winced. "Mouse."

Sharon chuckled. "I never thought you were small. In fact, as I fondly remember, I thought you fit just right."

Maas smiled.

"What's Nickel going to call me about?"

"He's going to offer you $50,000 to settle the case."

"He's crazy. I can't afford a deal like that."

"What if he offers more?"

Sharon didn't hesitate. "I want to at least break even. No way am I going to walk away losing money on this. I can't."

"I know how much this means to you, and me, but we may have to."

"You said women always win arbitration."

"They do, but they don't always win every dime on the table. The arbitration panel will decide who's more to blame for the error and divvy up the loss accordingly."

"The firm has no tape of my order and you said they're supposed to have it taped, so it's their fault. If they had done their job, they'd have a tape and it would be clear what my order had been."

"True, but they'll argue that you accepted a fill back from them for a buy, not a sell."

"I can say I thought you meant I had bought the seven contracts short."

Maas grinned. "You're learning fast. We have errors like that all the time."

"I got some books from the library."

Maas realized that she had not blindly trusted him. She had researched his scheme before calling him back, hence the delay. First love only went so far.

Maas said, "Either way, we may have to eat part of the loss."

"No. I have to come out ahead."

"Ahead?"

"It isn't just a $172,000 loss we're fighting to avoid. I'm pushing for some or all of the $172,000 profit I would have made if my order had been placed correctly to sell short. It could have been an even bigger profit if Nickel hadn't sold me out."

"I guess you're right," Maas said with great reluctance. "If we don't push for the profit, it'll look like even you don't believe you intended to sell short. But we have to be careful, something could still go wrong."

"Is Peter going to say anything?"

"No, but we should still try and wrap it up fast."

"Your firm already pushed for a hearing Monday. I'm flying down Sunday. Can you meet me?"

"I'd love to, but I better not."

"I really want to see you. I need you….for advice."

"I just don't think I can."

"Why not, Tony?"

"My wife overheard us on the phone."

"Oh, I'm sorry. Is she, what did she—"

"She was furious. Told me to finish this scheme with you and then never talk to you again."

"Is that what you plan to do?"

Maas let the question hang in the air as he considered his reply. Finally he said, "I really felt something for you when we met again. It brought back a lot of memories and a lot of what-might-have-beens and what might be. I think we have a future together."

Maas paused and Sharon said, "But?"

"But I have a wife and daughters, and a life down here."

"So you don't want to leave them." She sounded flat, as if every emotion had been drained from her.

"I don't want to leave them, but I also don't want to give up sculpting or a chance at a life with you. To be perfectly honest, Sharon, I don't want to choose."

"If your wife overheard us, I'd say you've run out of time to choose."

"I know."

"Then choose."

"I will."

"When?"

Maas pursed his lips and sighed.

"I won't wait forever," Sharon said. "I've already waited long enough."

"I know."

"Remember how depressed you were when we first talked about this scheme? Remember how much you wanted a change?"

Maas nodded, but said nothing.

"Remember how much fun we had when we were together? I think we could have a great future together. I don't want to wreck a happy home, but you certainly didn't sound happy. You don't sound happy now. I know it's hard to make a decision when you're down, but sometimes that's when you have to make the toughest decisions."

"I know."

"Don't abandon me again."

Chapter 40

Returning to the trading room, Maas found Peter checking the employee's cards in the metal rack on the wall beside the time clock. Peter stopped at one card, read the time and said, "Just as I thought. Genius thought he won the lottery last night, but he got up and came in to work right on time, 6:30 in the bloody morning."

"He is the most reliable of employees, if he remembers which elevator to take," Maas said, sitting at his portion of the counter.

"If I won the lottery I'd quit so fast, they could keep my last pay check and use it to light my chair on fire," Peter said.

Maas said, "I'd still come to work."

"Yeah, right."

"No, I would. I'd make them fire me," Maas said with a grin. "Show up in shorts and flip-flops with a case of beer under my arm and a stereo to listen to—loud."

"Nickel would fire you before you took your first sip," Peter predicted.

"I just read something about that," Frank said, reaching into his treasure trove of newspaper clippings on the windowsill before him.

"About being fired for having a beer on the job?" Peter asked.

"No, about quitting your job to do something else." Frank flipped through his clippings, raising puffs of dust as he burrowed like a Scottish terrier down a badger hole. "Ah, here it is." He pulled out a clipping, yellowed from the sunlight that streamed through the tall trading room windows every afternoon.

"Says here that 'Power professionals are just like everyone else—they'd rather be doing something else,'" Frank read.

"Are you a power professional, Mouse?" Peter asked with a look as if he was inspecting Maas under a microscope.

"'Although it was a decidedly unscientific survey,'" Frank read. "'Forty-one percent of lawyers said they would sacrifice seeing their children if it meant realizing their dream.'"

"Do sharks even have dreams?" Peter asked.

"Do sharks have children?" Maas countered, glad of an opportunity to shoot the breeze and not worry about Maria and Sharon, sculpting and brokering, Coop and S&P trades. "And what sort of sacrifice would it be?"

"Pagan? Druidic? Mayan?" Peter added. "Maybe the sacrifice of a virgin."

"Blonde or brunette?" Maas wondered. "Or maybe a nice redhead."

"Why are virgins always female? Why not a male virgin?"

"Much harder to find a male virgin who will admit to it when you're under the gun to appease a shark, or was it a god?"

"I thought we were talking about dreams and virgins," Peter said. "I've had my share of those."

"Virgins or dreams?"

"Both; often at the same time."

"'Forty-two percent of doctors said they would rather be broke and pursuing their dream than rich and practicing medicine,'" Frank read.

"And what, pray tell, were these anguished souls' dreams?" Peter asked.

"Why, thanks for asking. I just happen to have that information right here: 'Forty-seven percent of CEOs said their life-long aspiration was to sculpt.'"

Maas froze. A searing pain cut through his body as if from an old, unhealed wound.

"Nineteen percent longed to be musicians, while 13 percent wanted to run a marathon," Frank said. "For lawyers, many dreamed of writing a book, while 11 percent of CEOs wanted to write fairy tales."

"They already write fairy tales," Danny said, as he came in and sat at his desk. "I've read their profit projections."

"If they are power professionals, with all the money they make, they could take some time off to pursue any dream they wanted," Peter said.

"Problem is they'd be competing against sculptors who've been devoting every waking minute to sculpting their whole life, not just doing it as a sideline," Maas said.

"And those fairy-tale writers can be a competitive bunch, too," Peter added. "Send an ogre against you or bad mouth you to the fairy godmother if you step on their turf."

"Maybe the power professionals could just sculpt, play music or write a book as a hobby, and not try to be the best," Frank suggested.

"Right, 'Anything worth doing, is worth doing poorly,'" Hero said, overhearing the conversation as he strode in to check on a fill. "Lord Acton said that, or maybe G. K. Chesterton, or maybe it was my father. He did everything poorly."

"Who? Lord Acton?" Peter asked.

"No, my father."

"You're certainly evidence of his poor potential to procreate."

Hero glared at Peter.

"Lord Acton, whoever he was, was an ass," Old Man Winter said as he came in to hand a new account booklet to Frank. "I'll be transferring him in in a minute."

"Lord Acton?" Frank asked.

"No, Benny Edwards, my new client."

"No, he wasn't," Hero countered Old Man Winter. "If you enjoy doing something, why not do it poorly? You still get the enjoyment and the benefits. If it's a sport, you get the exercise whether you're good at it or not."

"I'd rather make some money," Winter called out as he hurried back to his desk.

Maas said, "I read somewhere that most self-made millionaires didn't set out to be a millionaire, but focused on what they loved doing."

"Then how'd they make the big bucks?" Peter asked.

"They did what they loved and the money followed."

"I love chasing women," Peter said. "Seems to cost more

money than it brings in, though."

"Eddie makes money on females all the time," Maas said. "They're horses, but some are female."

"Hugh Hefner made chasing women pay," Frank said.

"In more ways than one," Peter agreed with a leer.

Maas stretched, wondering how men became who they became. Life seemed to sneak up on you and before you knew it, you were something; a husband, a father, a broker. You rarely seemed to get to choose, or maybe if you did, you usually didn't realize at the time what a momentous decision you were making. The phone rang. Maas grabbed it; a fill from the New York Merc.

That afternoon, after the markets had closed and he had finished putting in his time in the trading room, Maas sat at his desk in the bullpen. The young broker who was using his desk during the day had left well before the markets closed, saving Maas the grief of seeing someone else at his desk. So much for Nickel's belief in the new blood's work ethic. The new broker's enthusiasm lasted all of three days.

After making a few half-hearted cold calls, Maas decided that Nickel had probably already called Sharon, so he wandered downstairs and outside to call Sharon.

"He went all the way up to $85,000," she reported. "Half the loss."

"That'd still leave us down about $86,000," Maas lamented, kicking repeatedly at the corner of a concrete planter. "Arbitration on Monday?"

"Arbitration on Monday. Can't you come see me Sunday at the hotel?"

Chapter 41

"The NFA's going home today," Danny announced Friday just before lunch.

Maas was relieved but, even so, he couldn't banish worry from his mind.

"Any major problems?" Peter asked, leaning back and stretching as he took a break from editing his article analyzing the precious metals markets.

"Oh, the usual nit-picking, but nothing worth pulling out the bribe money for." Danny chuckled at his own joke.

"New account verification," Eddie Weinstein announced as he rushed in. He handed the account booklet to Frank who was already on the phone with the client. Frank pulled out a binder containing a script and started verifying the account information with the new client.

"An Alaskan tour guide," Eddie whispered. "Makes 150 K a year." He pressed his hands together as if to thank God for making rich people who liked to lose money fast.

"A hundred and fifty K a year?" Peter asked, amazed. "What does he do, lead people out into Grizzly country and threaten to leave them there unless they pay him off?"

"I don't care how he makes his money," Eddie whispered, "just as long as he squanders it with me."

Frank completed the verification, much to Eddie's relief. It was one thing for a broker to tell a client the risks; quite another for Frank to state clearly and succinctly on a taped line that the client, in the worst case, could lose all or part of their investment. Brokers could sweeten the dire warning so it tasted like maple syrup. Frank gave it to the client straight, like the bitterest medicine known to man.

"I got a hot tip," Eddie whispered to Maas as the racing-addicted broker leaned over him.

"No, thanks," Maas said. "I'm taking a break from betting for a while."

Stunned, Eddie spun and staggered toward the door. "Let me know when this dread illness passes, Mouse. I'll avoid you until then. I would hate to catch whatever you've got. Don't you like gambling anymore?"

"Of course I do. I just can't devote much time to it right now."

Eddie flung his hands up and moaned. "If you love something, you have to devote yourself to it. You can't just forget about it. Your passion will start eating you up inside. It's bad for the digestion, not to mention the spirit and the soul."

"I don't think horse racing has ever been my passion," Maas said with a grin at Eddie's histrionics.

"It most surely is mine and I pursue it with all my time, body and soul."

"Don't let Nickel hear you say that; he'll take your desk if you aren't 100 percent devoted to brokering."

"As well he should," Eddie said, although he did lower his voice.

"You should pursue your dreams with all your heart," Frank agreed. "Look at Billy Elliot."

"Who?"

"That kid in the movie about an English coal miner's son who wants to be a ballet dancer."

"And Rocky," Peter chipped in.

"And William Wallace in *Braveheart,* the chess protégé in *Searching for Bobby Fischer,* and that rocket scientist from Appalachia in *October Sky,*" Danny added. He knew movies. "All of them pursued their dreams whole heartedly, at least in the movies."

"Pretty hard to do," Maas said.

"Watching a movie is hard?" Frank asked.

"It is if you get behind some tall bastard who blocks your view," Peter said.

"No, pursuing your dream wholeheartedly," Maas clarified. "Who has the time or money to pursue their dream and ignore everything else in their life?"

"*Dead Poets Society* showed that," Danny agreed.

"Showed what?" Frank asked, frowning.

"That going your own way has a price; a kid dies in it."

"That's a little higher price than I'd be willing to pay for any horse," Eddie said.

"*Irish Lady* paid the price," Maas said. "Why not you?"

Eddie glared at Maas.

Frank asked, "Wasn't *Searching for Bobby Fischer* about a kid who was really good at chess but his father wanted him to have a life beyond just playing chess every waking hour?"

"Yeah, it was about finding balance in your life," Danny said.

"I wouldn't want to die for a game of chess, either," Eddie said. "Although raising the stakes to death would certainly make the game more interesting. I wonder if it would increase betting on chess."

"Most people who pursue their dreams wholeheartedly fail anyway," Peter said.

"Not if they try hard enough," Frank asserted.

"Bull," Peter retorted. "I wanted to be a math professor, studied and worked like a demon, and I'm working here; not as a math prof at Princeton, Caltech or even Western Iowa Community College."

"That's just you," Frank said.

"When I was a kid I wanted to be a forward for Real Madrid, like Amancio Amaro Varela," Danny said, "but at 5 foot 7 with two left feet and slower than most girls, I never had a hope."

"If you had really tried, you could have made it. Look at Spud Webb or Mugsy Boggs in the NBA," Frank countered. "They're short, but they're great basketball players.

"They're famous because they're such one-in-a-billion exceptions," Peter said. "How big you are, who your parents were, how smart you are, and a million other things limit what you can be from the second you're born."

"Nonsense," Frank stated. "If you work hard enough, you can be anything you want to be."

"So you wanted to be a clerk in a crummy little brokerage firm in Los Angeles?" Peter asked.

Frank glared at him.

"How many guys want to play pro football, baseball, basketball or soccer?" Peter asked. "How many do? How many people want to act, paint, write or be a titan of industry? How many are? How many people do you meet who say, 'I'm a plumber, office drone or IT manager and that's what I've always wanted to be.' Not many. Hell, damn few."

"They just didn't try hard enough," Frank insisted. "Didn't seize the opportunity when they had the chance."

"*Carpe Diem*," Maas muttered.

"It is not crap," Frank countered, getting angry.

"No, I said, *Carpe Diem*. It's Latin for seize the day."

"Then the Latins were right," Frank said. "Seize the day and your chance."

Maas frowned. He muttered, "Which day? And which chance?"

Chapter 42

When Maas reached home that afternoon, he made some phone calls. When Maria arrived two hours later, he was ready. Maria stepped inside to behold Maas wearing the black dress shirt she loved. She said it matched his dark hair and set off his eyes, which appeared black yet, according to her, glinted like polished obsidian in a summer sun.

"You're bath is drawn," he announced with a flourish of a fluffy white towel.

She set her bag down and said, "You don't have to do this."

"I know. I want to. Besides, our anniversary sort of got lost amidst...."

"You made a mistake."

"I know."

"It won't work if you go through the rest of our lives thinking you have to make it up to me."

"Then how about just this weekend?"

"This weekend?" She tilted her head and, hearing no television, computer or voices, asked, "Where are the girls?"

"Your father consented to supervise our little princesses this weekend. We are free until 3 p.m. Monday. Your father agreed to take them to school Monday morning."

"That must have taken some convincing. If the Second Coming arrived before noon, he'd skip it in favor of sleeping in."

"He'll get up early for Dodgers' box seats."

"Baseball's his religion. I thought those were impossible to get."

"El Dorado has a box and I'm sure I can convince Sam to part with a pair of tickets."

She looked up at him with just a hint of a seductive smile. "You said something about a bath?"

A half-hour later they lay in the bath, suds up to their necks, the warm water beginning to cool even after several hot additions. Maas reached over and glanced at his watch, which sat on the dishevelled pile of his clothes on the floor.

"Got a hot date?" Maria asked, massaging his legs under the water.

"Already have one. But we should be going."

"Going?" she asked, surprised and disappointed.

"I think you'll find one thing even more relaxing than these waters."

Three hours later they were lounging in a sunken hot tub at the Miracle Hot Springs Hotel in Desert Hot Springs, just north of Palm Springs. They had iced drinks close at hand as the sun set over the mountains that separated them from Los Angeles. Almost all the other bathers who had been soaking, splashing and relaxing in the seven pools and hot tubs in the expansive, palm-shaded courtyard had slipped away to dinner. After moving from pool to pool, each a different temperature, Maria and Maas had settled in one that felt just right: not too hot, not too cold. They lay content, the bubbles from the hot tub's jets massaging their bodies as Maria reclined against her husband.

"Anthony, can I ask you something?"

"Of course."

She paused so long that Maas thought she hadn't heard him. Finally, she said, "Why did you think you wanted to leave me, and the girls?"

It was one of those times when he had to say precisely the right thing in the right tone of voice. He hated such times yet, if it went well, it would bring them closer together, suturing the rift that had opened between them. He knew from experience that the one thing never to say was, 'I don't know,' which was the response in the forefront of his mind. In reality, he did not know, so he thought about it. Maria waited. One of the reasons she loved him, he knew, was because he took time to try to answer honestly questions that he knew were important to her. He looked away at the stars as they began to appear in the clear, desert night sky above Mount San Jacinto as he considered his answer.

"When I was 10 years old, I wanted to be a shortstop," Maas began, choosing his words carefully, which led him to pause between each phrase. "I worked hard at it, played until it was dark, threw a ball against the garage and fielded rebounds for hours, day after day. I slowly and methodically, although unintentionally, destroyed the side of the garage until it disintegrated."

"You're dad must have loved that."

"I did help him replace the siding when one of my throws went right through the wall."

"You probably kept throwing the ball against it, though."

"We only replaced it twice more. When I was a teenager, I worked out to try and bulk up, but I was still small and, worse, I never could hit a curve ball, let alone a slider or a knuckleball. My eyes weren't good enough and my bat speed was just too slow. There are few things rarer than a shortstop who can't hit. They usually bat lead-off, first in the lineup. They have to be able to hit. I slowly and painfully realized that there was no hope for me. I would never be Ozzie Smith or Robin Yount."

"Who?"

"Hall of Fame shortstops." Maas paused to sip his Guinness from the side of the pool. "When I was in high school, I thought I'd be a sculptor. I sold one piece, but then ended up going to university and sculpting slipped onto the back burner, and then right off the range."

"That must have been hard," Maria said, stroking his arm where he held it around her.

Maas shrugged. "It happened gradually, like aging. There was never a day I decided to quit. It wasn't like baseball, where I knew if I skipped a season that would be it. I'll never forget the day I quit baseball. It hurt like an ember burning in my gut and it didn't go away. It still burns when I think about it, but there was never a day I quit sculpting. Unlike baseball, you can sculpt until you die. There's no time limit. I always thought I'd go back to it."

"You can now. We can finish the studio. You could sculpt for an hour or so after dinner, or after you come home from work and before you pick up the girls."

"I usually have errands or things to do around the house then."

"I'm sure we can figure something out."

Maas nodded, fearing his day was more full than Maria realized. Sharon just might be the only route to a life that included sculpting.

Taking a sip from his Guinness, Maas continued, "Then, when I met you, we had the girls and I slid into brokering. I never really liked it, but I thought that at least I could make a good living so we could all live well and not have to worry about money."

"And we have."

"You had to start working a few years ago."

"I wanted to."

"We needed the money."

"We were just going through a rough spot."

"We're still in the same rough spot." Maas stroked her wet hair. It felt silky between his fingers.

"Your dad was laid off, your mom broke her hip, and we had to help pay for your dad's heart operation, otherwise he would have died on a waiting list in Canada. None of it was your fault."

Taking a deep breath, he said, "To answer your question, I thought about leaving because I thought I had failed at everything I've ever done. I never became a shortstop. I never became a sculptor and I've failed as a broker. I thought maybe if I started fresh with someone who knew me when I was young, I might get a second chance at sculpting. I might finally succeed at something; something important to me."

Maria turned, kneeling on the sculpted bench in the circular tub. She held his face with her warm, wet hands and said, "Anthony, you're far from a failure. You're a loving, caring husband and father. I could never have asked for a better husband. There isn't anything you wouldn't do for the girls, or for me."

He thought that was the trait that had led him so far from sculpting, but did not voice the thought.

She kissed him and then, after shooting him a warm, reassuring smile, turned back to snuggle against his chest.

He muttered, "Anyone can be a good father or husband."

Maria whirled around, splashing hot water onto the deck by the tub. "No," she shouted, shaking her head, so water flew off her black hair. "Don't ever think that. Some husbands are horrible, most are average and only a very few are exceptional, like you. Why do you think I am even considering forgiving you? You have a lot of capital stored up with me and the girls; an awful lot."

"Being a husband or father is just something you do. It isn't something you work at like an athlete or an artist, or even a broker."

"Of course it is."

"No, isn't."

"That just shows what a good husband you are. You spend most of your free time taking care of me and the girls, and you think any husband would do that. They wouldn't. They don't. Most watch football, go off and play golf or hang out at work longer than they need to so they can avoid going home, especially the ones who talk all the time about how much they love their families. You just make it look easy without ever talking about it. A good husband or father is as rare as a good athlete, artist or broker." Maria stared at him, making sure her words had sunk in, and then said, "There's still time, you know."

"The Dodgers need a shortstop?"

"There's still a chance for you to become a sculptor."

Maas grinned with a melancholy smile as he marveled at her ability to dream. "Not if we go broke."

"What's going to happen at the arbitration?"

"Either they'll stick her, and me, with a $172,000 loss or have the company eat part or all of it. There's also a potential $172,000 profit Sharon's claiming. They could rule that the firm owes her $172,000, that she lost $172,000 or anything in between."

"How much of that loss would be ours?"

Maas did not fail to notice her use of the word 'ours.' "Half."

"Can we afford to lose that much?"

"I guess, with your investments. It's still a mammoth loss."

"If we lose, we'll just have to live very frugally," Maria announced with stoic determination. "Promise me you'll never, ever do such a stupid, moronic, criminal thing again."

"I promise." He did not ask if she meant his S&P scheme or his attempt to reconnect with Sharon. He assumed it applied to both.

"If you do, you can forget about me, and the girls." Their eyes locked, the depth of the threat clear to Maas.

Chapter 43

Since Maria had to be at work Monday morning, they drove back to Los Angeles late Sunday afternoon along the six-lane 10 freeway into the setting sun. Rested, relaxed and at peace, they planned a quiet, intimate evening at home with the girls still safe with Maria's father.

"Tony, it's Sharon." The voice on the answering machine filled the kitchen as Maas stood holding their bags in the doorway, staring at Maria as she stood at the machine, her finger still on the message button. "It's Sunday morning. I'm at the Airport Hilton. Can you come down this afternoon or this evening? The closer it gets, the more nervous I'm getting about the arbitration. I'd really like to go over what I should say and what they might ask. We have a lot riding on this." There was a long pause, and then Sharon added, "Sorry to leave a message on your home machine, but you haven't returned any of the messages I left on your cell." Maas had turned off his cell. Her father would call Maria's cell if anything happened with the girls.

Maria hit the delete button, holding it down for a long time after the beep signaled that the message was obliterated. Maas carefully set the bags down and waited in the doorway. Maria turned and looked at the clock on the wall. "You better get going."

Maas stared at her. He did not move.

She said, "I'd rather not lose $172,000."

Maas hesitated. What to say? "Are you sure?"

"Yes."

"I want to stay."

"Go."

"I don't—"

"Go."

Maas still hesitated.

"It's not like you're going to sleep with her....is it?" She looked at him, full of finely balanced hope.

"No."

"Then I have nothing to worry about."

Maas stared at her.

"Make sure she wins."

Chapter 44

Maas walked along the carpeted hall to Sharon's hotel room door and stopped. He stared at the numerals—604—on the door. He turned and retreated two steps back down the hall, then stopped. He walked back to the door, hesitated, turned away again and took three steps. He closed his eyes, let out a long, painful breath, returned to the door and knocked before he could change his mind yet again. There was still time to leave, he thought. Sharon opened the door. She was more beautiful than he remembered, even from just a few weeks ago. A tight, low-cut blouse accented her curves. Her hair, pulled back, revealed a perfect neck: graceful, firm and tanned. Memories of their shared past flooded through Maas's mind on a tidal wave of emotions.

"Hello," she said with a smile that embraced him. "Thanks for coming."

"I got you into this."

"Come in," she said, stepping aside.

He slipped carefully past her to avoid brushing against her and stood at the end of the bed. As she closed the door and approached him, he stepped over to the desk.

"Sit down. Would you like something to drink?"

He glanced at the mini-bar as he sat on a hard chair. "No, thanks. We should probably save our money in case we lose arbitration."

"We could go down and talk at the bar," Sharon offered, still standing on the edge of the bedroom at the end of the short hall that led to the door.

"Maybe that would be best."

"You don't trust me?" she asked with a wry grin.

"I don't trust me," he said, rising. He looked at her: the blonde hair, the bright eyes and the body that had filled his dreams in high school. And, in that body, a mind that knew him better than anyone; a mind that knew his dreams, the dreams of childhood, dreams unadulterated by reality, adulthood and responsibility.

She walked over to the bedside table and, picking up a small, black purse, said, "You really love her."

"I do." She stepped toward the door and he added, quietly, barely above a whisper, "But I loved you."

"And I loved you," she said. She turned and their eyes met for a moment in the past, full of love and longing. "I still love you." She took two steps toward him and, after a moment's pause, kissed him.

Chapter 45

Monday morning found Maas a wreck. Unable to sleep, he awoke with what felt like an avid gardener using a rake to till his stomach. He managed to force down four spoonfuls of cereal for breakfast, even though it tasted like soggy cardboard, before driving to the office in the dark. As the sun crested the smog-shrouded San Gabriel Mountains east of Los Angeles, he drove down the narrow ramp to the almost empty underground parking lot in the office tower that housed El Dorado. He was reassured by the routine nature of seeing Sam's silver Porsche, Danny's black SUV, Frank's cookie-cutter sedan, and Peter's ancient, rust-spotted, graduate student-special subcompact in their usual spots. Everyone had "their" spot since they were always the first to arrive at the building. It was nice to exchange the same greeting with the same security guard, take the same ride up the elevator and walk down the same carpeted hall toward the bull pen and the trading room just as he had done every workday for years.

"What up, boys?" Maas asked Frank, Danny and Peter as he strode into the trading room and set his bag on his part of the counter.

Danny said, "Sam wants to see you."

Maas walked across the hall to Sam's office. As Maas sat in the chair beside Sam's desk, he saw that the big man was scowling.

Without preamble, Sam said, "You're fired."

Maas stared at the manager.

"We'll be informing the NFA that you knew Sharon Calloway before she opened her account," Sam said, his voice clear and even as he kept his eyes locked on Maas in a frigid glare. "We don't have any direct evidence that you colluded with her to defraud the firm, but we'll be passing what information we do have along to the police."

"Sam—"

"You son-of-a-bitch. What the hell were you thinking, Mouse?"

"My name is Maas, Anthony Maas, not Mouse, damn it," Maas yelled, springing up from his chair. "After all the money I made Nickel and Vinny and you, Nickel was going to kick me out the damn door!"

"Get out!"

"My pleasure." Maas stalked across the hall to the trading room. He grabbed his bag and turned to leave but stopped. It hit him. Looming over Peter, he roared, "You stupid bastard. All you had to do was keep your mouth shut."

"It was a gamble whether she'd win her case," Peter said, glancing back at Danny and Frank, who listened with unabashed curiosity. "Nickel offered a 25 percent raise; no risk."

"So much for your new firm."

"As you said, it would have been a hell of a lot of work."

"You lazy, naïve bastard. In three months Nickel will find someone to replace you for a quarter what he's paying you, just like Al."

Maas stormed out. He had to call Sharon.

He tried to call from the elevator lobby but his phone had no signal. He waited for the elevator, but it was slow in coming, so he took the stairs down 14 floors two at a time. Panting, he rushed outside and called her cell.

"Hello," she answered groggily. He had woken her.

"They know. Peter told Nickel that you knew me before you opened the account."

"My God." She was fully awake. "How much do they know?"

"Enough to fire me."

"Oh no. I'm so sorry, Tony. The arbitration; I can't face them alone. You have to come with me, Tony."

"I can't. It would cripple our case." He rubbed his knees and shins. They throbbed from his punishing run down the stairs. His shirt was stuck to his back with sweat.

"Tony, I don't want to walk in there alone."

"If I go with you, it'll just confirm the firm's argument that we're colluding. It'll look as if I screwed up your order on purpose, so you would win in arbitration."

There was a long silence. Maas wished he could see her and read her face, but all he heard were her short, quick breaths, as if she was panting.

"You can do it, Sharon," he said. "Stick to the story we went over last night and you'll be fine. You—we—can still win."

"They could arrest us."

"I doubt it. They don't have anything more than their suspicions."

"They know I knew you."

"Tell them the truth. Tell them we grew up together in Vancouver; nothing more, nothing less."

"Nothing more?"

"Not for the case; just keep it simple—the truth. We knew each other growing up, hadn't seen each other in 20 years, but met at my mom's funeral a few weeks ago. You asked what I did, we got talking about commodities and you called to open an account. You'd traded them before, a few years back."

"But I didn't."

"You said you did on your application. If they ask what firm you traded with, say you can't remember. Your husband handled it all."

"My husband handled it all. Okay." She sounded far from convinced.

"Sharon, if you go in there sounding guilty, we could walk out of there eating that $172,000 loss or worse. Pull yourself together. I know you can do this."

"I'll try," Sharon said, her voice was steady again, but still weak and uncertain.

"Stick to the story and you'll do fine."

"You really think so?"

"It's a story and you can sell it. They'll believe it, if you do."

"Okay."

"Come on, get fired up. You were right and they were wrong.

You placed the trade correctly, right?"

"Right."

"They should have taped the trade, right?"

"Right."

"They screwed up, not you, right?"

"Right."

"They deserve to eat the error and give you the $172,000 you would have made if their incompetent clerk had been on the ball and taken your order correctly, right?"

"Right."

"Then convince them of that. You can do it. I know you can."

"I'll try."

"You will. You've always been a salesman. Go in there and sell your story. You'll win—for you, for me, for your gallery, for my sculpting, for our future together. Sell it."

Chapter 46

Maas sipped milk in an attempt to calm his churning stomach as he waited at a coffee shop near El Dorado for Sharon's call. All the little aches and pains he had accumulated over the years seemed far worse today. His neck hurt whenever he turned to the right. His left shoulder burned and his left ankle, where he had twisted it once playing golf, ached. His knees and shins still throbbed from his run down the stairs.

The arbitration would start at 8 a.m. and would take an hour or two, so he faced a long, worry filled wait. His cell phone rang. It was 7:40.

"I just peeked in the room. There are two women and three men on the arbitration panel," Sharon reported, anguish and desperation fighting for predominance in her voice. "Tony, we're going to lose. Women won't buy my story. Women hate weak women."

Maas reeled, the world swirling before his eyes. He steadied himself with a hand on the cold, metal table at which he was sitting. "Calm down, Sharon. There have been women on arbitration panels before and they're just as likely to rule in favor of female plaintiffs as all-male panels, if not more so." He had no idea what the real statistics were, but this was no time to let a paucity of information get in the way of reassuring Sharon. "You're going to win. You're the wronged party. The firm screwed up. They entered your order incorrectly and cost you a $172,000 profit. It could have been much more. They sold you out when the market was moving down. If you had been short, you could have made even more money if they hadn't sold you out on the margin call."

"I—"

"No. That's it. They took your money, opened an account and took your order wrong so that you lost money. You want your money back plus the profit you would have earned if they had placed your order correctly. It's their responsibility to tape orders and they didn't. They can't prove they placed the order correctly, so it's their fault. It's as simple as that." Maas took a deep breath, hoping his tirade had broken through her self-doubt.

After a long pause, she said, "You're right. We should win. They messed up."

"They did."

"I can do this," Sharon said, more to herself than to Maas.

"I know you can."

"They're calling us in."

"Knock 'em dead."

She clicked off. Maas stared at his cell phone. He wished he could be there. It was as if he had $172,000 on a horse race, yet could not see the race or even hear the call.

Chapter 47

A half hour later at home Maas had a second breakfast, forcing the cereal down more as something to do than because he was the least bit hungry. He sauntered into the backyard to watch the workmen, who had new orders from Maria, as they put the finishing touches on the exterior of the studio. It was going to be nice. There was plenty of room to create and, from an aesthetic perspective the studio was in a style that complimented the house as if the two had been designed by the same architect.

On his way inside, Maas glanced at his watch for the thousandth time. How was it going?

He finally called Maria and after some delaying small talk told her he had been fired.

"I guess I'm not surprised," she said, her voice far calmer than he had expected. "I thought they'd figure it out. I just didn't think it would be this soon."

"I can probably get a job with another firm."

"Do you want to? As far as I can see, you undertook this whole scheme to avoid having to be a broker anymore. Sharon said you wanted to make a pile of money so you could stop brokering, which you never overly liked, and become a sculptor."

"You talked to Sharon?"

"Of course."

Maas was speechless. When did they talk?

"I think you should try sculpting." Maria sounded as if she was recommending he try a sandwich on rye instead of white bread for lunch.

"I doubt I'd make any money at it."

"There's a bunch of ways to make money as an artist. Get a job in an art gallery or at an art museum. Go back to school, get a degree in art and teach at a high school or a college. We don't need that much money if the girls and I cut back."

Maas stared off into space, shocked.

Maria asked, "What do you think?"

"I think I married the right woman."

"Never forget it. What about sculpting?"

"I'll think about it."

"What's there to think about? Sculpt."

"It's not that simple."

"Why not?"

"I won't be making any money."

"We can survive on my salary for a while."

"If anything breaks or goes wrong, we'll have to dip into our savings."

"That's why we have savings."

"If we lose the case, we may not have any savings left."

"Then we better hope Sharon wins."

Chapter 48

It was another two restless, interminable hours before Maas's cell rang. He stared at it. It had to be Sharon. What had the panel ruled? What would be his future? Their future?

"Hello?" Maas asked, his voice tentative, hoping for the best but fearing the worst. He looked out at his studio as the workmen gave it shape.

"It's me," Sharon said.

"Have they ruled?" Maas closed his eyes, even as he tilted his head toward the floor, preparing to hear that they had lost $172,000 or, worse, faced criminal charges.

"I thought it went rather well, really." Excited, she spoke rapidly.

"What did they rule?"

"They certainly asked a lot of questions and spent forever reading over my account booklet and the company's rules and regulations."

"What did they rule?"

"They haven't, yet. The panel kicked us out while they discuss the case and make their decision."

Maas opened his eyes and sat down in a kitchen chair. He had steeled himself for bad news and now, no news was far worse. "How long?"

"Half an hour; maybe more, maybe less."

Maas sighed. Why couldn't they be quick and be done with it?

"Wait a minute," Sharon said. "Nickel's gesturing at me to come over. I'll call you right back."

"Don't hang—" Maas listened to silence, wishing she had just kept him on the line. He put the phone down and stared at it. What could Nickel want now? The arbitration hearing was over. The panel was deliberating. Maas looked around, his gaze flitting from the backyard to the empty living room to a painting in the hall of a weeping willow shading a tranquil pond. He looked at his watch, at the painting again and then back at his watch. When would she call? What could Nickel possibly have to talk about?

The phone rang. He snatched it up. "What did he want?"

"Tony?"

"Yeah, what did he want?"

"He made a final offer."

"What was it?"

"A hundred grand. We'd still lose $71,500."

"What did you say?"

"No."

The agony of waiting would continue.

She said, "He must have felt the hearing went our way or why would he have made the offer now?"

"You're probably right."

"They're calling us back in. I'll call you as soon as they announce their decision."

Maas set the phone down. Jail lurked in the back of his mind like a malevolent stalker, and he worried about Sharon. Would she lose her gallery? And what would he do? He had told Maria he wanted to stay with her, that going to Victoria and living with Sharon to sculpt had just been one dream among many. He had not admitted to Maria that sculpting was his greatest dream and had been since he was a teenager. All the other dreams paled in significance compared to sculpting. Although he loved Maria and the girls, he also still loved Sharon. Love did not expire like an option contract on a set date. Worse in a way, his love for Sharon did not mean that he loved Maria any less, just that he could see a future with both. Two futures, but he had only one option.

The phone rang.

"They ruled," Sharon reported.

Maas waited for the news that would determine their futures.

"It could have been worse."

"What was the ruling?"

"I think it went well, all things considered."

"The ruling?"

"They said they were suspicious of our previous relationship, but had no evidence to suggest any wrongdoing on your part or mine."

Maas felt tension ease from his shoulders, although as soon as it eased, it returned far worse, as if a boulder had been set squarely between his shoulder blades. "The ruling?" he asked again, desperate for her to just spit it out.

"They ruled that the company probably did take my order wrong."

"Good."

"And that they should have had a tape of my order and of the fill."

"Neither of which they had."

"They had your affidavit, though."

"They would have fired me if I hadn't signed it. What did they rule?"

"The company didn't have any proof they placed the order correctly, but I didn't have any proof they placed it incorrectly."

"What did they rule?" Maas had to control himself to not yell the question at her.

"The panel ruled that the company was responsible for the $171,500 loss, while I would have to forego the $171,500 profit that I claimed."

"Nickel must have been livid."

"He left in rather a hurry."

"I'm sorry we didn't make a profit, but at least we didn't lose anything. Will you be able to keep your gallery?"

"I doubt it. I still have the same bills and now more debt, and I need money to attract new artists. My current ones just aren't selling."

"There's a chance I know someone who might be able to help. At least we can close the account and get all our money back; no profit, no loss."

"Well, not quite."

Chapter 49

"Once I realized your S&P scheme was falling apart," Sharon said, "I invested some of our money in the grains."

"You spent our money on grain contracts?"

"Not spent, invested."

Maas was about to say, 'threw away,' when Sharon said, "Don't worry. Danny's been watching the technicals and he said the grains should move up fast in the next little while."

"Should? I don't believe this; grains? They're even more of a crap shoot than the indices."

"But the return can be so much more. A big move on the S&P is maybe 40 points, a measly $10,000 per contract."

"Measly?"

"It's only a $10,000 return on a contract that you have to put up almost $30,000 in margin for. Barely a 33 percent return."

"Barely? It *is* a 33 percent return."

"Corn can rocket up from $2.50 to six or seven dollars, doubling or tripling your money. And, best of all, the margin is less than $500."

"Nickel let you trade again?"

"He made me put in protective stops, and made sure Danny took my orders and taped them. He was extremely polite about it."

"Nickel's polite to anyone paying him to trade. Where are your stops?"

"Danny suggested 20 cents below where I bought in, but I did 30 below."

"How many contracts did you buy?"

"Two hundred and forty six."

Maas dropped the phone. He could not breathe. His chest felt tight. He struggled to breathe and then, hoping his heart would not erupt from his chest, he snatched the phone off the kitchen floor. "How many contracts?" He could not have heard correctly.

"Two hundred and forty six. Danny said it's the second largest order he's ever taken."

"With a 30 cent protective stop, that's…that's a hundred grand loss."

"We'd still have a bit left, even in the worst case."

"We'd lose a hundred thousand dollars!"

"It's not like it's going to go down that far anyway. I just didn't want to get stopped out on a wildly fluctuating day."

Maas rested his head in his hand to calm the turmoil within. He was having trouble grasping the enormity of what Sharon had done. Maybe he should start with something simple. "What commission is Danny charging you?"

"I told him I knew you, so just the discount fee; $9 a trade."

Appalled, Maas asked, "When did you tell him that?"

"Early last week. Peter already knew anyway, and aren't client-broker conversations confidential, like a priest's confessional?"

"Not really." Danny at least, Maas realized, had kept the secret. He was a good man. "We need to get out, now. We could lose a fortune."

"We could make a fortune."

"We were out of this mess, free and clear. Why did you go back in? I want out. You—we should be out."

"You led me into this, Tony. You can stick with me until it's done."

"It was done. Arbitration was over. We got out of it in one piece and we didn't go to jail. Then you dumped our money back into an even riskier gamble without even asking me."

"What choice did I have? I have to make some money or I'll lose everything I care about: my gallery, my house, my chance with you, and your chance to sculpt."

Maas groaned.

"It'll be alright. You'll see. Danny's been great. He's been keeping me up to date. He said he does it for another client, too, so it's no trouble."

They argued another 10 minutes to no avail. Reeling from the devastating news, Maas said goodbye and set the phone down on the table.

When Maria arrived home at 5:30 p.m., Maas still sat by the phone. He had tried calling her several times, but she had been in meetings all day.

"Where are the girls?" she asked, setting her bag down on the kitchen counter.

"Your father picked them up and took them out for dinner," Maas said, his eyes glazed over as he stared, unmoving at the phone.

"What's wrong?" Maria kneeled before him as he sat slumped in a kitchen chair. "Did the arbitration panel rule against us?"

"No," Maas said, coming out of his stupor at the memory of the good news that had started it all. "They ruled against the firm, pretty much. We don't get any of the profit, but the firm eats the error."

"That's fantastic. It's over then."

"Not quite."

Maria frowned, not following him.

"Sharon took all our remaining money and bought 246 corn contracts. Danny's been talking with her and his analysis of the technicals led him to believe that corn is going to move up significantly real soon."

"I agree," Maria said. She stood and took a salmon out of the fridge to start preparing dinner.

Maas stared at her.

"I've been talking to Danny, too," she said. "I really liked his analysis, so I got into corn, too."

"After all the years I've been a broker, you decide to play the commodities market?" Maas asked, aghast. "You know 99 percent of people lose money in commodities. No one wins. The institutional investors make all the money. What were you thinking?"

"My other investments have done well," she said, offended, as she took out soy sauce, ginger, garlic and oil to mix into a marinade. "Besides, you always said that if you ever invested in the markets, you'd invest with Danny."

"If I was suddenly struck stupid. How many contracts did you buy?"

"I kept some of my money back, so I only bought 300."

Stunned, Maas asked slowly, "Three hundred? One hundred and fifty thousand dollars margin?"

"Yes," Maria said, taking a pan out for the fish. "It's not worth the risk to only invest a few thousand; you can only make a few hundred dollars."

Maas stared at her. "Did you at least put in a protective stop?"

"Yes, of course."

"Where?"

"Danny and Nickel insisted on 20 cents below, but after I said how much equity we had in the house, I convinced them to do 30 cents below. The market is fluctuating, so I didn't want to get stopped out on a wild day."

"How could…I don't….," Maas stuttered. "We could have been free and clear. We could have paid off our credit card debt, refunded our IRAs and had some money to cover our expenses for a while, as well as pay for Dad's cook for months."

"I already paid off our credit cards," Maria said, pouring the marinade over the Coho salmon. "I didn't want to bother you since you were preoccupied with this scheme of yours, so I just called the companies and sent them checks from my investment accounts to cover the balances."

"Thank God." Maas rested his elbows on the table to cradle his aching head. Images of Cooper flashed across his mind accompanied by a shooting pain in his ribs. "Corn?"

"At least it's not criminal," she said with a smile to soften the words.

"We could still go broke."

"Don't worry, dear," Maria said, coming over to run her hand through his short hair. "Corn will go up soon, then we can get out with a nice profit and we'll be set. Danny's predicting a nice run up. We should double or even triple our money. Then you can take a few years off and sculpt."

"If I had a dollar for every time I told a client the same thing, we'd be rich."

"We will be."

"If corn plummets, we'll be facing a yellow death."

Chapter 50

"Why did you put Maria into corn?" Maas demanded as Danny ambled out the front door of El Dorado's building the next morning.

"Good morning to you, too," Danny said. He stared at Maas for a moment and then turned serious. "She was interested in a little play to invest some of her money in commodities."

"Three hundred contracts is a little play?" Maas demanded, stalking back and forth before the clerk.

"She bought a lot more than I recommended, but I really like the technicals." He held up a chart. "I thought you'd want to talk about it. Look," he said, pointing with his index finger. "This is the first wave. Here's the second and the third. It's due for a major move up soon."

Maas glared at the chart. His life held in the balance by lines on a page. "It's Maria, my wife, not some anonymous hick from Missouri with too much money on their hands. How could you?"

"She said it was just a small play."

"One hundred and fifty thousand dollars?"

"You've made that in six months. I figured you have tons of money."

Maas sat down heavily on the edge of a stone planter. His head drooped low.

"Maria's an adult," Danny said, standing before Maas. "She opened an account and knew a lot about commodities, including the risks. I didn't sell her on the idea in the least. I wouldn't do that."

Maas looked up, confused. "She knew a lot about commodities?"

"She knew all about margin, the different types of contracts and how the grains often go up in the fall if the harvest is less than expected."

"Where'd she learn that?"

"She listened to you."

"What a time to start listening. Can you get her out?"

"She doesn't want to get out. I just called her and Sharon. Both are up seven cents, but they want to wait for a bigger move."

Maas looked up. "You knew Sharon Calloway and I knew each other before she opened an account."

"She mentioned it," Danny said, looking over at the morning traffic on Century Park East.

"You didn't tell anyone."

"None of my business." Danny looked back at Maas and added, "Besides, there's no crime in knowing a client before they open an account, is there?" He stared at Maas, waiting for a friendship to be affirmed by the truth.

Maas dropped his gaze to the ground. After a long moment, he said, "She was my girlfriend in high school. If things had worked out differently, we would have got married. We saw each other again when I went up to Vancouver and it was like we'd never been apart." Maas stopped and looked up intently at Danny. "We needed some money so we could restart our lives together and give me a chance to pursue an old dream."

Danny frowned. "What about Maria, and your daughters?"

"I was tired, frustrated and looking at another 20 years the same as the past 20. Sharon offered me a second chance."

"Don't you love Maria and the girls?"

"Of course, but I also love Sharon and sculpting."

"Sculpting?"

"Something I used to do."

"Sculpt with Maria."

"No time. No money."

Danny stared at Maas a long time before he said, "You're a fool, Mouse. You don't have the foggiest idea what you've got."

"It's not what I want."

"Everyone wants what you have."

"Some people want more than that."

Danny shook his head. "Make sure you don't lose everything you have reaching for something you think you want. Know when to exit the market."

Maas looked up at his old friend, wishing he could make him understand, but realizing his words were not up to the task.

"I better get back to it. Take care of yourself, Mouse. It's been fun. Sorry it ended this way." He turned to go.

Maas could not let him walk away without even attempting a better explanation. "They were forcing me out the door, Danny."

"I know," Danny called out, not looking back.

"I was in a slump and they were kicking me out. They weren't giving me a chance to get back on my feet."

"I know," Danny said, but he kept walking back toward the building.

"After all I did for them, all the money I made them."

"I know," Danny replied. He waved goodbye over his shoulder and then stepped back through the front door into the building and was gone.

"The thing about capital punishment is," Hero was saying as he gestured at Chisel Chest with his cigarette just down the patio from Maas, "is that when you kill a man, you take everything he ever was, everything he is, and everything he'll ever be from him. That's a hell of a thing to do to a man, whoever it is; one hell of a thing."

"Thanks for the *Unforgiven* dialogue," Chisel Chest said. Maas looked over at the bickering pair. Chisel Chest stared at Hero. He frowned, scratched his nose and then, jabbing the tall, spindly Hero in the chest with his index finger, said, "You know what, Hero?"

"I'm a bleeding heart, super-liberal, pencil-necked pansy?"

"No, you're right."

"Huh?"

"I've been wrong all along. Capital punishment is wrong."

"No kidding?"

"No kidding. I see it now. You've convinced me. A choice like that is too difficult to ever make for sure. You can never be certain you have all the information, it's irreversible and there's always a chance you're wrong. You're right. We should never execute anyone." Chisel Chest stuck out his hand and shook with the bewildered Hero.

As they stubbed out their cancer sticks and walked back toward the building, Chisel Chest said, "Of course, murderers and rapists should be put away for their entire unnatural vile life without ever being let out. It's the only way to protect society."

"Forever?" Hero exclaimed. "You can't do that. It's inhumane, it's uncivilized, and I'll tell you why...."

Chapter 51

Maas drove the girls to school and returned half an hour later to the empty house. Even though he had been sleeping in, at least compared to his brokerage-firm days, he felt tired. His legs were sore, his left shoulder ached and his stomach had been unsettled for days. No matter how much he slept, he still felt worn out, depressed and irritable.

"Have you done any sculpting?" Maria asked when she called later that morning.

"I don't feel like it right now," Maas said, sitting in a kitchen chair where he had been lingering over a late breakfast. "Maybe later."

"Worried?"

"I've applied to a hundred jobs and haven't got a nibble. Maybe I should go back to brokering, although I wasn't making much money as a broker."

"You did."

"A long time ago."

"Anthony, you can sell. You're a good broker."

"Nickel didn't think so."

"He doesn't know you."

"He's known me for years." Maas turned and looked out at the studio. "I just don't have the drive and energy I had when I was younger."

"It's not like your 90," Maria said, angry at his attitude. Then her voice softened again as she said, "Something will turn up. We'll get by; we always have. I have to go. Take it easy and let me know if there's anything I can do, okay?"

Maas finished his second, late breakfast, moped for a time, watched some dumb television and then wandered out to the studio. He had only been out to it once when Maria gave him the grand tour. He opened the sliding glass door.

In high school, Maas had been an eclectic artist, using metal, stone, wood, and assorted other materials for his sculpted creations, and the studio reflected that eclectic streak. He meandered around touching the gas cylinder Maria had purchased, with a torch for working with metal. He ran his hand over the potter's wheel and idly rotated it back and forth. He crouched to inspect the electric kiln she had bought from a firm in Eugene, Oregon, after she learned they made the finest pottery kilns in the world. Assorted pieces of wood clustered in one corner beside a pile of neatly stacked metal sheets and bars. A furnace for blowing glass was wedged in another corner. He had never even seen glass blown, but he had mentioned once that he might want to learn how to work with glass. Maria had included the equipment in his studio. As he stood in the center of the room, he marveled at Maria's thoroughness. Not many professional artists had a studio as well equipped as this one, let alone a studio equipped to perform so many different types of art. He had everything he needed, except a fire in his belly to create.

He heard a knock on the sliding glass door and looked over to see Maria at the door. Smiling, she held up her lunch bag.

Maas grinned and let her in. She hugged and kissed him. "You sounded so down on the phone, I thought I'd come home and make sure you were alright," she said, looking up at him with a searching gaze.

"I'm fine."

"We aim for a little better than fine. Don't worry, corn will go up. Danny thinks it'll double. Hail in the Midwest or Argentina or somewhere. Care to share a couple of wiches?"

They sat at the pristine spinning wheel, each on a stool, munching their sandwiches.

"You certainly equipped this place to the nines," Maas marveled, gesturing around the studio. "Must have cost a bit more than you planned."

"A bit," Maria said with a mischievous grin. "But nothing we can't afford. Try not to worry. Do some sculpting. You may as well, while you have the chance."

Maas nodded, but had difficulty mustering the energy—or was it courage?—to sculpt.

She looked at him, reached across and, holding his chin in her hand, looked into his eyes and said, "Anthony, I'd spend every penny we had on this studio to make you happy."

Maas turned and, looking around the studio, said, "I think you knew what I wanted more than I did."

"Then sculpt."

Chapter 52

For his first project, Maas decided to work in metal, since he had always been most comfortable with that material. The sculpture he had sold in high school had been metal. As he spent his days working on his new sculpture, he secretly used part of Maria's paycheck to cover Coop's weekly vig. Her check also covered the mortgages, but there was almost nothing left over for food, gas, the phones, or the dozens of other necessities required by a family of five, let alone any to pay for his father's help. Maas sold some stocks he had bought years before and had largely forgotten about. He also was happy to see a final, sizable check from El Dorado for half the commissions from some trades Old Man Winter convinced Maas's clients to make. Maas was happy to see the money, but it only reinforced his belief that he had lost his ability to be a successful broker. He had been unable to cajole his clients into making any more trades, yet Old Man Winter had convinced almost all of them to trade a little more. Part of it was the influence of a new voice and style, but Maas knew much of it was the plain fact that Old Man Winter was a better salesman.

Luckily Maria and the girls were cutting back. Eating out was a thing of the past. Clothing purchases and spending on everything from CDs to movies, shoes to gourmet coffee, car washes to downloaded music had dropped to zero. Maria, as clever as ever, had made it a game with the girls to see who could avoid spending money the longest. She called it a Spending Fast. Robyn had managed nine days in one stretch, which earned her a new volleyball, since her current ball had been hit against the garage so often it was coming apart at one of the seams.

Maas doggedly looked for a job, but there were few that fit his background in the financial sector. There were plenty of broker positions, but he had little confidence he could ever succeed cold calling again and he did not want to be a broker again. Increasingly, he spent his time sculpting. He had not created any art in decades but, after he forced himself to get started, the old skills returned. The activity stoked a growing fire in his belly.

When he finally finished his newest creation, he liked what he had done but was as nervous as he had been on their first date when he brought Maria to the studio to see it. He paused at the sliding door.

"Maybe I should wait," he said, stopping Maria at the door and blocking her view of the interior with his body. "It's not ready yet. I want to put another coat of paint on the frame and one of the panels needs to be worked a little more to get the texture just right."

"Anthony, I'd love to see it, but if you don't think it's ready, I'll wait. I am at your disposal."

Maas hesitated, glanced back over his shoulder into the studio, steeled himself and said, "Okay." He slid open the door and they stepped inside.

Maria stopped, stared, walked around the six-foot sculpture and then, smiling, turned to her husband and said, "I like it."

"What's going on?" Robyn asked from the doorway.

"It's the premiere of your father's first sculpture," Maria said. "Come in."

Robyn stepped inside, quickly followed by Malena and Coralea.

"Cool," Malena said, peering at the black metal frame that held a triangle, a square, a circle, and a rectangle.

"I like the rough texture," Robyn said, running her hand over the frame.

Coralea asked, "It's not finished, is it?"

They all looked at the little girl.

She stepped toward the sculpture and thrust her tiny fist through the center of the hollow triangle. "You *are* going to put something in the shapes, aren't you?"

Maas stopped, stunned. She was right; but what to put in the geometric shapes? Then it hit him.

Three days later he was ready. This time, as his girls trouped into the studio, their eyes lit up.

Maas had obtained different colored glass—he wasn't up to blowing it himself, yet—cut it and inserted the pieces into the center of the geometric shapes within the black, textured frame. He had also set up a light behind the sculpture so it shone through the beveled pieces of colored glass.

"It's meant to be set up outside in a position so sunlight streams through it," Maas explained as his girls and Maria inspected his creation. "The light just approximates what sunlight would look like at a certain time each day."

"It's great," Maria said, hugging Maas.

"Not bad, Dad," Robyn admitted.

"It's neat," Malena said.

All eyes turned on Coralea. After a moment's further inspection, she answered with a big, little-girl smile, "Now it's finished."

Chapter 53

Maas watched the bills mount over the weeks, even as corn meandered up and down in an irritatingly narrow range. The crop reports were mixed, some predicting a bumper crop, others offering dire warnings of the effects of a drought in the Mid-West and storms in Argentina. No one knew what to believe, so the grains jumped up five cents, down seven and then up again in an infuriating dance of irresolution. As he worked, Maas idly dreamed that his first piece of art would sell in a few days, more sales and commissions would quickly follow and he would never have to get a real job again. It seemed a blissful possibility. Even with such dreaming, he still applied for more jobs—anything remotely related to the financial world that was not brokering.

"Lindhe told me, but I couldn't damn well believe it," Cooper announced one morning when he appeared at the door to Maas's studio.

Startled, Maas turned off the torch he had been using to start his second project. He flicked his welding visor up and, still clad in his thick leather apron and gloves, turned to face the loan shark. Coop stepped into the studio followed by his impeccably dressed accountant.

"Lindhe said I should leave you alone, even if you were canned from El Dorado," Cooper said, stalking around the studio, peering at the potter's wheel, the kiln, the scrap metal against one wall, and the bench laden with tools. "Said you'd taken up art or something."

"He is paying on time, just like a government bond," Lindhe observed. He tilted his head to one side to peer at Maas's first creation, which stood in a corner.

"How long's that going to last with him wasting his time doing....doing whatever the hell he's doing?" Coop demanded, looking around with an exasperated expression. He clearly had never been in a studio, and probably never would be again.

"My wife's working, and we expect an investment to make us a fair amount of money any day now," Maas reported, feeling trapped in what now felt like an exceedingly small, enclosed space as Cooper prowled around the studio like a tiger in a cage designed for a house cat.

Cooper stopped and peered at Maas. "If you mean your corn investment, I wouldn't stake your ribs on that returning even a tenth of the money you sank into it." Then, noticing Maas's surprised look, Coop added, "My other clients at El Dorado keep me up on what's going on—with everyone."

"Know your client is a cardinal rule in the loan trade," Lindhe said, looking as relaxed as ever.

"Damn right," Coop agreed. "What I want to know is when you're going to get off your ass and get back to brokering to make some real money. I don't want my payments resting on you making any money selling this...this junk." Coop prodded Maas's newest work with the toe of his black dress shoe.

"Lot of money in art," Lindhe observed, still standing rock still near the doorway.

"In this?" Coop asked in disbelief, gesturing around the studio.

"You never know," Lindhe replied.

"Well, I don't know if there is or if there isn't," Coop said as he advanced on Maas and jabbed his right index finger into Maas's chest. "But one thing I do know; you will pay what you owe me." The leather apron did not prevent Maas from involuntarily stepping back.

"I have been making my payments. I was actually wondering about the possibility of another small loan."

"What for?" Coop asked, his eyes narrowing.

"Just to tide us over."

"Until your corn comes in?" Coop sneered. Then he glanced

at his accountant.

"They have some equity in their house," Lindhe reported, consulting his palm pilot. "His wife makes almost enough to live on. He got a nice check from El Dorado a few weeks ago, and Mr. Maas has disability insurance, should he be injured, as well as life insurance."

"How the hell did you know all that?" Maas demanded, forgetting, if only for an instant, to whom he was speaking.

"Know your client," Lindhe repeated his rule with a solemn look. "Credit checks and old fraternity brothers at various banks are crucial assets in this trade."

Coop looked at the floor for a moment considering and then looked up at Maas. "How much you need?"

Chapter 54

Maas was working on his second metal piece, 'Eye of the Cyclops,' when he heard a knock on the studio's door.

"Danny said you were sculpting, but I didn't believe him," Frank said, stepping inside. He looked around, eyeing the kiln, bellows and metal-working equipment. "Looks like Dr. Frankenstein's lab."

Maas chuckled. "Come in, come in." He moved a book on sculpting he had been perusing that morning from a stool and offered the seat to Frank.

"What brings you here?" Maas asked, as he checked his watch and realized the markets had just closed. Engrossed in sculpting, the morning had flown by. "You're off work a little early."

"Actually, I'm off work at El Dorado permanently."

"You didn't get fired, did you?" Maas asked, fearing that something he had done with Sharon's account had cost Frank his job.

"No, no," Frank reassured Maas, shaking his head and waving his hands. "I quit."

"I'm sorry to hear that. I can tell you from personal experience, it's not a good time to be out of work."

"I've actually already found other employment," Frank said, beaming. He paused and announced with great pride, "I started my own brokerage firm."

Maas stared at Frank. The older man had always been quiet,

unassuming and most of the time faded into the woodwork. He was not a talker like the brokers or a practical joker like the clerks. He also did not, given his age, seem to Maas to be a man to embark on the arduous and risky adventure of starting a brokerage firm.

"I decided to stop working for other people," Frank explained. "I spent three years working on the floor in Chicago as a young man and I have more experience in the financial markets than Nickel, Vinny and Sam combined."

"I have no doubt," Maas said, still trying to get his mind around the idea of Frank starting a firm. "Peter was thinking of starting his own firm, too."

"He's the one who put the idea in my head. He asked me to come aboard to train new brokers, but I'm not really the salesman type. I'm more a back room manager. That's where most of my experience has been."

It hit Maas that Peter's offer had been less than unique to him. Had Maas been Peter's first or second choice? Or had he asked several other brokers before Maas and Frank? It really didn't matter, yet a part of Maas cared deeply.

"I ran Lim, Lo and Short's trading room for seven years back in the eighties."

"I didn't know that," Maas said, surprised again. Lim, Lo and Short was one of the largest brokerages in North America. "When are you going to be up and running?"

"We already are." Frank stood and walked over to Maas's only completed sculpture. He peered through the thick, blue glass in the triangle. "Peter had a bunch of stuff he didn't need, so he offered to sell it all to me; rock bottom prices, too."

Maas winced. Peter had involved Frank in his thefts. How much time did you get for receiving stolen property?

"I should tell you something about Peter," Maas began.

"Nickel was happy to get rid of the stuff, too."

"Nickel?"

"Yeah," Frank said, turning back from the sculpture. "Peter found boxes full of all the missing stuff down in the storeroom when Danny sent him down to find some file the NFA wanted. The account booklets and tickets were scuffed up and water damaged, and some were missing covers. Someone must have put them down there thinking they were too messed up to use."

Maas nodded, relieved that Peter had not sold Frank stolen goods.

"Most of them were usable if you sorted through them, and it was easy enough to put a sticker for my new company on them; cheap, too. I also got the old phone system from Nickel, real cheap."

"What's your company's name?"

"Jefferson Adams Financial," Frank said, standing tall, as if announcing the birth of his first born. He handed Maas a new business card. "The guy who founded Kennedy-Cabot used good, patriotic-sounding American names. His last name was something totally different. If it worked for him, why not for me?"

Frank sat on the stool opposite Maas and, leaning forward said, "The reason I stopped by wasn't to shoot the shit or admire your sculptures, although I like that one over there," he said, gesturing at Maas's only completed work. "I came by to ask if you wanted to get back into brokering. I need someone to hire new brokers, train 'em and teach 'em to sell. Someone to instill a work ethic in the lazy bastards."

Maas had never heard Frank talk so forcefully. Being an owner had changed him. Apparently working for someone else had turned him into a mouse, sapping him of his passion—until now.

"I'm sort of busy here," Maas said, gesturing around his studio.

"I need someone like you," Frank insisted, his eyes intense and clear, locked on Maas. "You have years of experience and the younger brokers listen to you."

"I wasn't exactly opening many accounts the past few years."

"You just lost the fire in the belly. El Dorado was getting old hat for you, stale as a year-old affair. Get you teaching the new bloods and you'll feel like you just got into the business again, fresh as Boatin' Bob's fish. It worked for me. I know you can do it, that's why I'm offering you a partnership: 70/30. I set up the firm and did all the heavy lifting, so I get the 70."

"Sounds generous, Frank."

"It just shows how much I want you aboard." He leaned toward Maas and whispered, as if fearing being overheard, "You and I could make a fortune. Not this year, maybe not next but within four, five years we should be making mid-six figures."

"Sounds tempting, but I don't really want to get back into brokering right now."

Frank leaned back and pursed his lips. "This is an opportunity of a lifetime, Mouse. I have an FCM license, a dozen brokers already hitting the phones, and I hired Al to handle the trading room."

"Al?"

"Yeah, he's far from cheap, but he's worth it. I cut him in for a share of the profits to keep his ass in a chair in my trading room for the rest of his life. He can do the work of any other three clerks and he doesn't make more than one error a year, two in leap years."

Maas nodded. Al was the best. Maas stood. He walked over to his sculpture, tapped the metal as he considered the proposal and turned back to Frank. "Thank you very much for the offer, but the timing's not right for me. A few months ago, maybe, but now.... now's not the right time."

Frank stared at Maas from his perch on the stool, then pursed his lips in disappointment and nodded. "Alright." Frank stood. "The offer's on the table as long as you like, though we'll have to see about the percentages. Your share may go down a good bit if you only decide to join after my firm is running full throttle. Decide soon and you can make a killing. Decide later and you just might be left on the dock waving goodbye to me on a new yacht."

"I'll decide soon."

"You keep an eye on Jefferson Adams Financial. Give me six months and we'll be showing a profit. In a year, we'll be comfortable."

They shook hands and Frank walked to the door to leave. He stopped and, his hand on the door, said, "I hope I see you at my door some time soon." Then Frank left.

"I hope not," Maas whispered. "I sincerely hope not."

Chapter 55

"Maybe I should broaden my job search," Maas suggested as he ate lunch with Maria in the studio. She now regularly came home for lunch. It was nice seeing each other in the middle of the day.

"Corn will go up soon," Maria predicted, blowing on a spoonful of steaming country vegetable soup. "Danny is sure it'll blip up. He just isn't sure when."

"Is blip the technical term?" Maas asked with a grin. "Good soup."

"I think so," Maria said with a smile. "It was on sale; four cans for a buck." She looked around the studio and added, "In any case, you should sculpt. You're good at it. I like your first piece. I think you have a creative flair."

"Hopefully someone will be willing to pay for my flair. Just have to figure out how to sell it."

"Call Sharon."

Maas looked at Maria, remembering her threat that he must never talk to her again. "I don't think I should."

"You should."

"Are you sure?"

"I'm sure. If she can win at arbitration, she can sell art; besides, we need the money."

Later that day, Maas called Sharon.

He nervously announced, "I finished my first piece."

"When do I get to see it?"

Relief flooded Maas's body. "Now, if you want me to send you some photos."

"Email them to me today. I want to see it. I need some fresh, hot new artists to attract customers."

Maas emailed images of his sculpture to Sharon, who replied moments later. She wanted him to ship his sculpture to Victoria for her to sell. She recommended a shipping company. The next morning an overjoyed Maas met the shippers at the door and kept a paternal eye on them as they carted his creation into a wood crate and trundled it to the truck. Then it was gone. He walked back inside, feeling for the first time as if he was an artist. His work was out in the world. People would see it, criticize it, loath it, love it or, worst of all, feel nothing at all at the sight of it. Feeling full of passion and vitality, he returned to work on his next piece, 'Eye of the Cyclops.' He was sitting on a stool, considering how to proceed when the phone rang. Without looking, his mind on his new work, he picked up the cordless phone from the workbench.

"Anthony," Maria said. "Corn dropped today."

Maas froze. His mind snapped back from his world of art to reality. "How far?"

"I got stopped out."

Maas closed his eyes. He felt a pain in his chest. The world went silent. His mouth went dry. "We lost $90,000?"

"Roughly." Her voice was low with an edge that was on the verge of tears.

"Sharon will have been stopped out, too."

"How much will she have lost?"

"Together we'll have about $25,000 left." Maas closed his eyes. He now had a depleted IRA, a second mortgage, and Cooper— his dark eyes on Maas's now larger loan—circling ever closer and smelling blood given his information network. Sharon would lose her gallery. Maas would never have a chance to sculpt again. He would not be able to help his father any more. What was he going to do? His head suddenly felt far too heavy for his spine.

"I need to find a job," he said, even as he wondered, 'Here or in Victoria?'

"What about sculpting?" Maria asked, concern engraved on every word.

"I can do it in the evenings, weekends," Maas said, but even he didn't believe his words. He had never been able to do it before. "I'll work something out."

"*We'll* work something out. We can make some time for you; you've always made time for us. And Anthony....I'm sorry about the corn."

"We'll get through it."

"I know, but I'm still sorry. I screwed up."

"So did I."

Maas sat on the stool in his studio, shoulders slumped, as he scanned his beautiful studio. He loved it. He loved shaping metal into pleasing forms. He loved releasing the images in his head and turning them into reality. The images had been fighting to get out for decades and now, finally, they were being freed one by one. He glanced at a pad on the workbench on which he had sketched a dozen ideas for sculptures that he planned to create. Now, would he ever create any of them? Brokering or sculpting? Maria or Sharon?

Maas rose and, taking one last look around his studio, walked to the door. He slid open the glass door and just as he was about to close the door, the phone rang, staying his hand.

It was Sharon. "Danny was so sure, so certain."

"Brokers are always certain with other people's money," Maas said. Then, realizing he was being unfair to his old friend, added, "Danny's the best technical analyst I know. He's right more often than he's wrong, by a wide margin."

"Not this time."

"Are you going to be able to keep your gallery?"

"I doubt it, unless a fairy godmother appears with a pumpkin stuffed full of money."

"How about a fairy godfather?" Maas asked.

"I'm way past being particular."

Lindhe had called. He heard Maas knew a gallery owner and was interested in getting involved in the art world. Maas decided to introduce him to Sharon, but only after Lindhe promised no loan-shark loans. Lindhe had always kept his word. With the Internet, Sharon could show art to Lindhe's wealthy friends and colleagues in Los Angeles almost as easily as she could to someone in Victoria and, if they wanted a closer look, the flight to Victoria cost little compared to the price of most of the art she sold.

"Now all I need is a new hot young artist to bring in the customers."

"Although I'm far from young, I'd love to be hot. I shipped my sculpture to you this morning." He sighed. "It may be my last."

"I'm so sorry, Tony, I never meant Maria to get involved in the corn...."

"In a way she was doing it for me. She took a shot at making enough so I could quit working and sculpt full time."

"You're going to have to go back to work for Nickel?"

"No." Maas snorted at the thought. "I'll need to find something else, somewhere."

"What about sculpting?"

"I'll have to make time to do it around a day job."

"You need time to create good pieces."

"Most of us don't have the luxury of devoting their entire life to their dreams."

"You could, if you came up here. We'd make a great team. I just had to let my assistant go, so you could help me out in the gallery evenings and weekends, and spend most of your time sculpting. We could be together again. Please come."

The words hung there, tempting and beautiful, as Maas stared at the metal that he had been shaping into his 'Eye of the Cyclops.'

"Will you?"

Chapter 56

Late that afternoon, Maas stood in his driveway securing his 'Eye of the Cyclops' to a rented flatbed trailer. Boxes filled the backseat of his car as he tied his creation down to the trailer.

Maria pulled up in her car and parked on the street, since Maas's car and trailer filled the driveway. She walked across the grass.

"You finished it," she said, eyeing the circular, rusted metal of the sculpture with the dark blue glass eye in the center.

Maas nodded as he tied down another rope. "I had a burst of energy this afternoon."

He finished tying his sculpture down and stood back, beside her but not looking at her.

"Are you alright, Anthony?"

As he stared at his sculpture, he felt the glimmer of a smile forming. "Yeah, I think I am." After a long pause, he turned to her and said, "Thank you for all your support. I'm sorry it didn't work out." He hugged and kissed her. "Goodbye, Maria."

She glanced at the boxes in the back seat of the car and a look of great pain flashed across her face. He was about to slide behind the wheel when she asked, struggling against her emotions, "Where are you going?" The words were forced, as if she did not want to ask the question, let alone hear the answer.

He looked back at her and said, "To take up an old friend's offer."

Maria's face fell, tears forming around her eyes. "We could

have worked it out. We could have made time for you to sculpt," she pleaded, crying.

"What's wrong?"

"You're going to her?"

"To Frank. I'm going to see Frank."

She ran to him and held him tight. He wondered if she would ever let go. Her tears moistened the shoulder of his shirt.

"Frank agreed to trade my sculpture for box seats to a Dodgers game. I had to pay your father back somehow or he'd never baby-sit again."

"You're going to work for Frank?"

"We'll be partners."

"What about sculpting?"

"I tried it full time and we ran out of money."

"You're giving up?"

"I'll work four days a week, have two weekend days with you and the girls, and on the seventh day I will create art."

Chapter 57

Three weeks later the email arrived as Maas sat at his desk at Bill's new firm.

Anthony,

You might think I'm bitter, but I'm not. Deep down, I knew it would end this way. If you were someone else, you would have joined me in the world of art all those years ago. You didn't then and you wouldn't now. People don't change who they are. Maybe that's why I loved you—you were always dreaming, and dreams are always better than reality.

Looking back, I should never have been surprised by your choices. If anything, I was shocked when you told me about your scheme. It was such a risk—or so it seemed to me. Now I realize that to you it was no risk at all; if you had thought there was any risk, you would never have even mentioned it.

Please don't blame yourself. It is as much my fault for hoping, as yours for thinking you just might.

Thanks for introducing me to Lindhe. My gallery just might survive.

I decided to keep the piece you sent me. I think it will be your last work. I hope it will not be, but deep down I know it will, just as I knew you would never leave your wife, girls and brokering for art, or for me.

Take care and at least keep dreaming.

Love,

Sharon

Maas stared at the screen. She was wrong—it hadn't been like that. It hadn't been that predetermined, either time. He hadn't known what he would decide either time. His life could have been completely different. The fact that he'd made the same decision meant...meant...He loved Maria more than Sharon? He loved his daughters? He loved his life as it was more than sculpting? He did not know. Did it matter? Whatever the reasons, he was still himself.

Three months later, Mass finished his second sculpture, shipped it to Sharon, and started on his third. Sharon was wrong.

Chapter 58

The following spring, Maas opened his front door and froze at the sight of the two men on his doorstep.

Cooper, without a hint of emotion in his voice, announced, "You owe me," then snapped his stubby, nicotine-stained fingers and closed his black eyes, waiting for the number to come to him.

"Nine thousand, four hundred sixty-six dollars and seven cents," Lindhe read off his personal assistant. "Principle only."

"It's Sunday," Maas wailed, raising his hands in supplication. After a furtive glance inside to make sure his family was not in sight, he closed the door gently behind him.

"We work seven days a week," Cooper said. "A habit you might consider adopting."

"I switched to full time a few weeks ago. I'm working all the time."

"No more of that sculpting nonsense?"

"Some of it pays," Lindhe said with clinical detachment.

"Not much, and not his," Cooper said.

Maas sighed and said, "You'll get your money."

"I always do," Cooper said with a malevolent grin. "Whatever it takes, I always do."

The End

About the Author

K. Scot Macdonald is the author of the novels, *The Shakespeare Drug* and *In Justice Found*, two non-fiction books, *Rolling the Iron Dice* and *Propaganda and Information Warfare in the 21st Century*, and has contributed to two edited volumes. His work has also appeared in *The Writers' Journal*. He lives in California with his wife, daughter and two Scottish terriers. To find out more about him, visit KScotMacdonald.com.

About Kerrera House Press

Kerrera House Press is an independent press dedicated to publishing the books you keep. Visit us at KerreraHousePress.com for more information about our authors and our latest books.

Reader Resources

For a reader's guide, character bios, and more about the story and writing of *Mouse's Dream*, please visit KerreraHousePress.com.

www.ingramcontent.com/pod-product-compliance
Lightning Source LLC
Chambersburg PA
CBHW031943240626

47153CB00003B/839